WHISTLE (?)

IN THE DARK

SUSANNA M. NEWSTEAD

HERESY PUBLISHING

First Published in 2021
by HERESY PUBLISHING
Newbury RG14 5JG
www.heresypublishing.co.uk

© Susanna M. Newstead 2021
Susanna M. Newstead has asserted her right under the Copyright, Designs and
Patents Act 1988 to be identified as the author of this work.

Cover design by Charlie Farrow

This is a work of fiction. Names and characters are the product of the author's
imagination and any resemblance to actual persons, living or dead,
is entirely coincidental.

All rights reserved. No part of this publication may be reproduced or transmitted
in any form or by any means, electronic or mechanical, including photocopying,
recording, or any information storage or retrieval sustem, without prior permission
in writing from the publishers.

A CIP catalogue record for this book is available from the British Library.

ISBN 978-1-909237-09-4

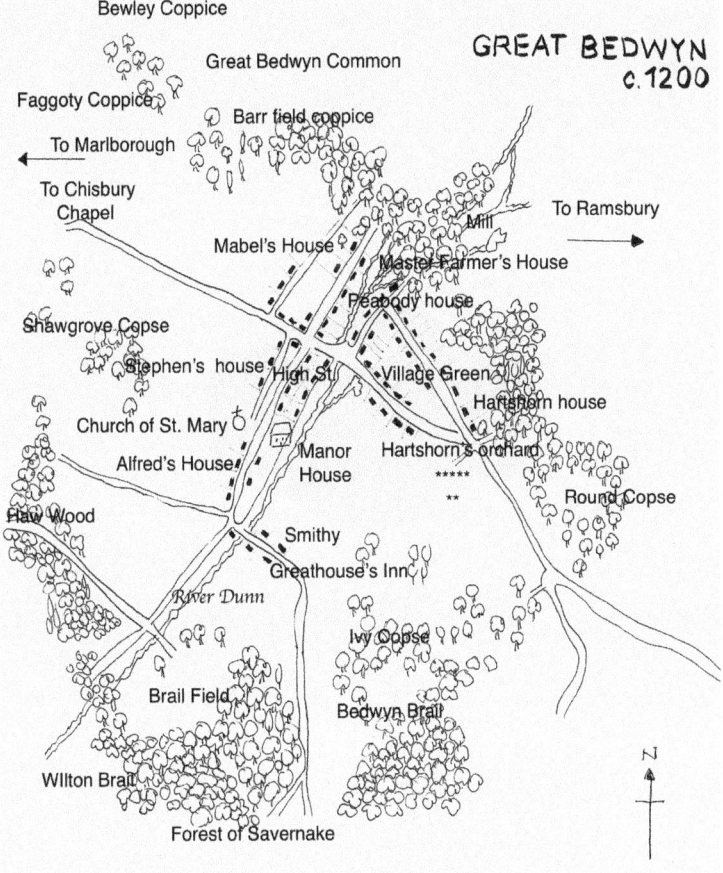

CHAPTER ONE ~ MABEL
GREAT BEDWYN WILTSHIRE
1200 -1212

It was at the thirteenth hour of the thirteenth day upon her thirteenth birthday that Mabel Wetherspring realised that she was very different from her friends and what was left of her family.

She had dropped out of the village ring dance because she'd begun to get too hot, nauseous and dizzy. John Swineherd had hold of her right hand and Stephen Meadow her left.

She'd let go of them and spun off into the trees.

Those trees were tall silver birches, their white bark glowing in the moonlight. It grew dark early in December and the only light was from the full moon and the bonfire which they'd lit. As she stumbled on, the light diminished.

'Oh... I have had too much mead,' she said to herself. 'I will have an unholy headache tomorrow.' But somehow she knew that it wasn't true. She hadn't drunk enough to piss into a thimble.

She was so dizzy. It was so dark. And to combat the feeling of the forest spinning around her, she stood as still as she could with her arms out, her eyes closed and spun withershynnes three times whilst saying to herself, 'Oh how I wish I could be a little black bat and see in the dark.'

She liked bats. They were clever little things. They could hang upside down and the blood never rushed to their heads. She'd tried it a few times herself, her knees hooked over a low branch of a beech tree and blood *always* rushed to her head, making her ears thump and her face turn red. It was most uncomfortable!

Her ears were thumping now, but differently.

She felt her eyes widening even though she had not told them to do so.

She straightened out her arms and felt the sleeves of her kirtle stretching tight. She watched as her fingers changed shape and colour, lengthening and darkening and growing a webbing between them. Her ears wriggled through her hair. She hadn't been aware of them until that moment when she picked up the sound of something small rushing through the undergrowth.

Her shoulders pulled back, her arms twisted and the stitching of her kirtle snapped with a popping sound. Her elbows doubled up and her teeth lengthened. She ran her tongue along them. Oh how sharp they were suddenly.

Then all at once she was on the ground and everything around her was much, much bigger.

Her body was tiny; her arms were enormous and where her sleeves should be, were membranous wings. She tried to take a hand to her ears; there was a strange buzzing in them, but her arms wouldn't reach.

She tried walking. That was very difficult because her legs were so short.

Eventually she clambered up onto a sarsen rock, many of which were littered around the locality, and launched herself from the edge.

The air held her up. She flapped. She twisted. She gained height.

She flapped some more.

"Wheeee!" she yelled at the top of her voice—only her voice was tiny.

"Oh. My. God," she said. "Mabel, you're a bat!"

*****

This was the first time Mabel realised that she was a shapeshifter.

She'd heard the legends about these people, of course. They all had. Women who changed from ordinary females into seal-like creatures, adept at plummeting into the waves encouraging their lovers to follow; men who had the ability to turn themselves into hares and run wild with the wind across the downs. Other not so friendly sorts who were men by day and wolves by night.

That night on her thirteenth birthday was a frightening but exhilarating surprise. And as she wheeled over the trees of Savernake Forest in the light of the moon, she began to realise that this was no accident. It was meant to be. She was in control. This thing had not been done to her; she had done it to herself.

And if she had done it, could she undo it?

Oh but not yet!

It was wonderful to skim the treetops and dash between the branches. Never, not even in her best dreams did she feel so liberated. Had she been a human on the ground she would have been blundering about, hitting the twigs and missing her footing. Up in the air as a bat, she was totally free, fast and utterly manoeuvrable. She tried landing on a twig. It hardly bent with her weight. She was upside down, staring at a world which was grey and silver and full of night sounds. Sounds she'd never heard before as a human, but as a bat, she recognised them all.

Then she panicked.

Could she ever be a girl again?

Turn with the sun, left to right. Fly and spin. This instruction went through her head.

She had just begun to lift off again when a nasty thought entered her bat head. 'Ah if I am in the air and I become a girl again, I will fall to my death.'

She lifted off from her twig and tried to find her sarsen stone again. Not the same one but one she recognised as being a boundary stone to the village in which she lived. Bedwyn.

She landed on it with a bit of a thump and sat. At least, she thought that she sat. It was hard to know how a bat sat. It didn't feel the same as how a young lady sat.

Then she started to worry. If she could get back to being a young lady again, would she still have clothes? She couldn't run naked through the village to get back to her cott!

Mabel looked around her in this strange half-light, everything black, white and silver but perfectly formed and detailed.

'Think Mabel. What exactly did you do to turn yourself into a bat? If you do the same again, can you get back to how you were?'

With her tiny heart thumping, she lifted herself to the little claws of what passed for her hands and the tiny toes protruding from the edge of her large wings. She stretched and began to revolve slowly, following her left shoulder. Withershynnes. Three times. Ah no... that was wrong. She needed to undo it, so she turned deosil—with the sun.

In her head and in her human voice she said, 'I want to be a girl again.'

Part of her was thinking, 'Oh please, let no one see me. If they do, I am doomed.'

And the other part of her brain was saying, 'Oh that winter moth looks so juicy!'

"Moths! Moths? I do not eat moths, I am a girl," she said out loud.

She stared down at her hands; pink, four fingered, one thumb with short nails.

She stared at her feet, encased in their brown shoes. She felt for her ears. There they were, normal size.

Except.

They were still a little papery.

"Oh no... let them please go back to normal. I will have to wear a head cloth or grow my hair a little more if they remain papery. No, no, no that can't happen."

She needn't have worried, for a moment later they were smooth and hairless. She gave a sigh and patted her light brown hair into place.

Mabel sat for a while, as a girl, turning over in her mind what had just happened to her. Must it always be the same? Must she always turn withershynnes—against the sun—and speak the words, "I want to be a... whatever," for this thing to work?

She needed one more practice just to be sure.

And then she would go home to think upon her new found skill.

She had really enjoyed the sensation of flying. It had been wonderful. Might she try that again?

In haste, and whilst she turned withershynnes three times she said, 'I want to fly.'

*****

Again there was a strange sound in her ears. Her eyes widened once more. Her mouth stretched and her tongue protruded. Her two legs divided into four and grew minute hairs. Tiny claws clung to the rock upon which she sat.

'Ah no... this isn't what I wanted,' her human brain said.

'Too late Mabel,' said the voice in her head. 'You're a fly! Next time you'll take your time and remember to be succinct!'

She fell to what passed for knees and stretched out on the rock. Once again everything was huge around her and this time it was REALLY huge.

She moved an arm. A hairy green stick waved in front of her eyes. She felt something wriggling on her back and realised it was her wings unfurling. She raised what passed for a leg and smoothed them down.

How beautiful those wings were, silvery and almost transparent.

Her eyes now began to focus and her vision shrank to the few feet around her—vision which was rather fragmented and mosaic-like.

Her ears did not work properly. But her nose, if she still had a nose, was incredibly sensitive.

'What is that delicious smell?' she said to herself. 'Oh it's like the best rabbit stew my mother used to make.'

As quickly as a swooping swift, (now there, thought Mabel, was an animal I should like to try), she lifted off from her perch on the rock and followed the lovely smell.

It was difficult not to rely on her usual senses, her eyes and ears but somehow she knew that smell was her primary perception and she gave herself up to it completely.

Her wings were incredible, beating so fast she was sure they would be a blur. And she heard a faint buzzing sound. Ah yes... it was those wings moving, lifting her here and there.

There was an overwhelming urge to follow the smell. She simply could not help it.

As she travelled further away from the village, the smell became overpowering and even more enticing.

Her fly brain wondered why there was no other of her compatriots flying with her. Then her human brain said, 'It's a winter's night, there will be few around.'

'Good, more lovely stew for me,' said her Mabel brain.

Mabel landed on a sticky mess, not unlike one of her mother's bag puddings and she stretched out her tongue to lick the sauce.

'Oh it was going to be so good.'

What made her stop, she'd never know. Suddenly a voice in her ear said.

'No... NO! Mabel, this isn't a bag pudding. This is a body. A dead body!'

*****

It was a dead rabbit, lying in a ditch. Back in her own body again, Mabel looked down at it and was almost sick. 'However could I think *that* delicious? It's only delicious if it's cooked and then not if it's days old.'

It looked as if the rabbit had been nibbled by foxes and other forest creatures.

'I shall have to watch that,' she said to herself. 'I don't want to make myself ill by eating putrid food. It's fine for a fly but for me...?'

She turned to make for home.

And as she walked she thought about what had happened to her that night. She had almost managed to convince herself that it had been a figment of her imagination, when she bumped straight into Stephen Meadow. Had she been a bat, she'd have been able to miss him by a mile.

"Oh thank God!" he said. "Where have you been? We have all been out looking for you."

"I am sorry. I... felt a bit ill and had to go and sit in the quiet of the forest for a bit."

"We were all so worried about you. You've been gone for such a long time."

"Oh surely not. It was not past the thirteenth hour of the day when I left you."

"Mabel..." Stephen leaned forward and whispered, "You know how dangerous the night is. You know what creatures lurk out there..." He lifted his arm and pointed further into the trees. "Devils and demons..."

"And bats and foxes and badgers."

"Oh... don't be such a know all! You know what I mean. The dark is dangerous."

Mabel skipped forward, away from him. "The dark isn't dangerous in itself. It's dangerous because you can't see where you are going." 'Unless you are a bat or a fly,' said the voice inside her head.

Stephen tutted. "You always were an annoying littl..."

"Shall we go home?" she said.

*****

That night Mabel lay on her palliasse on the bed in the cott which she had once shared with her mother and thought about her life. Her father had died when she was three. One day he'd gone out to his work in the lord's barn where he was supervising the building of a new stone wall. The lord of the village needed a new barn to store produce and so the builders were called in to extend it. Mabel's father was the bailiff of the estate and amongst other things, it was his job to oversee the men as they worked.

He was standing waving his arms about, berating a stone worker for not using the right mix of mortar when he accidentally struck the unfinished wall with his bailiff's staff. The wall was only one stone thick and badly built.

It complained by falling on him.

When they dug him out he was well and truly dead and Mabel's mother became a widow.

Luckily, her mother had some land and property of her own and so they vacated the spacious bailiff's cottage for a smaller but nicer house in the village. They lost the best cow to heriot and Mabel went to work in the manor. All had been well. They were not poor, for the lord had made sure that a pension was paid to his bailiff's wife—after all her man had been killed in his service –and they managed well. Better than some other villagers.

But this just served to set up petty jealousies in the people of Bedwyn, especially in the children with whom Mabel was acquainted.

They called her Snobby Mabel. Or Mistress Toogood or another half a dozen names.

Mabel was a bright girl, not particularly pretty with a snub nose and freckles. She wouldn't have been considered a catch, despite the family's wealth, for she was a little unruly and more of a boy than a girl.

Her mother had despaired of her.

"Why can't you behave like a girl. You're a woman now. You need more decorum..."

"What's that?" Mabel had said, as she loaded her catapult and took a pot shot at one of the wood pigeons strutting about on the roof.

"Dignity. Femininity. Gentleness. Warmth,"

Mabel's sandy brows drew together. "I can be warm... and gentle."

"How do you expect to attract a husband when you are so... so...?"

"Unattractive?"

"Mabel for the fortieth time, you are not unattractive just..."

"Plain."

"No, not plain either. You have lovely hair. You have a good figure. You're of a delicate size."

"You mean I'm stunted?"

"Don't purposely misunderstand me." It was true. Mabel was petite.

She loaded her catapult again.

"Put that down and listen to me."

Mabel sighed and faced her mother.

"You are only days off being twelve. That means you will shortly be out of childhood. Silly behaviour will not be tolerated in a woman."

"I'm not silly. My catapult has furnished us with many a dinner..."

"Do not argue with me!" Her mother snatched her catapult from her hands.

"You are a mistress know-all. You always have an answer. You know best."

"Perhaps I do."

"How could you? Have you lived a long life? Have you learned everything there is to learn?"

"Well... I have learned more than some people. I can read for a start."

Her mother harrumphed.

"And what good will that do you?"

"It has already done me some good."

"Oh yes?"

"I saw the Lord Stokke the other day and he was very interested that I could read and write. He said that I might come and read to his old mother who's bedridden."

Her mother had blinked in surprise.

"Read to her? And will he pay you? I doubt it."

"Oh yes, he'll pay me."

Mabel flounced off. She'd had enough. That's what happens when you educate a child out of her class and her environment. They became cuckoos. Cuckoos in a nest that didn't recognise her.

And now her mother too was gone.

Her last words to Mabel had been, "You wait here. I want to complain to Master Farmer across the lane. Every morning even before it's light, his large cock wakes me up and it's getting too much for me. Every morning!"

Mabel couldn't help it. She giggled when she remembered it.

But it was no laughing matter for her mother had forced her way into the neighbour's enclosure, tripped over his large cockerel, banged her head on a pile of tiles waiting to be used on the barn roof and... wallop! Dead in an instant.

And Mabel at twelve had been alone. She had cousins in the next village but they were much younger than she was and she didn't really see them socially.

Her aunt and uncle were just humble farmers and couldn't really understand Mabel's desire for a better life. They'd laughed at her need for an education when she'd enrolled in the church school run by the priest, at the age of eight and told her, like her mother had, that it would do her no good.

She'd show them!

And now she was thirteen, a woman and her own mistress. She had a good job at the manor, working with the napery and bedlinen; one of the laundresses and hoping for more and better roles as she aged.

And now, she found she could shift her shape to any animal she wished. Tomorrow she'd try another animal and she fell asleep wondering which one she should try.

She woke early. It was Sunday and she must dress in her finery and attend church. Then the day was her own.

She had recently been busy of an evening, weaving on her tablet loom, a green, brown and yellow band to attach to her new kirtle. A pleasing pattern of zig-zags. She realised that the colours and configuration looked a little like a snake. The adder of the forest floor. That was an interesting animal to be. However she realised that they were all hidden deep in the forest litter at this season; perhaps she'd try that one between March and October when they were prevalent in the woodlands.

She finished attaching the band to the neck and sleeves of her cotte and thrust her arms up into it.

Taking up her cloak - she'd need it for it had gone very chilly - she set off the little way to the church of St. Mary.

She would give thanks to God today for this special gift of hers.

Then, as Mabel exited the cottage, she was brought up short. What if this was *not* a gift from God? What if this was something the Devil had planned?

Oh no. She'd just discovered this amazing skill and now she was afraid to use it, in case the Devil was tempting her with it.

She dragged her heels to church.

Looking up at the clouds hanging in the bright blue sky, the sun shining but with no warmth in it, the trees by the churchyard rustling in the intermittent breeze, she decided she would ask God to give her a sign.

She stood at the back of the church and wrapped her cloak around her. Her feet were already cold and she was wearing her thickest hose.

Ah no. She couldn't ask God directly. No one but the priest was able to speak to God, they said.

She couldn't possibly tell the priest what had been happening to her. He would not be pleased at all.

Then she would ask someone else—someone associated with the forest, all green things, the living denizens of the woods. A God of a different kind. One which personified the animals into which she was able to change.

She'd ask Herne the Hunter.

*****

Three times withershynnes... "I wish I was a pigeon."

Mabel realised that she'd need to travel fast if she was to get to the glade with its little pool, where she heard Herne the Hunter had been often seen.

Three miles. It must be three miles and she wasn't going to tire herself out with walking.

Her nose hardened. She felt it grow and change colour. Her vision widened as her eyes moved sideways and grew larger. Now she could see further and in more detail than she had ever done before. The colours were amazing.

"Good Lord!" she said and it came out as a soft and croaky 'coo.'

Her arms shortened and bowed backwards and feathers began to sprout on them. They felt incredibly strong. Her legs and feet shrank and as they did, she noticed her toes becoming scaly and clawed.

She flexed them. And almost fell over.

Ah yes. That was something she was going to have to watch. A human hand was at rest when folded but it was unable to grip. A bird's was able to grip when it was curled around a branch. She knew she'd be able to sleep with her claws fixed and relaxed.

With her powerful legs she lifted off.

Wheep, wheep, wheep. Her muscular wings ploughed through the air like a warm knife cutting through a soft green cheese.

It seemed odd to be flying through the air in broad daylight but here she was, the air rippling over her feathers feeling like she was flying through a soft brush.

She looked down. She was directly over Master Hogman's property. She could see his little pigs, fewer of them now since slaughter day, rootling around in the bushes surrounding his barn.

The man came out from his house. Oh! The language... and on a Sunday too! Yes, he was fighting with his wife again.

She left them behind and veered towards the forest trees. At the edge of them she just caught a glimpse of a bare leg and bare bottom. Now who might that be? Ah yes. Master Greathouse. It was well known that he was tupping his neighbour's wife, Emilia Stockman. On a Holy day? Fie on them. She gave a little chuckle and it came out as a soft 'prrrrp'.

She flew higher, all the while learning how to control her wings and tail, trying to understand how flying worked. What kept her in the air? How could she turn left and right?

She was amazed at her pace. It seemed to her that she was able to pick up speed with very little effort. If she'd been a human, it wouldn't have been possible to run so fast, even if the legs were at full capacity.

And she was not out of breath. How could that be? Again if she were human, she'd be panting like Master Greathouse was, on top of Mistress Stockman!

She gave another 'prrrrp'-like chuckle.

She was approaching the pond and she slowed, choosing a wide willow tree upon which to land.

By gauging her desired perch and then flying at a speed which was approaching a standstill, slightly above the area, she landed. Her legs and feet served the simple function of grasping the perch. She felt her legs absorb a fair amount of the force of the motion but there was no hurt as she thought there might be.

'I am getting used to this flying,' she thought.

She turned her head in a jerky kind of movement. No matter how she tried it would not move smoothly.

It was then she saw several other woodpigeons. Their evil yellow-white eyes followed her as she slid up the branch nearer to the trunk of the tree. I suppose she too would be giving them an evil yellow eyed stare. It seemed they knew she was an interloper.

She dropped to the ground and picked up a fallen ivy berry. She was missing dinner at home. Might as well fill up here.

Her pigeon brain was dedicated to finding food, she realised. Her Mabel brain said, 'Find Herne.'

Her stumpy little feet stamped as she waddled round three times and said to herself, 'I wish I was a girl again.'

She knew that she'd achieved human form when the wood pigeons, hitherto not bothered by her presence, lifted off in panic and disappeared over the further ash trees.

Now she was here, she hadn't the faintest idea how she might speak to the God of the forest and its inhabitants.

Tentatively she stepped forward closer to the water and peered out across the rippling surface. Many folk had been there and attached ribbons and pieces of cloth to the trees. There were other gifts to the God, in the form of flowers, now decayed and food of which there was little left.

Here and there, Mabel saw a different kind of gift. A small knife stuck into the mud of the edge; a brooch suspended by a thread from a reed. That would drop into the water next time there was a storm.

She bent to see what else had been placed in the mud at the edge of the pool.

Her eye lighted on a whole silver penny.

A WHOLE PENNY. Pushed into the silt.

That person must have been desperate to pay so much to have an answer to a question or a deed done or undone. That was a lot of money.

How come it was still here? Why had no one stolen it?

Her hand stretched out to touch it. No. She had no desperate need for it and it was there for a purpose.

"I see you have seen it, daughter," said a low voice.

Mabel spun around. She'd not heard him approach. If she'd been a bat she'd have heard him yards away. Even her pigeon ears would have picked up his tread.

"I am not going to steal it."

"No, of course not." The voice was kindly and soft. "You have no need, I suppose."

Mabel licked her lips. "I've come to... seek out Herne the Hunter and ask him a question."

The man came out of the trees.

He was a man like any other. He wore a short tunic of an indeterminate green with a hood of the same colour. His eyes twinkled and his face was rather dirty. He was not Herne.

Herne was half man, half deer and a spirit as old as time itself.

"Cernunnos?" said the man. "Or Odin with his Wild Hunt?" He tutted through stumpy teeth, "You'll not find him here though many have sought him."

"But people have seen him, haven't they? They have. Master Torode has seen him. He said so. And Mistress Comfort, she came here with her daughter and..."

"Aye, in the forest but not here."

"Oh." Mabel felt very deflated.

"Then why *do* people come here?"

"To offer to the old gods. So that they won't be forgotten. They'll come in their droves on Midwinter night."

"In seven days' time? The solstice?"

The man nodded and his greasy hair fell over his face.

Mabel began to feel just a little uncomfortable.

"What did you wish to ask, mistress?"

"I thought that a God like Herne would be able to tell me if something... something I have experienced, is sent from God or the Devil," she said with great confidence.

"Oh, my. That is an important question."

"It is to me."

"Maybe one you could ask your priest?"

"Ah... no."

"And what is this thing you have experienced?"

The man came closer. Mabel stepped back.

"I cannot tell you."

"But I too may have had this experience. In my life, I have seen many things. I might be able to help you."

Mabel tittered. "I doubt it." She looked him up and down. What if this man was also a shapeshifter? What if he could do what she could do? Was she in danger?

She decided to take Herne by the horns. After all, he'd either know what she meant or he'd be astonished and think she was mad.

As she formulated what she was going to say, she thought, 'Or he will think me evil and want to kill me.'

Her brain worked out the best way to flee should she need to.

"I can change myself into any animal I wish... and back again and I wondered if God wished me to do this, or if the Devil..."

The man's laughter rang out in the glade and bounced over the water to the bare trees.

"I am a shapeshifter."

He folded his arms. "Are you indeed?"

"So I wanted to ask Herne if it was something that I could do without getting my soul into deadly peril. He is part animal. He would know."

The man's eyes narrowed. "Where do you live? Where do you come from?"

She almost told him but stopped herself at the last moment. "I cannot tell you."

"How did you get here?"

That was easy. It would not be a lie. "I flew."

The man couldn't stop laughing. He clutched his middle and roared.

"Aw c'mon. Why are you really here?"

She tried to look coy. "I was practising my flying. I told you."

Again he took a step towards her.

Mabel retreated. "Ah well, I have to be off. I need to get home to my Da." It was a lie to make him think she wasn't alone in the world.

"Does *he* know you can fly?"

"Of course he does. He can do it too."

The man stroked the side of his head. "I think you're touched, young lady."

"Maybe I am," she smiled sweetly as she started to walk away.

The man pursued.

Out of the corner of her eye she saw him put on a spurt of speed.

'Oh God, if this is what you want me to do,' she said to herself, 'let this work and me escape. If it's the devil's work, then no doubt, I will not be aided.'

Three times she spun as quickly as she could.

"I would like to be a peregrine," she said out loud. "PLEASE!"

There was a strong fizzing in her ears. Once again she felt her nose and mouth fuse and grow. This time it was to a wicked point.

The wings grew fast. Pointed and sleek.

Her eyes grew large and yellow. Her vision was staggering. She could not conceive of how amazingly detailed everything became.

Her feet once again grew but this time the claws were as deadly as sword points.

Her eyes swivelled to the man who'd fallen to the ground in sheer terror. He scrambled backwards away from her.

"You ask if it's God or the Devil?" he said at a shriek. He crossed himself.

"It's the DEVIL!"

But Mabel was far above him by then, building up speed, racing across the treetops, her little falcon heart beating at a fantastic rate. Her falcon eyes seeing everything for miles and miles and miles.

CHAPTER TWO ~ THE BODY

God had spoken.
At least Mabel believed he had. She had escaped. And as she landed on the oak tree growing in the plot which lay around her house she felt whole and unsullied, free in mind and body. And safe.

Yes, God was with her. It was alright.

She flew down to the ground, after making sure that none of her neighbours could see her, though their cotts were not very close, turned three times sunwise or deosil and there she was, a girl again.

Then she must have some dinner. She was starving. She would learn over time that changing back and forth would make her both hungry and tired.

She removed the turves from her hearth and blew the little embers into a fire. Brrr. She was suddenly cold. She stopped and looked up at the rafters, imagining the blue skies through which she had streamed that morning. She had not been cold then. Her peregrine-self had been as snug as if she'd been wearing a fur lined cloak. But of course, in a way she had. She realised that feathers were warm!

Mabel would find out many things as she tried out her new skill over the next year.

She realised that the feet of a fox fell silently upon the forest floor; that an owl could turn its head right round and see backwards, (she loved being an owl,) and that, as an owl, she could see as efficiently in the night as the peregrine could in the day.

She learned that mice, rabbits and voles lived in perpetual fear. They were endlessly driven to search for food but at the same time were constantly afraid for their lives. She had to concentrate hard if she became a mouse and not lose herself in fear of the sounds which came into her huge ears. She knew that she was fast but she knew that the animals which preyed upon her were just as fast. She was also amazed to learn that mice could not control their bladders. THAT was embarrassing!

In the spring of 1201, she became a robin; a cheeky little minx with a bright eye. She menaced Master Stockman senior as he dug his plot one Saturday morning and laughed, albeit internally, as he spoke to her about nice juicy worms and crunchy beetles. Ack no! She wouldn't eat those, unless she was very, very hungry.

She was sitting on the handle of his spade that day, when there was an almighty clucking and a red breasted creature came hurtling across the ground and hit her with force. She fell from the spade and landed on the earth with a splutter.

This creature then proceeded to grab her with its claws and stab her with its beak.

Another robin!

Oh dear. She had unwittingly trespassed on another's territory.

'Terribly sorry,' she squeaked and as quickly as she could she fled into the trees and changed into a girl again.

"I'll have to watch that too," she said. "I can't afford to be injured." She sucked at a scratch on her wrist.

As time wore on she began to gain confidence and her animals became larger. The greatest fun was had when she became one of Master Hogman's pigs. She was a small, red, bristly, flat nosed hog who loved running around the field on perky little black trotters and she adored rolling in the mud. She hoped this would come off when she changed back to a girl.

The other pigs didn't seem to mind her. But that evening when Master Hogman came to count his animals back into their little wicker fold, he was puzzled.

He took off his coif and scratched his thinning hair.

"Well, I got twelve... and now I got thirteen and it ain't breeding season, even though that one there looks a bit small and scrawny."

He tried to catch hold of Mabel but she squealed and bucked and he couldn't get a purchase on her.

"Ah well... So what! If I got another eh?" His wife was screeching from the open doorway about his supper and so he reluctantly went into the house. They were STILL arguing, thought Mabel, laughing.

Through the summer she tried a dog and a cat. Everyone was sweet to her as a dog and gave her little bits of their dinner ham or cheese but as a cat she was not quite so welcome.

Some of the younger children threw stones at her until Mistress Mosspath stomped down her garden and stopped them telling them that they should be ashamed of themselves. Cats were useful creatures for keeping down vermin. Fie on those evil children!

Mabel had no intention of chasing rats and mice. She scurried away quickly. Maybe not a cat eh?

*****

As time wore on, Mabel had such an overwhelming desire to be a horse.

But that was going to be really difficult as no one in the village owned a horse, except the lord, his marshall and his steward. One more horse would be very noticeable there.

Nevertheless she was determined to do it.

She thought carefully about what kind of horse she might be. She knew it wouldn't be a good idea to be one of the lord's beautiful fast, sleek beasts. How about a utilitarian rouncey? No one could complain at that and if she went far into the forest where she knew there would be no people to spy on her, that would be a possibility and sensible.

She rode over the treetops as a fast forest hawk—a sparrowhawk; lustrous, graceful and streamlined and chose a large glade into which she stooped.

She was a little upset that her descent had frightened a charm of goldfinches and they fled into the bushes in panic.

She preened her feathers, sitting on a low branch of a hazel tree and thought. No, I am not hungry, I do not need goldfinch for my supper.

Now for a horse.

Should she change back into a girl first? Well, she'd never know until she tried it, would she? Straight from a bird to a horse. That would be a first.

Moving her claws along the branch, she hopped to the ground.

She turned withershynnes three times, "I would like to be a rouncey horse."

Now, bearing in mind that Mabel was a sparrowhawk of about two feet and she wanted to be a horse of about five feet at the withers—the top of its back—there was a lot of changing to do.

She realised that day, that it was easier and quicker to go from a big animal to a smaller one; so after a few writhings and poppings, where she tried to resist the movements, Mabel let nature take its course and watched as her legs lengthened and became powerful and her little body elongated. Her nose too, lengthened and her nostrils flared and grew huge. She took an experimental breath through them; oh my, how well she could breathe! When she exhaled there was a powerful snort. The feathers all disappeared to be replaced by sleek, glossy brown hair. She felt the feathers on her head retreat to be replaced by a thick mane, which extended down her arched neck. But the best thing... oh by far the best, was the tail. How she loved swishing it from side to side. And she was overjoyed how her ears worked independently, first one flicking and then the other.

She dipped her head. She now had hooves where moments before she'd had scaly sharp claws. She pawed the earth.

"Oh my!" she yelled, happy to have managed such a transformation and in her pert little brown ears the sound registered as 'neeeeigh!'

Slowly she found her feet, as it were and began to walk around the field. Then she picked up speed. Oh how magnificent it was! She tossed her head just so she could feel the whip of her lovely mane brushing her. Mabel felt beautiful for the first time in her life. Now she was trotting, her hooves striking the ground in a particular pattern over which she had no control. It simply came to her naturally to speed up to a canter and then when she had got the feel of that, she began to gallop. Oh my! She was fast. The trees went by in a blur of green; the blackthorn blossoms whizzed past in a cloud of dirty white; the primroses in a streak of pale yellow.

Suddenly she felt she needed to stop running and she came abruptly to a halt rearing up on her hind legs. Once more she yelled with pure pleasure. "Neigh!"

Once she had been round the whole glade, she slowed and eyed the new spring grass, lush, bright green and plentiful.

It took a lot of willpower not to sink her horsey teeth into it more than once with a satisfying crunch. No! She was a girl. She didn't eat grass.

She became aware of a fox staring at her from the edge of the glade. Its keen amber yellow eyes flashed in the sunlight and she walked forward to stare at it kindly.

When she was a few feet from it, it turned and melted into the bushes, with a swish of its fine, red tail.

The little goldfinches had returned, unafraid of the horse she had become.

The horse was the biggest animal Mabel had ever tried and she knew that it would tire her and that she needed to get home.

She looked up at the sky.

"Oh my! I had better fly! I will be late for church."

Fly she did, this time as one of her favourites, a pigeon. This was an unassuming creature of which no one took any notice but it was fast over the treetops and made light work of eating up the miles, without tiring her too much.

Even so, she fell asleep in church.

*****

The years passed and Mabel matured. In 1208, after working her way up the ladder, she was promoted in the manor. She became the housekeeper in charge of all the workings of the grand home; she was to supervise the storage of food; she was responsible for the staff who ran the laundry but also the kitchen, the hall and the bedchamber. It was a responsible job which she took seriously and thoroughly enjoyed. She did not feel the need to marry and besides there was no one she *wanted* to marry. Or who wanted to marry her. It might be a dangerous thing to let another into her strange life.

And as the years whizzed by Mabel had become adept at her transformations as she liked to call them. She spent many happy hours investigating the lives of her subjects. Fox, badger, mole (she tried that just once, but she didn't like being in the dark and reliant only on her nose.) Birds were her favourite and she'd tried everything from the tiniest of titmice to the majestic heron.

But there was one animal, even eight years after she had discovered her skill, which she had not tried. A deer.

She had to admit that she was a little afraid to become a deer, for this was the King's forest and the deer belonged to him. He hunted there and allowed others to hunt the roe and the fallow, for a fee.

She had no intention of providing someone with a good supper, even if she was to be eaten by the King.

But one fine day in the summer of 1208 when she knew that there would be no hunting because the forest was in what was known as 'defence'; this meant that no one was allowed to disturb the deer, for the pregnant does and hinds were about to give birth and they must be allowed to do so in peace, she had a hankering to be a deer. Once more she sought a quiet spot, well hidden from prying eyes. She turned and muttered, "I wish to be a fallow deer."

Instantly her nose lengthened and became an elegant shape. Her legs splayed, her arms dropped and now she walked on four legs. Her skin became dappled and soft red brown. She had no antlers for as she knew fallow females were not horned. Her feet and hands grew into delicate little hooves and Mabel high stepped through the grass to the stream bank to dip her tongue into its crystal surface. A sweet face looked up at her, reflected in the water. This was the first time she had seen herself as any of the animals she had grown into and she was quite surprised to see that, even though she was without doubt a deer, she still recognised herself as Mabel Wetherspring. She chuckled. She was sure no one else would though.

Delicately she sipped from the water and even though she knew she was safe, she scanned the furthest bank with her ravishing large brown eyes.

Plop! A water vole entered the river opposite her and she was momentarily startled.

'Foolish Mabel,' she said to herself. 'You could have fallen in.'

Her hooves skittered in the mud of the edge of the little river and she backed quickly onto the grass again, her heart pounding. Another animal who was nervous and jittery, then. She had learned over the years which animals were confident and unafraid and which would jump at shadows.

She felt best at home in the long grasses of the meadow where she would be hidden by her colouration and her pattern or in the bushes which littered the edge of the meadow. Slowly she made her way across the open glade.

All at once something *really* frightened her. It sped past her and disappeared into the bushes. Mabel's human brain recognised it as an arrow.

A voice said, "Bugger!"

Mabel didn't wait to hear what other expletives the man was about to utter but fled on swift feet into the bushes, lay down and tried to stop panting in fear.

The man came out into the glade.

Stephen Meadow hunched his shoulders and took a firmer grip on his bow.

"Stephen is a poacher?" said Mabel to herself. "Well, well. Naughty man." It was expressly forbidden to hunt deer in the forest particularly as a common man. The King owned every beast and the fines for being found with a carcass or even horn from a deer, were horrendous. It could break a man for life.

Was Stephen Meadow alone?

It looked like it. Her deer eyes scanned the glade, No one had followed him and no one had gone out to meet him. However he was making for the bush directly where Mabel lay. Soon he'd tread on her.

She made the instant decision to change.

Wriggling further into the bush she cleared a space for herself and turned. This wasn't easy as a deer but it was even more difficult, she realised as a girl, for she wasn't used to standing upright in dense prickly bushes.

"Ah no. I must change again quickly."

Once more she turned. "I want to be a fly."

There was no way on earth Stephen would discover her as a fly.

Transformation complete, she crawled under a leaf and stayed perfectly still. Stephen passed her, muttering under his breath and drumming his fingers in frustration on his small hunting bow which was slung over his shoulder.

He disappeared in the large oak trees to the edge of a copse and was lost to sight.

Still Mabel did not move.

It was high summer. There were many insects of all kinds, buzzing around the bushes. Some were bees at their daily round of collecting nectar from the flowers of the blackberry. Some were ladybirds hunting the green aphids abundant on the soft leaves of the bindweed.

There were grasshoppers hiding deep in the roots of the grass and hoverflies visiting the bindweed flowers.

There were also predators. This was not winter when there were few animals to eat the juicy fly that Mabel had become. This was the height of the season for... everything. Birds, other insects, spiders. Mabel wished she hadn't made a snap decision to be a fly in summer.

She peered out from under her nettle leaf.

It was, she thought, all clear.

She would buzz out into the meadow and change to her pigeon again.

In the next instant all thought of transformation was gone from her fly brain.

Mabel realised that flies were not terribly clever. She was a girl, of that there was no doubt and she still had her human brain... somewhere inside her. But for some reason her fly brain was trying to get the better of it.

She flew out and landed on a stalk of grass. Mabel was looking up at the sunny sky, her legs wrapped around a stalk of meadow grass when her nose, or what passed for it, started to twitch.

She tried to ignore it as she had trained herself to do many times but today, somehow, it was not to be ignored.

She set off across the meadow, flying low and rather erratically, making for a ditch at the furthest side.

She flew into a sticky mass strung between two blades of grass.

"No!" she cried, "it's a spider's web!"

She struggled. It didn't feel as if she was caught too tightly. She pulled first one leg, then another free and saw the threads holding her, break.

It was then she spotted the eyes of the spider approaching. In a blind panic, she struggled with another leg.

'Whatever you do, you must not allow it to bite you," said her Mabel head. "If it does that, then you are finished."

Two legs now. She was caught only by two legs.

The spider was confident of catching Mabel and did not make the swift approach she'd seen spiders make at other times when in her human body.

Mabel struggled again. The web broke its moorings and swung down.

But just before the spider reached her, a black shadow approached from above and the sun was blotted momentarily.

Mabel's fly eyes were unable to catch the movement but her human brain knew what it was; that it was a starling. A starling adept at flying and catching prey on the wing.

The spider disappeared from her sight and the sun returned.

Mabel tried to close her eyes. Close her protuberant rust brown, fragmented eyes but she was unable. She realised flies have no eyelids.

'That was close. Too close.'

She crawled for a heartbeat under another leaf, this time a many fronded vetch plant and sat to think.

Her fly brain took over again.

'Oh that delicious smell!'

She lifted off and was guided by the fabulously appetizing fragrance emanating from the small dip of a ditch.

She landed on a nettle two inches from an eye. An open eye where a little white maggot crawled and wriggled.

She looked around, bearing in mind that her vision was limited to a few feet and was not highly coloured like human vision.

There were other maggots. "Oh, hello little ones," said her fly self. "Oh don't be ridiculous," said her human one.

Then her human brain took over.

'Oh. My. God.'

It was a corpse!

*****

It had been dead for a while, she thought. And her next thought was, 'I need to be a woman again. This is just impossible as a fly.'

She flew to the ground and turned three times deosil.

"I wish to be a woman again."

"Ah... she had misjudged the distance and she was almost on top of the corpse with its company of maggots and its staring eyes.

She gave a slight shriek and then looked round quickly to make sure no one had heard her.

A nosy magpie came within a few feet of her, his dark, blue black eye trained upon the wriggling maggots. This had been dinner for him until this girl had appeared from nowhere!

She shooed him away and bent to see the corpse.

An awful smell hit her nose and she put her hand over her mouth.

"Ugh! It smelled much better as a fly."

She twisted her head to look at the face. Did she know this poor unfortunate?

She did.

It was Master Greathouse.

*****

Edward Greathouse had been a tall good looking man of thirty four who owned an inn on the road to Ramsbury, though he did not run it by himself. He was relatively affluent as many folk passed his establishment on their way to Hungerford, a large town nearby and it was a bustling thriving business.

Mabel searched for his purse. If this had been a roadside robbery, his purse would be missing as, no doubt would his clothes but they were all there.

She thought back to the man she'd met by the pool in the forest all those years ago. Had this man been a wolfshead, a felon escaped to the forest? Was he or someone like him responsible for Master Greathouse's death? If so, she'd had a lucky escape all that time ago. Surely he could not still be here? She knew that the warden of the forest and his men moved the masterless felons out of the forest regularly.

Covering her nose and mouth with her hand, Mabel leaned over to look at the back of the man's head. It had been caved in and the skull broken.

"Well if it's not a robbery then it's certainly murder, for he didn't do *that* to himself. And what's more this is the result of a few blows," she said out loud.

She realised that she'd have to report the death to the authorities and was about to change and fly off when...

Ah... perhaps... not.

It was well known that the person who found and reported a body was often taken up for the crime, regardless of their innocence.

She walked up and down thinking.

'I need to tell someone else... but how not to implicate myself?' She stopped still.

'Stephen. Yes, *Stephen*.'

He couldn't be far away. She ran towards the copse of trees where she'd last seen him.

'Ah wait!' she said to herself. 'He too might think that I am a murderer.'

Before she reached the trees, Mabel turned withershynnes three times and said, 'I wish to be a peregrine.'

With the speed of that bird and its superior sight she'd soon spot Stephen trundling across the forest floor.

And yes, there he was, tramping through the long grass. How to make him turn back?

Mabel took herself off into a dive and pulled up at the last minute with a menacing croak.

Stephen Meadow yelled and fell to the ground. "What the hell!"

Mabel veered and turned again and this time she managed to catch him lightly on the top of his head with her claws.

"Argh!" His hand went up to his thinning sandy hair and he

dropped his small bow.

With stretched legs and even more stretched talons, Mabel picked up the bow, and with a crafty look over her falcon shoulder, she rose and sped off across the ground.

She couldn't fly *too* fast or Stephen would not be able to follow, of that she was sure. She circled a couple of times to make sure he was lurching along behind her and took off again towards the glade they'd just left.

"Oi, you thieving bird! " shouted Stephen, "You drop that, do you hear!"

Mabel ignored the expletives.

She came back to him and gave him another buffet with the power of her body's draught.

"Argh!" He fell to the grass again but was soon up, shaking his fist at her. Oh how she was enjoying this. 'That is for all the times you pulled my hair when I was a girl!'

At last they came to the ditch and Mabel dropped the bow a foot from the corpse.

The stupid man started to search around.

'Oh for Heaven's sake,' said Mabel to herself in her human brain. 'It's right in front of you. Can't you see?'

But of course, her peregrine vision was much superior to his and her sense of smell ten times as powerful as his own. It was only when he was right on top of the body that he realised it was there.

He reached for his discarded bow.

"Ergh. Oh… Hell's fires! What?"

The man backed off muttering expletives. Mabel laughed to herself, sat in the branches of the ash tree above him. If only Father Ignatius could hear him, he'd be doing penances from now till Christmas!

"Bloody bird. What does it want to do that for?"

Mabel had always thought Stephen a little dim. 'Right on top of a bloody corpse.'

It was then that Stephen Meadow realised that this was the corpse of a *man*, and not merely an animal. Oh yes, he'd been covered over with leaves and detritus but it was obvious, from the yellow tunic the man wore, that this was a murder victim.

Indeed it was a bloody corpse and Stephen prodded it with his foot.

The man's head flopped to the side.

"Argh!" It then became obvious to Mabel that Stephen had realised who the man was.

"Edward?"

There was no answer of course.

"Edward... are you dead?"

'Of course he's dead, you simpleton,' said Mabel. But all she really said was 'kack, kack, kack.'

Stephen looked up.

"Bloody bird!"

Mabel lifted off from her lofty perch. She had done what she could. Now it was up to Stephen to report the death of his friend and neighbour, if he would. If not, she'd have to think again.

She didn't suppose that he would be able to resist talking about his experience to someone. He was always a bit of an idiot. Had been from childhood. A runaway mouth.

Stephen wiped his hand across that mouth and backed off.

"Oh... oh..." he turned and ran. Then thought better of carrying his illegal hunting bow and bent to secrete it in a thorn bush along the way.

"Oh... wait till I tell me mam... she'll never believe me!"

He had an inane grin on his face and Mabel grinned an inane peregrine grin too.

'Oh he'll tell...he won't be able to help himself...'

What's more, he wouldn't even think twice about the fact that he'd found the body and might be accused of the murder.

'Silly Stephen.'

CHAPTER THREE ~ SUSPECTS

Mabel kept pace with Stephen all the way to the village and up to the reeve's house. She sat on the roof of the substantial building and watched the little birds dive for cover.

"Oh no... that's not fair," said Mabel in a croak. So she turned withershynnes and wished herself into a pigeon. The smaller birds wouldn't be worried about her now.

She heard a breathless Stephen relate the fact that he'd found the body of Master Greathouse in the forest, to Master Head, the village reeve.

"What were you doing out there Stephen?" said Henry Head. "You sure it wasn't you?"

"Aw c'mon Henry. Would I run all this way to tell you if I'd done it? I'd bury him, cover him over and keep quiet wouldn't I?"

The reeve's eyes narrowed into a 'I don't believe you' stare, though Mabel couldn't see it up on her perch.

"Well I would, wouldn't I?"

"You got a problem with Edward Greathouse, son?"

"No... no…!" said Stephen Meadow at a squeal. "Of course I bloody don't!"

There was a silence in the conversation and Mabel had to hop to the edge of the thatch and peer down to see what was happening.

They'd walked out into the yard.

"Phil...? Whatsup?" said the reeve's wife, coming up with a basket tucked under her arm.

"Looks like ol' Greathouse has been done away with," said Head, never one to mince his words. "Bashed over the head. Dead as yesterday's dinner."

"Oh Lord!" cried his wife, dropping the basket, her hand going to her mouth.

'Aha!' thought the pigeon. 'Is this another of Edward Greathouse's conquests?'

"What shall we do Master Reeve?" asked Stephen, hopping from foot to foot.

"We'll have to tell the coroner's office. Then when he's been we'll have to recover the body and send to the constable. He'll have to have a look."

"His head is all bashed in!"

"The constable?"

"Nooo! Edward!"

"Ah."

"I'll go to Durley shall I and tell the constable?" said Stephen in a helpful voice.

"No, you go to the coroner in Ramsbury. You're the first finder."

Stephen didn't seem so keen on that.

"I'll send Gibso to Durley." This was the reeve's youngest son, Gilbert. "Meanwhile I suppose we'd better go out and have a look at him. Where exactly is he?"

Stephen thought hard.

The pigeon on the roof said, 'Chisbury Copse - in the ditch to the southern side.'

It came out as 'coo, coo, prrrp, coooooo, coo coo. Prrrrrp.'

They both looked up.

"Chisbury Copse, in the ditch on the southern side," said Stephen confidently.

'Well I never!' said Mabel to herself.

The reeve took Stephen's shoulder and turned him to walk away.

"I gotta go and tell me mam first," said Stephen excitedly.

"Well hurry then."

And they walked away.

Mabel flew to the ground and peered into the darkness of the open door to the reeve's house.

Looking around quickly, she turned and said "I wish to be a woodlouse?"

It took a few heartbeats but she managed it and watched as her legs split into several little stumpy ones and her nose grew feathery. Her back arched and grew many hard plates and her vision shrank to the few inches before her.

'Damn!' Mabel hadn't thought very carefully about this. All she'd thought about was that she wanted to get into the house and be undetected so that she could spy on Mistress Head. A woodlouse had seemed a good idea.

Mabel scuttled on fleet feet to the side of the door jamb and peered round. Ah, there was Alys Head, weeping into her apron. She could just see her though the picture was a little blurry.

She scurried further in, keeping to the space where the beaten earth floor met the wall.

Suddenly Mistress Head picked up a mug and hurled it at the wall. There was the sound of shattering pottery. Now, why had she felt the need to throw a perfectly good piece of crockery at the wall?

Mabel uncurled herself. She'd realised that her instinct as a woodlouse was to curl up tightly at the first sign of danger.

It wasn't going to help her though with the chicken which was attached to the scaly legs which she saw approaching through the bright doorway.

"Oh fiddle faddle!" It had its beady eye trained on her and it looked hungry.

Suddenly Mistress Head screeched angrily.

"OUT!" and the chicken flew out of the cott with a startled high pitched chuckle.

"Phew."

Next Mabel knew, she was travelling through the air along with a lot of dust and bits of seed.

Mistress Head had taken a broom to the chicken and was now sweeping the floor frantically.

Out went Mabel, curled in a ball and as she landed, she quickly made for what looked like a water butt situated at the side of the doorhole. Yes, her Mabel brain remembered it was there.

She burrowed deep under it and peered out.

It was several heartbeats before she dared come out again.

*****

Sitting in her house, shelling the peas she grew in the plot behind her home, she began to think through all the women she'd seen with Edward Greathouse over the years. She threw the peas into a pot and followed them with some spring onions.

Well, there was Mistress Stockman. Mabel had seen her with him quite a few times.

She wondered if Mistress Peabody was another of his lovers. They were often to be seen walking about together, though Mabel had not seen them actually engaging in any naughty business. She threw some dried ham into the pot.

Would a woman do that? Bash his head in like that?

Might it be a jealous lover?

Might it be a vengeful husband fed up of playing the cuckold?

A delicious feeling of nosiness overtook her. She wanted to know. Suddenly, she wanted to know who was responsible. Not because she cared particularly about Master Greathouse but because she was interested in the truth. And, she realised, she was uniquely placed to find out the truth.

Right... the evenings are longer at this time of year. Eat your supper and then go and do a little digging.

She didn't count it as spying on her neighbours. It was much more than that. It was... it was.... Mabel searched for a term which would justify her poking into the lives of her friends and neighbours.

Justice... that was it. JUSTICE.

She was looking for justice.

She added some cabbage and a little fennel to her pot, then topped it up with a few dried mushrooms which she had sitting in a jar on her shelf. As she stirred it all, Mabel listed in her mind the people she thought most likely to want Greathouse dead.

Master Peabody... Ah no, he'd died the year the pestilence had come to the village.

Master Stockman senior, one of the lord's cattle men, must be a possibility. He was the first in the queue. She tipped some wild strawberries into her pottage. And now Master Head. His wife was definitely upset by the murder.

Then, as Mabel spooned the pottage into her mouth, she thought there would be people who were dissatisfied with Master Greathouse's accommodation at the inn. There might be a few of those. However, she thought as she chewed through the tough cabbage, they were unlikely to be local.

Hmm. She wiped her bowl and began to take in the enormity of her task. There might be dozens of people with whom the man had had arguments or people who felt a grievance against Greathouse. How was she to find those?

She must start in the village. She'd once heard the constable say that most murders were perpetrated by those who knew the victim well. Family and friends. She'd begin with those.

What animal to be? How could she gain access to people's homes without arousing suspicion? She didn't wish, however, to place herself in danger as she had done that day. Not an insect - too risky. Oh but what about a wasp...? She could fly into houses then and no other animal would try to eat her... Ah no! She'd seen a blackbird eat a wasp once. Maybe not. And people didn't like wasps. She was very likely to get walloped.

As a peregrine, where flying was quick and easy, she wouldn't be welcome in the house.

What other bird was quick and might be allowed into the house?

She had it in a flash. Yes...an actual flash!

'Oh pay attention Mabel!' In her distraction, she'd set fire to her polishing cloth!

*****

She glided on glossy blue wings into the barn where Master Stockman was forking up hay and made for a central beam. She landed on the edge settling her wings which formed two perfect points behind her.

Her tail made two little 'v' shapes behind her and she looked at her shadow. Oh how very pleasing.

Dark blue-black above and bright white below, with a blood red forehead and throat, and a black band across her chest, as a swallow she felt really pretty. The sexes were alike and, as she looked at the little sparrows squabbling in the dirt below her, she realised that it must be very dull to be a female sparrow.

But she wasn't here to admire her plumage.

Stockman was alone. Did he seem to her to be feeling any guilt? How would she tell?

She flew around a bit, as close as she dared to get to Master Stockman at his work.

He was muttering.

What was he saying?

At that moment, in came another man.

"Hey! Alain!"

"John."

"Have you heard the news?"

"Oh? What's that then?"

"Old man Greathouse is dead."

Stockman ceased to fork his hay.

"Dead? No?"

"Aye... someone killed him."

Stockman leaned on his fork.

"Well, that's no surprise is it?"

The other man whom Mabel recognised as John Fordman, gave a forced laugh.

"Someone he's filched off, I suppose."

Stockman nonchalantly picked up a dried straw of grass and chewed on it.

"Filched in more ways than one."

"Grasping bastard."

Mabel realised that the village only had one reaction to anyone who made a success of themselves. Envy. This, she thought, was envy talking.

The man named John came closer and lowered his voice.

'Damn,' thought Mabel. I can't hear. She flew down and dug her claws into an upright beam in the barn's wall.

"Won't be making a fool of you any longer will he?"

Stockman bridled.

"Whadaya mean by that?"

"Weeell..." said the other. "Obvious i'n't it?"

"Why you... foul mouthed snake..." Alain Stockman made a feint for John Fordman.

"Aw c'mon, you know what I mean. You can't deny it."

"I'll have the skin off yer..."

'Oh...' thought Mabel. 'Stockman has a temper.'

John backed away. Mabel lifted off from her perch and flew between them. John ducked.

"Bloody bird," said Stockman.

WITHERSHYNNES: IN THE DARK

"Give Edward the back of a spade did you?"

"No, I did not."

"Ah well." John stood in the barn doorway. "There's many a folk will be pleased if you did." And he left.

Stockman swore, threw down his fork and lifted a flask to his lips. "Wish I had... bloody wish I had," he said.

*****

'Ah,' thought Mabel. 'Maybe it wasn't Stockman.'

He didn't look pleased with himself; he didn't look guilty; he didn't look ... anything.

He sat down in the hay and proceeded to drink his flask dry.

There was a spade lying against the barn wall. Mabel made a few passes across it. As far as she could see there was no blood on it.

Eventually Stockman stood up, wiped his mouth with the back of his hand, picked up both the spade and the fork and left the barn.

Now where?

She flew out of the barn, over the head of Master Stockman and over the village towards the Crofton Road where there were several cottages lining the pools of the river Kennet.

She executed a reconnoitering pass over the first cott and ducked in the open doorway. How fortuitous that village folk left their doors open all day in the summer.

Mistress Peabody was at her trestle, pounding some oats into a powder, peering at it.

Mabel swooped up to the beam where she had, in the past, noticed there had been a swallow's nest. She snuggled into it.

Mistress Peabody, whose first name was Matilda, looked up quickly.

"Oh no. I was going to get that down, wasn't I?" she said out loud. She swiped her hands across her apron, got hold of the handle of her besom and tried to knock the nest from the beam. She failed.

She held the very end of the stick and jumped. Mabel flew free just as the nest tumbled.

"Now, out of here you rent dodging bird. No free accommodation here for you. Go to the barn."

Mabel squeaked 'I've just been there you silly woman,' but it came out as 'wee, wee, splink, splink!'

She relocated to the highest beam and warbled down at Matilda Peabody who gave her a surprised stare and then went on with her pulverising. Mabel thought she seemed angry and not just because a stray swallow had taken up residence in her house.

She'd been there a while when the Peabody eldest son came in and threw down his boots.

Matilda gave him an evil stare.

"I've been in the river setting the traps. They're wet."

"Stick 'em by the fire then and don't get in the way."

"Eels are in the trough."

"Alright."

Her son, whose name was Thomas, threw himself down on the bed by the wall.

"Heard the news?"

"No... What?"

"Master Greathouse is dead!"

Matilda spun round as if her son had poked her in the back

"What?"

"Dead...Your little bit on the side is dead."

"How dare you?"

"Or rather, YOU were *his* little bit weren't you?"

Matilda Peabody slumped down on a stool.

"Dead? How?"

Her son was enjoying himself. "Someone swiped him with a hard and nasty sharp object, I'm told. Got no back to his head now."

Matilda eyed her eldest son with contempt.

"You're enjoying this aren't you?"

"Yeah!" Thomas lay down fully on his bed and put his hands behind his head.

"Nasty sight, by all accounts."

"You are a wicked boy!"

Thomas jumped up.

"Oh nothing about you being a wicked woman then?"

"Wha...?"

"Doing the jig-jig with Master Greathouse when Da was slaving his guts out keeping this house going...eh...?"

Matilda turned from him.

"Get out!"

"You forget. It's my house now."

Mabel could see Matilda working herself up. Her bosom heaving, she turned, her eyes full of tears.

"I loved him... You know I loved him..."

"Father? Nah... You never did."

"I loved Edward... you know I did. In fact, for your information, I was going to go and live with him. In his house. Help him in his business. Leave you, you selfish clod headed bastard. We had talked about getting married."

"Well if I'm a bastard, you know who's to blame for that don't you?"

Matilda shrieked and launched herself at her son with fists designed to hurt him.

They didn't, he merely got hold of her wrists and forced her to her knees.

Then he took a hand to her face.

Slap!

"So now you've nowhere else to go but here. Better be nice to me."

Mabel had seen enough. She launched herself from her perch and flew at Thomas, feet outstretched. She quickly realised that this wasn't a very swallow-like manoeuvre. She wasn't a peregrine or a sparrowhawk. This was a swallow preparing to land, not fight or kill.

But it was enough, the man stepped back.

"Bloody bird! Curse you!"

Mabel kept flying, until he reached for his mother's besom and gave her a mighty thwack.

The back draught knocked her down and he made for her, with outstretched murderous hands as she lay on the beaten floor, dazed.

Suddenly, he folded, his eyes rolled up in his head and he fell.

"If I've killed you, so be it," said a very tearful Matilda Peabody, a rolling pin in her hand.

She picked up poor Mabel's stunned body and stroked her smooth blue-black back.

"Oh poor little thing."

Mabel struggled.

"Thank you," said Matilda. Then she walked out into the sunshine and threw up her hands letting Mabel go.

"Thank you..." she said once more.

"Thank *you*," said Mabel.

But all Matilda heard was "chuckerchuckerchucker."

*****

That was pretty conclusive. Mistress Peabody wouldn't kill Master Greathouse. Her future happiness depended on him. They were going to be married. Did Mabel believe this?

Well, it was certain that Mistress Peabody was upset at the death of Edward Greathouse. And *she* believed it.

But... it all depended upon the truthfulness of the man. Did he intend to do right by Mistress Peabody when it seemed he had quite a few other lovers in the village?

More eavesdropping was necessary.

Should she do it this evening? Mabel was feeling a little frail now after her argument with a brush.

She vowed to fly the quickest route home but for some reason she didn't manage to get there.

She landed on a tree close by the Peabody cott and preened her feathers. What was wrong? Had some of them been damaged in the tussle?

Her wing muscles hurt and she decided she must have sustained an injury when she fell to the ground. No doubt it was bruised and she'd find a nasty spot on her arm when she changed back into a woman.

In rather an absent way, she watched as Mistress Peabody exited the cottage. She walked like a woman in a dream, looking neither right nor left.

No... she hadn't killed Edward. Of that Mabel was sure.

She decided to follow at a distance and see where the woman was going.

Matilda made for the river. Mabel puzzled. She had no bucket, jug or dish in which to collect water.

The swallow landed on a dead tree, which was all twiggy and spiky and kept very still.

She watched as Matilda searched around for some large stones. What did she want with those? Mabel hopped nearer.

Now the woman had closed her eyes and was praying or it looked like it.

This lasted a little while. Mabel looked round. It was a lonely place. There was no one out and about within a furlong or more. She had a terrible feeling she knew what the woman was about to do.

And she was right.

Matilda, with her skirt full of rocks, walked into the river, heading for the deepest pool. The river in itself wasn't very deep over most of its length but here and there were deeper pools where lived fish like pike and the eels which Thomas had been collecting that day. She saw one of his traps still hiding there.

Matilda waded in deeper.

"Oh God... What shall I do?" said Mabel with an anguished 'chuckerchuckerchucker.'

Mabel flew down and made a few passes above the drowning woman but it was no good, she couldn't be deterred.

"Right." Mabel landed on the bank, took a quick look round and spun. "I want to be a powerful swan."

Bubbles were now showing where Matilda Peabody had gone.

Mabel's neck grew gracefully arched, sprouting exquisite white feathers. Her nose grew a horny hood of black and her mouth turned to a bill of yellow red. Her feet became webbed. Even before she had completed her transformation, Mabel waded—or more correctly waddled—into the river and dived. Mabel knew that swans didn't really dive. They merely upended themselves but this was an emergency.

"Where was she?"

Mabel called her name. "Matilda..?" But it simply came out as a rasping 'prrrow.'

She dived again and realised she could see so amazingly well under the grey green water.

There was Matilda, on the bottom, clutching her rocks to her, bubbles rising from her mouth and nose.

"Oh... God... let me be able to help her." Mabel could not swim as a human.

She took Matilda's clothes in her strong brightly coloured beak and pulled. And pulled again. Matilda was not in any state to argue with her.

The rocks fell from her clothes and Mabel managed to get a purchase on her skirt, pulling for all she was worth. The woman rose a little in the water for she was not totally saturated and there was still some air in her blue kirtle to hold her up.

Mabel managed to get herself underneath Matilda's body and every sinew screaming, she lifted her in the water.

They broke the surface with a splash.

Now Mabel changed her hold and began to pull Matilda to the bank. It was hard work.

She towed and waited, holding the woman up whilst she recovered to do it again.

And at last they made the plant strewn bank.

It was not enough though. Matilda needed help.

Panting with her exertions and very tired with all her transformations of the day, Mabel looked around quickly, spun and said, "I wish to be a woman again."

*****

She left Mistress Peabody on the bank and ran to the nearest cottage.

She tripped over the threshold and burst in on Master Miller and his wife and children eating their supper.

"Oh Master Geoffrey... come quickly, please."

Geoffrey Miller bounced up from his seat.

"Mabel?"

"I have just seen Mistress Peabody fall into the river and I didn't know what to do."

"Fall into the river?" He looked at his wife. "Where?"

"The other side, sir, of your water wheel. About one hundred yards."

"Oh," said his wife Eleanora, "It's deep there."

"I think she was suddenly taken ill and she fell."

The miller took up a long staff and rushed out through the door.

"We must fish her out."

"I got her out." Mabel realised that she was not at all wet but even though Geoffrey looked at her oddly, he didn't take issue with her and ran on. "But she doesn't look good, sir."

Mabel could not tell anyone that she had seen Mistress Peabody try to take her own life. It was expressly forbidden by the church and those who did were committing the terrible sin of *felo de se*. Not only that but it was against the law. You could be hanged for it. And you certainly would not be allowed to be buried in consecrated ground, were it known you had killed yourself.

They reached the woman quickly and the miller turned her over and started to hit her back with loud thwacks. "Come on Matty, there now... let's get that horrible river from out of your lungs."

"Here," said Mistress Miller, breathily. "A drink of water." She offered a cup to Matilda's lips.

Mabel and Master Geoffrey looked at each other in undisguised disbelief.

"Water, woman? She's had a surfeit of water!"

"Yes, Geoffrey."

Eleanora Miller looked at the water in the cup.

"Oh..." She looked surprised. "My water is a funny colour. I don't think it's fit to drink!"

Her husband smirked. He was used to her stupidities.

"What happened Mabel?"

"I was taking an evening stroll along the river bank when I saw Mistress Peabody put her hand to her head and simply keel over and fall in."

"Where? Show me."

Mabel was worried. What if Master Miller realised that Matilda had stepped from the bank into the water and waded out of her own volition? She took him to a part of the bank which was clear of any footprints.

"Hmm."

"And you took her out...?"

Mabel stared at the man.

"I waded in here..." Mabel did exactly that and was soon very wet, "and I grabbed her clothes and pulled her out... here." Here was where the bank was wet with her attempt at rescue as a swan.

"Hmm." He picked up the limp woman.

"We had better get her home and into dry clothes and warm by a fire."

"Yes."

As he carried the unconscious but alive Matilda to the lane, Miller looked back at Mabel.

"He doesn't believe me," said Mabel to herself out loud.

"Well done, Mabel," he cried as he staggered off with his burden.

CHAPTER FOUR
~ THE DEAD MAN'S LOVES? ~

As Mabel had predicted, her arm was painful and showed a bruise from where she had been hit by Thomas Peabody.

Upon the next day she had to go to work at the manor and she dragged herself from bed with wobbly legs and looked at the new day with bleary eyes. She was so tired and could hardly put one foot in front of the other. What's more she couldn't put her arms above her head; a legacy of her tussle as a swan, with the limp body of Mistress Peabody, she guessed.

On her way across the green, she met Master Smitan, the local blacksmith.

"Ah Mabel... our heroine!"

"What?" said Mabel, a little sharply.

"Mistress Peabody. You saved her life with your quick thinking."

He swiped at a fly passing his face.

"Oh..." he jumped back, startled. "I thought it was a bee."

"No... simply a fly." Mabel was puzzled why such a simple thing would rattle him so.

He recovered quickly.

"I hate bees..."

"Oh? Why's that."

"I just do. You managed to save her life I hear?"

"Oh... oh... yes... Yes. I'm glad she's recovered."

"She's apparently a little befuddled about what happened to her. She says..."Simon Smitan chuckled, "that a swan rescued her."

"Oh..."

"She thinks you are a swan, Mabel! Fancy that."

"Haha." Mabel forced out a merry laugh. "The mind plays tricks you know, Master Smitan, when you have a head full of water."

"Indeed it must." And he went on his way.

'I must be careful,' said Mabel to herself. 'One of these days someone will spot me.'

Things were quiet at work that day... good job it was, for Mabel found herself nodding a couple of times, over her records. She was glad when her tasks were done and she could go home.

A good meal of some cheese and sallet and some more little strawberries which she grew in her garden plot and Mabel was feeling better.

Now, who else was on her suspect list?

She needed to see how Mistress Head was this fine evening. Might she give anything away about a relationship with the dead man?

Mabel stood in her yard and turned three times. "I wish to be a sparrow."

She had noticed that no one took much notice of sparrows. They could hop around in doorways and peck at spilled grain but no one chased them away.

Off she went to the house of the reeve.

He was away but Mistress Head was there, sitting in the doorway shelling boiled eggs as she chatted to her neighbour, Amicia Hardhand.

"They're out getting the body now. To bring it home. The coroner wouldn't let it be moved until he'd seen it," said the reeve's wife, Alys. She sniffed. "It can be buried but not in consecrated ground of course because of the Pope's ban..."

Amicia nodded, twirling her distaff with practised fingers.

"Sad he has no family."

"No..." Alys sniffled and gulped back a sob, "No, none at all."

"What will happen to his property now, do you think?"

Alys finished her eggs and wiped her fingers. She strode out into the yard and threw the shells out onto the midden, narrowly missing treading on a small brown sparrow called Mabel.

"I don't know. Maybe there's a will. Maybe someone from another place will take it."

"I always thought of him as a bit of an idiot," said Amicia. "But I'm surprised he never married. Some woman surely would be very happy to take on his large portion, idiot or no."

Alys Head's eyebrows flew up. "How did you know...?"

"Rich and an idiot..."

The reeve's wife let that go. "You know of course that he was tupping every woman from Chisbury to Chilton?" said Amicia Hardhand.

Alys swallowed, Mabel crept nearer.

"Ah... really?"

"He had *such* a reputation..."

Suddenly Alys turned and said with her back to her prey, "You were never tempted then? You with your puny husband and hardly a penny to your name?"

Amicia Hardhand stepped back.

"No, I most certainly was not."

There was a stony silence.

"And you...?"

Mistress Head turned back. "Absolutely not."

Haha! Haha! Mabel noticed that Alys Head had her fingers crossed close to her back. Everyone knew that meant you were telling a lie.

Mistress Head took the eggs into the house and with no goodbye, she shut the door.

'Well that's another one,' said Mabel. "I knew there was something fishy there.'

She lifted off and rose up into a hawthorn bush to think.

'There must be quite a few husbands in the area wanting this man dead,' she thought. She watched as Mistress Hardhand floated off up the lane. 'Was *she* another one, despite her protestations?'

Mabel flew off in a rather haphazard way, not really knowing where she was going. She'd noticed before that sparrows flew in short bursts, here, there and everywhere without any real purpose to their flying. Except for finding food of course. And they were always in company.

Landing with a bit of a bounce on an outstretched briar protruding from a hedge, Mabel came face to face with a rather smart male sparrow. He was a very handsome specimen with bright black and brown plumage.

"Cheep, cheep. Cheepcheepcheep?"

"Cheep off," said Mabel, looking fierce.

"Cheep? CHEEP!"

"Most certainly not!"

She flew off in the direction of Master Greathouse's home which was the last building in the village.

The male sparrow followed.

"CHEEP! Cheepycheepycheepy... cheeeep?"

Mabel thought that sounded rather lascivious.

"Look, I know what your game is. But I'm not interested, alright?"

This came out as a high pitched, 'Tweet, tweety tweet.'

Master Sparrow took a flying leap at her.

"Oh no you don't, mate!"

Out came her claws. Peck, peck went her beak. They tumbled over and over on the dusty earth, screeching.

Eventually he got the message and retired to fluff up his feathers.

Mabel beat a hasty exit to the overhang of Master Greathouse's dwelling and looked round. The door was closed. All the windows were shuttered but if she was clever she could get in.

There was no smoke coming from the smoke hole. This meant no fire was lit.

She took herself up to the apex of the thatch and sidled up to the gap.

No one could see. In she went.

It was very dark in the house and she'd never been in here before. This was a building of two stories with a hall between two wings, the upper floor of which was accessed by rudimentary stairs and a gallery.

She flew down and shook her feathers. Ack! A strong smell of soot was coming from her! She gave a sparrow sneeze.

Mabel stood on the table which lay at one end of the hall and poked about with her beak.

"Yum..." There were a few crumbs of bread there. She pecked at them. They were as hard as filberts.

And so was the loaf which had been left out. Mabel realised that the bread was days old. And yet it was only yesterday she'd found the body. Was this his dinner of that day? Or was it older? She needed to find out when he'd last been seen.

Then another thing struck her.

His body.

The man had been lying out in the forest for a while, she thought. She had no expert knowledge of how to gauge when a man had died but she was fairly certain that maggots did not suddenly appear on a dead body.

The flies had to find the decomposing corpse; that admittedly could take mere moments, but then they needed to lay eggs and *then* the maggots hatched. That she was sure, took a little time.

Interesting. She needed to find out where all her suspects were when Edward had been killed.

She needed to know when he'd last been seen.

When had *she* last seen him?

In the churchyard on Sunday. Hale and hearty and making eyes at Mistress Peabody. Upon reflection, perhaps *her* story was true.

Hmm. She flew up to the smoke hole. Ah it was easier to get in than out. There was a slight overhang. She was just trying to claw her way over it when the door opened and four men came in.

Mabel froze.

The four men were carrying the body of Master Greathouse on a blanket.

*****

The reeve was directing proceedings.

"Alf, swipe that off the table. We'll lie him there."

The foremost carrier pushed a cup and the stale loaf onto the floor. The loaf bounced like a football. The cup clattered and rolled under the table.

Master Greathouse was manhandled onto the board.

"Phew!" Stephen Meadow wiped his perspiring brow.

One man, whom Mabel recognised as the chap who dug the graves in the churchyard, Alard Pickup, began to unfold the cloth wrapping the body.

"Oh no you don't!" shouted the reeve, leaping forward. "He's been dead five days; he stinks like a cabbage fart! Leave him where he is."

"Five days?" thought Mabel. "That makes it Monday when he was killed."

"Did the coroner say that?" asked Peter Corngold, the blond headed ploughman.

"No, the Constable's doctor friend from the town. He's a clever bugger. He can work out how long someone has been dead and if they've been moved."

"And was he?"

"Yes... was he?" chirped Mabel from her lofty perch. "I want to know." They took no notice of her.

"Aye he was. He wasn't killed where he lay."

"So where do we think he was killed?"

"The doctor seemed to think it was probably here in the village."

"What? And someone got him all the way out to Chisbury Copse?"

"You'd need a cart for that," said the fourth man; the only man present who owned a cart.

They all looked at him.

"AH... Archard... trust you to think of that," said the reeve sarcastically.

"I'm only sayin'."

'Hmm. Who has a cart besides Archard Carter?' said Mabel with a cheep, cheep.

"How many carts in the village, Archard?" asked Corngold.

The man sucked his teeth.

"I got two. Miller's got one. The church has one... you do, don't you, Alard?"

"Yep... we have one, a handcart, in the old shed at the back of the priest's house. Bit ramshackle though."

"Get a body to the forest?" asked the reeve.

"Get a body anywhere in the *churchyard*," laughed Alard. "I doubt if it'll manage into the forest."

The men moved off.

"Course... ol' Simon Smitan has got one."

"Aw c'mon!" said Stephen Meadow. "Theym'z best friends. Edward and Simon. He wouldn't hurt him."

"Nah... you're right."

"They've been the best of chums since they were lads."

"Nope. Hard to see Simon Smitan taking a chunk outta Ed's head."

They were making for the door and Mabel saw her chance. Off she flew and squeezed herself between Alard and Stephen and rose up into the hawthorn.

"The bloody birds round here are getting mighty frisky," said Stephen.

"Season for friskiness ain't it?" said Corngold.

"Cheepy cheepy cheep," said Mabel's admirer from the branch above her.

"Oh cheep off!" shouted Mabel in her most authoritative sparrow voice.

There was a glint in the cock's eye.

The hen called Mabel waited for the men to round the corner, looked around, flew to the floor, turned deosil three times and gave the cock sparrow the fright of his life! He fell off his perch!

*****

On her way home, because she wasn't really looking where she was going with her head down and thinking, watching the swish of her kirtle, Mabel bumped into Master Simon Smitan again, the village farrier and blacksmith.

"Oooh. Mistress Mabel. I am so sorry."

"No. No, my fault. I wasn't watching where I was going." She'd always thought this man a rather savoury dish, with his height, his curly dark auburn hair and muscles on muscles.

She cleared her throat. "I am so sorry about your friend."

His tanned face lost its smile.

"Aye. It was a shock, I can tell you."

"They've just brought his body back to his house. I saw them."

"Ah... yes..."

Simon turned and walked with Mabel towards her cottage.

"He's my best friend you know...? *Was* my best friend. Since we were young. We did everything together."

"Oh that is sad." Mabel was a little younger than these men and so didn't remember them as children.

"And the saddest thing is, I am getting married soon, next week in fact and... poor Ed won't be there to..."

Mabel hadn't heard about any wedding plans but then she was a bit of a loner. Who would tell her? And no banns had been published in church which was how she usually got to find out, because of the Pope's prohibition.

Mabel walked along beside him trying to think who he might be going to marry.

"Of course with the Pope's proscriptions, we can't have a proper wedding at the church but Emma and I are going to do it anyway."

"Ah, you're going to marry Emma Hartshorn?"

"Yes, that's right. Soon—and now, Edward won't be—there to see it." His voice wavered and Mabel thought he was close to tears.

"Well, I wish you every happiness... despite the... sadness you have experienced, Master Simon."

"Thank you. Thank you." He wiped his eye.

"In fact it was Ed who introduced me to Emma."

"Oh did he?"

"Yes. She worked at the inn and Ed thought it would be nice if we..." This time he turned away from her in his grief.

"You will be at his funeral? Such as it will be."

"I'll help carry the bier."

"That would be a nice gesture."

"It's a pity that he can't be buried in consecrated ground and we can't say a mass for the repose of his soul but... we can still do him proud."

"I'm sure." What else could she say?

But one thing which she desperately wanted to say just popped out.

"Have you any idea who killed him, Master Simon?"

"Oh I have an idea."

"Oh my! Really?"

He turned to face her.

"You'll hear a lot of gossip about Edward. How he had been involved with many women in the forest..."

"From Chisbury to Chilton, I've heard it said."

"Ah well. That would be about right. Ed could never stay faithful to one woman. Why he'd never married you see. He thought it unfair to withhold himself from so many women."

"Oh... rather a high opinion of himself then? " said Mabel with no stopper to her mouth. "Oh forgive me, Master Simon... to speak so ill of him when..."

"No you're quite right." He laughed through his nose, "he had several lovers and none of them had any cause to be upset about it."

"They all knew that they weren't the only one?" said Mabel.

"Oh no... I don't think so... I don't think that was the case... all bar... no I can't say."

"Who? Who knew about the others?"

"Ah no... it wouldn't be fair."

"Fair to whom? Edward or the woman?"

They were approaching Mabel's house and Master Simon stopped a few feet from the door.

"Surely if you know something you ought to tell the authorities."

'Oh no... Tell me... tell me first,' said Mabel to herself with an excited skip of her heart.

"Well... he was having difficulty with one woman in particular who thought that he ought to marry her. She was getting very possessive and..."

"Mistress Peabody."

"How did you know?"

"A lucky guess."

Simon took her upper arm in his considerable grasp and bowed his head to Mabel's, whispering.

"It may be nothing and I have no wish to accuse her of anything but..."

"You think she may have found out that she was not the only one and killed him in a wild passion?"

He straightened up. He towered over little Mabel.

"It's not impossible."

"It's hard to see Mistress Peabody in a wild passion."

"Who knows?"

"Hmm," said Mabel as he walked away. She looked up at the

darkening sky and mouthed.

"Something isn't right here. I can feel it in my bones."

*****

Next day after her work at the manor, she had a little weeding and preparation to do in her garden. Bending her back she did not hear Mistress Peabody slowly come up behind her.

"Ooh!" Mabel jumped. "You gave me a fright."

"I'm so sorry. I didn't mean to…"

Mabel slapped her hands together to rid them of earth. "Come, come and sit with me in the house. I have just finished making my last elderflower concoction and I need to try it out. Would you like to try it?"

Matilda gave her a shy smile, "I would very much like that."

Sitting in Mabel's little hall by the light of the fire, Mistress Peabody wrung her hands together.

"I came to thank you for rescuing me the other day. I am so sorry it has taken me so long but I wasn't feeling well and this is the first time…"

"It's alright. I understand."

"This is a very good elderflower drink."

"Thank you. As you know we have many elder trees here surrounding the village and even though they're considered unlucky, I feel I'm lucky to be able to gather their blossoms just feet from my door."

"Is that what you were doing when you found me? Looking for blossoms?"

Mabel thought she'd better stick to the story she'd given to the reeve.

"No, I'd just walked by the river, that's all. And I saw you fall in."

Mistress Peabody's mouth twitched as if she'd smile but it came to nothing.

"Except I didn't."

"You didn't drown, no. I fished you out."

"Mabel..." Matilda looked down at her locked hands. "You know that I did not fall."

"Did not fall? Then... how?"

"I walked into the river because I didn't want to live. I wanted to drown."

Mabel again had to appear as if she was shocked.

"Oh no, Mistress Matilda... Please..." She crossed herself. "You mustn't say that."

"You know I did because you must have seen me walking into the water."

Mabel's heart began to pound. 'No...Please don't let her have seen me change into a swan.'

The woman chuckled, a sound very much at odds with her facial expression.

"I thought that a white swan rescued me but it must have been you."

"I did throw off my kirtle and was down to my white shift... so that might be what you saw..." lied Mabel.

"Ah... of course."

Matilda took another sip of her cordial.

"You have added honey I think?"

"I have. I have a few hives you see. I love my bees."

"It's very nice."

"Please do not tell anyone that you tried to take your own life. Yes, *I* know it, but no one else needs to know," said Mabel, taking Matilda's hand. "It's our secret."

"You are so kind."

Mabel decided, if she could, to get a confession from Mistress Peabody.

"Why did you decide to kill yourself? It seemed to me a very sudden decision."

"Edward."

Mabel's heart jumped and a rush of blood made her light headed. "His murder? Do you know something about it?"

"No, no nothing at all... but I felt that now he's gone... I *feel* that now he's gone there is nothing more left for me to live for."

"Oh no... That can't be true."

"You know that he and I were... lovers...?"

'You and half the village,' said Mabel's brain but she kept her mouth closed.

Mabel patted her hair. "No... no I didn't." She got up to pour more elderflower mixture.

"But surely that was not a terrible thing because neither of you were married. You are a widow and he was a bachelor."

"We were planning on marrying."

"Oh what a shame... I mean a shame that you didn't get a chance."

"No."

"Had he actually asked you?"

"He was about to. It was going to happen any time soon."

"Oh how sad."

"And now... now I have nothing to live for."

"Oh please don't say that."

The woman shrugged. "You are a very sweet girl."

"I am twenty four now. A girl no longer. And we are friends. I can help you through this."

Matilda shook her head. "No one can help me."

Mabel made a grab for both her hands.

"Mistress Matilda... tell me... did *you* kill Master Edward?"

The woman made a sort of squeal. "I couldn't kill him. I couldn't, no. How could you think that?"

"Not even if you were very angry with him for...for seeing another woman?"

Tears sprang to Mistress Peabody's eyes. "I know that he had been seeing others. I know it but lately he had given them up. It was just me."

"Are you certain of that?"

"As certain as any woman can be of any man."

'Ah well, not very certain then,' said Mabel to herself.

Matilda Peabody stood up.

"I must go home. I have food to prepare."

"For your son?"

"Yes, for my son."

"*He* didn't like the idea of you marrying again, did he?"

"How do you know ...?"

"A guess. Because you are still a young woman. If you married you might have had children and..."

"No... no... it will not happen now, will it?"

'No. It won't,' thought Mabel.

There was someone else with a motive for killing Edward Greathouse. Young Peabody. If his mother had had children...where would that leave him?

Mabel watched the woman walk up the path.

Then a thought came to her. Why now? Why was Edward Greathouse murdered now? He'd been having affairs for a long time. Was there something that had happened recently which made him a target now and not before?

She watched as Stephen Meadow strolled past. "Ah, our water baby."

"Hello Stephen."

He stopped and cocked his head. "Something puzzles me."

"A lot puzzles you, Stephen. It's the size of your brain compared to the size of your pizzle."

He grimaced and poked out his tongue.

"You can't swim, Mabel!"

"I learned."

"Pah!" he said and walked on by.

*****

That night Mabel decided that she would venture out for a short while and become an owl so that she could listen in to the conversations in the Hartshorn family home.

Emma Hartshorn was a pretty blonde girl with apple cheeks and sweet red lips. Many men in the village had had designs on her but whilst she made eyes at them all, she had chosen no one, as far as Mabel was aware, to marry. Until now. She wanted to make sure that Simon was telling the truth.

If they were being married as soon as Simon had intimated, then talk would all be about the wedding, thought Mabel.

Shortly after dusk, a brown little owl lighted upon a fence at the back of the Hartshorn family home and sunk its claws into the wood.

Creeping nearer to the open door, Mabel stretched her already marvellous ears.

Four people were sitting inside chatting.

Master Hartshorn was a forester, like all his extended and forest wide family. His wife was a weaver and worked at home for someone in the town of Ramsbury. The son was the younger child about ten, who tended their plot and Emma was a laundress in the manor. Mabel knew her quite well for she was in charge of all the cloth in the manor.

Mistress Hartshorn was speaking.

"That's right Em. Just sew that bit there and then we'll try it."

"Ma, we won't see very well. It's going dark."

"There's enough light to see by. Come over here to the fire."

"How many more times are you going to alter that dress?" said a bored young voice. Thierry Hartshorn.

"Leave the girls alone, Ti. They're enjoying themselves. We'll all be in bed soon anyway."

"Aw the bloody gnats!"

"Shut the door then, Ti," said his father, Wilfred. "They're coming in attracted to the light."

The door banged shut.

Damn! Now Mabel could hear very little.

On silent wings she glided up to the thatch and walked carefully down on her talons.

There was a small gap between the thatch and the door and Mabel clung to it, listening and peering into the house.

"Isn't this too long, ma?"

"I'll take it up a bit more."

"You know that pink doesn't suit you. Why do you want to be married in pink?" said Thierry.

"Oh for goodness sake. It's her wedding. She'll have what she wants. What would you know anyway?"

Ti giggled. "I hope Si fancies you in pink. It makes you look like a boiled crayfish!"

So they *were* to be married.

"Will you stop being so unkind," said the elder Hartshorn. "Push off."

Suddenly there was a swishing sound and the door opened outwards.

"Pushing off, I'm going for a piss in the privy."

Mabel was flattened behind the door between the wood panels and the hard daub of the wall, as the door banged.

"Poof! That'll teach me to eavesdrop." True eavesdropping, she realised, laughing from her position on the ground and the sound came out as "gwook!"

CHAPTER FIVE ~ EAVESDROPPING

The next day was the manor's wash day and there was much to do. Mabel didn't, of course, do the washing herself but she had to supervise and oversee it all.

At dinner time she went to sit under the large oak tree which grew by the gate of the manor to eat her bread and cheese. It was a very warm day. She pulled her fingers through her hair and watched as a cloud of gnats hovered just above her. There must have been a hundred of them and never once did they bump into each other in their jiggling about. How clever. It was as if they were all dancing. She must try being a gnat one day and see if she could work out how they did it.

Into her vision came John Swineherd driving a couple of his pigs along the lane. She lifted a hand in greeting. He reciprocated. As her eye absentmindedly travelled along the road, she saw a furtive Tom Peabody, dash into the house of the Hartshorn's.

Now what was he doing looking so guilty?

Tom was the same age as Mabel. She had been born in December and he had come into the world a few days later. To her mind, he'd always been a selfish boy and, from what she'd seen lately, it looked as if he'd made a selfish man.

Mabel cast a quick look round. She stood nonchalantly, went

behind the tree, turned three times and said, "I wish to be a butterfly." In her mind she was imagining the lovely peacock or the pretty little blues which dotted about the village.

However, she had misjudged the season and as her body began to change, she realised that she was growing sooty brown wings with little yellow rings on them.

Ah well... it didn't matter what kind of butterfly she was, really. In fact it was probably better to be a ringlet than a peacock because it would be easier for her to blend into her surroundings.

She fluttered off to the open door of the cottage and landed on the jamb. Ah no! She knew how dangerous doors could be. She had a sore nose and forehead from last night to prove it, so she flew just a few feet into the cottage and landed on a shelf.

Tom was there in the shadows with his arm around the waist of Emma Hartshorn.

"Aw, Em. You can't do it. Please... don't do it..." he was saying.

Emma pulled away. "I'm doing it so you'd better get used to it."

"Em..."

"No! Tom!"

"You're going ahead with it even though Si's best friend has just been murdered?"

"What's that got to do with it?"

"Well... I thought as a mark of respect..."

"Of course we're thinking of Edward. But we are still alive and he wouldn't have wanted us to be unhappy."

"Oh you know that for certain do you?"

Emma gave Tom a strange look. As a butterfly, Mabel was puzzled by it. But her human brain said, 'that is sarcastic disbelief.'

"What do you mean? You're just jealous."

"Too right, I'm just jealous. *I* want you for my wife."

"We've been through this time and time again, Tom. Simon can give me a much better life than you. What have you got? Nothing."

'Ah,' said the little brown butterfly, 'She is marrying one man and is in love with another.'

"I might have... one day."

Emma flounced off. "No, Tom!"

"You know I'll never give up."

Emma grimaced at Tom. It was the most ugly expression. "Oh... so you'll pester me just as your silly mother pestered Edward, eh?"

"My mother is stupid. Edward was never going to marry her. Not in a month of Sundays."

"Just as I am not going to marry *you*."

"So you are saying that what we had... have, is not a... relationship."

"It was a relationship. Now it isn't."

"You can't throw away four years like that... that's not fair."

"Of course I can."

Tom backed away and looked deeply at his erstwhile love. "And you'll do the same to Simon?"

Emma flounced off, flicking her long blonde hair. "Whatever do you mean?"

"Me... and Simon... got anyone else in tow? Someone with whom you might have an extra marital affair eh? Once you marry Simon."

"Of course not. Don't be foolish. I love Simon."

"PAH! You love who is going to be the right person to give you what you want at any one time."

Tom had moved quite close to the shelf on which Mabel hid. She quickly scurried behind a jar of pickled cucumbers.

"That is a wicked thing to say... take it back."

"I will not."

"I have to get back to work."

"Go then."

"I will."

Emma gave Tom one last scathing look and flounced out of the door. She was a good flouncer, thought Mabel. I must practice that! Flouncing.

Tom bunched up his fists.

Mabel peered around the jar.

Suddenly one of those fists came punching out of nowhere and the pottery jar of pickled cucumbers, a jug of oil and a wooden butter pat went flying.

"Argh!" cried Mabel in her butterfly voice as she flew up into the rafters. It took her quite a while to come down again.

By which time everyone had gone.

She too needed to get back to work.

*****

"Oh Mabel, what have you done?"

Once Mabel turned back into herself, she realised that as a butterfly she had sustained damage to one of her eyes. She must have been hit or got verjuice from the pickle in her eye for it was painful and sore. She was bathing it at the riverbank and trying to get a good look at it in the water's reflective surface. Elinor Poorgrass, the young daughter of the Lord's Marshal, was looking over her shoulder.

"Oh I just had a bit of an accident that's all."

"Here let me look." She took Mabel's head between two hands. This girl was the closest Mabel had to a real friend in the village.

"Oh dear...you'll have a black eye ere long. What happened?"

"You won't believe it but I dropped a jar of pickled cucumbers and one flew up and hit me."

"Then your cucumbers are way too hard!"

Mabel laughed.

She got up from her knees and walked slowly back with Elinor to the manor.

"You're friends with Emma Hartshorn aren't you?" she said.

"Well, I know her. She's about the same age as me except of course her father is a humble forester and mine is..."

"In charge of the lord's travel arrangements...yes I know."

"Why?"

"You know she's getting married soon."

"I had heard she was marrying the farrier. Yes." Now, this was said in a certain indefinable undertone which piqued Mabel's interest.

She peered at Elinor with her one good eye. "Meaning what?"

"Meaning she is marrying Master Smitan."

"Marrying Master Smitan... when... she'd actually rather have....?"

A sly smile crossed Elinor's mouth. "Ah, yes I see what you mean."

"Well then?"

"There was talk that she would marry Alfred Stockman."

Mabel coughed. "Stockman?"

"Yes. They were walking out for a long time last year."

"Oh I must have missed that. I thought that she had a penchant for Tom Peabody."

Elinor scoffed. "Well yes... she did rather like him for a while but her father soon put paid to that."

"Oh?"

"He'd never allow her to marry a Peabody."

"He wouldn't?"

"The Hartshorn men hate the Peabody men... don't you know that?"

"Ah... well... I keep myself to myself."

"Her father caught them kissing behind the barn and that was that. It cooled."

'Aha... I don't think so, somehow,' said Mabel to herself. I think it's a little more recent and much hotter than that!'

"So what does Alfred think about Emma marrying Master Smitan?"

"I dunno. Can't say much though can he?"

"Perhaps not. He's just a servant whereas Simon is free and his own man."

"Precisely. Personally, I think she's making the right decision."

"Oh you do? Marry for money and not for love?" Elinor gave her such a look as if to say, 'Well... wouldn't you?'

"Alfred is much older than her, isn't he?"

"He is, by nearly ten years, I think," said Elinor. She came close to

Mabel's head and whispered. "I caught him kissing her once."

"Alfred kissing...?"

"...Emma. My oh my, it was a passionate embrace. It made the blood rush to my cheeks."

"You saw Alfred kissing Emma? Where... when?"

"In the manor garden about a week ago."

"Oh my! So recently?"

"Well... yes... come to think of it."

They were now entering the manor gates and Mabel was about to run down the stairs to the storeroom where she was off to check the supplies of spices for the kitchens.

"And you think that this relationship is over...?"

"Well... she IS marrying Master Smitan."

"Oh dear... there may be trouble ahead..."

"Mabel! You don't think that Alfred murdered Master Greathouse?"

"Oh Elinor... what possible reason could *he* have for killing Master Greathouse?"

"Well, it's well known Edward was a bit of a, you know... a bit of a..."

"Philanderer? Have you any reason to think that Greathouse has also kissed Emma?"

Elinor shrugged.

A voice rode over their conversation.

"Mistress Elinor. You'll have to let this drop."

"I beg your pardon?" said Elinor.

The voice came from behind the door to a storeshed.

Master Smitan stepped out.

Mabel looked up quickly. "Master Blacksmith. It's rude to listen to others' conversations, you know." As she said this her cheeks flushed. Well, what had she been doing this very day?

He smiled a very winning smile. "But if it concerns my beloved then, I must overhear and then say something. All this speculation does no good."

"Well then, you may have your say."

"Emma and Master Stockman. You must let it go, Mistress Elinor. There's nothing in it. I spoke to him the other day and he apologised."

They all looked at each other for a heartbeat then Mabel said, "You *knew* about it?"

"I saw them. I saw them together and I saw the kiss you are referring to, Mistress Elinor, and it was not really a problem."

Elinor bridled. "Well, I think it would be."

"Alfred was drunk. He always gets like that when he's drunk. He's an idiot."

"Perhaps that's why he wasn't successful with Emma. He's an idiot," said Mabel.

"Well you can be a bit of an idiot too, Simon," said Elinor as she walked round him. He kept her in his gaze.

"Yeah... yeah I can," he admitted.

Elinor pointed at him. "He can't stand anyone as much as looking at Emma."

Simon Smitan's handsome face creased. "Well yes... I admit it. She is my love and I can't bear to think of any man looking at her."

Mabel threw Elinor a glance and the girl shrugged. "You're an idiot too."

"Yeah... yeah I am, I know. I am an idiot some of the time. I am. But I'm trying to conquer it and... Emma knows how I feel. She has a bit of a chequered past. So do I to be honest. But from now on... it's just Emma and me."

The two girls looked at each other.

"We had it out... me and Alfred. We did. We're good friends. We've been friends for years. We are not going to let it spoil the friendship. We have been through too many years and things for us not to sort it out... me and Alf."

Elinor looked relieved. "Well, thank Heavens for that!"

The blacksmith nodded and went on his way again.

Elinor ran off up the stairs and Mabel stepped down into the darkness of the undercroft.

"*That* was interesting," she said to herself.

*****

Her head was thumping by the end of the working day and so she took herself off home a little early.

There was no need to go out tonight and frankly she had had enough of playing the investigator for a while. She washed her hair, donned a clean shift and sat with some of her elderflower concoction by the light of her fire.

Cross legged on her bed, her back against the wall, she dozed a little.

And inevitably, she fell asleep.

The fire died down and flickered out. The moon and the stars rose in the sky. The tawny owls in the tree behind her cottage hooted their love song.

Then she woke to a screaming and yelling close by.

Jumping off her bed, she fell to her knees. Her legs had given way and pins and needles began to torment her. She stamped up and down. Too long sitting cross legged.

"Mama!"

She heard an agonised voice repeating, "Mama... mama... No," over and over.

Opening her shutter, she peered out into the darkness.

In the light of the moon, and a couple of flares held by her neighbours, Mabel saw that the fuss and bother was being made by the youngest girl of the Peabody family, Jonetta, who was eight. Her mother, Mistress Peabody, was being held up by the village reeve, Master Head and several people had collected around them.

Then Mabel saw Tom Peabody swagger up. "What's going on?"

Mabel couldn't quite see what was happening and so she decided quickly to change into something which would have the best chance of a good view.

Three turns withershynnes later and Mabel was a barn owl, gliding swiftly out of her window up into an oak tree.

She blinked languorously and looked down.

She heard Tom say, "But it can't be. No..."

"She's admitted to it. I can't do anything but take her and lock her up if she admits to it, can I?" said Master Head.

"Whadaya mean she's admitted to it?"

Master Head rounded on Thomas Peabody. "She admitted, in front of witnesses, that she killed Master Greathouse. In her own words."

"But... she can't have done."

"Why not? Why can't she?"

"Well for a start she loved the bloody man. She'd hardly kill him now, would she?"

Some of the neighbours took in hissing breaths of disbelief. Others groaned. Some shook their heads as if they did believe it but considered it impossible at the same time. Some gave one another knowing looks and winks.

Master Head too was shaking his grey head. "The man was killed around the time of dinner on Sunday. I asked your mother where she was at dinner time."

"She was with us at home."

"And she said she wasn't sure."

"Well, now you know. We're sure. She was with us wasn't she? We were all together. She can't have walked out to Chisbury Copse and killed him."

"Well you would say that... wouldn't you?"

"And what do you mean by that?"

"She says she killed him. You all say she didn't. You're bound to want to lie to save her, aren't you?"

The elder Peabody girl folded her arms under her bosom. "How dare you! We are not liars."

WITHERSHYNNES: IN THE DARK

Mabel sidled along the branch to take in the growing crowd of people collecting around the small family group.

"She was with us, I tell you... no matter what she says," said Tom. "Aw c'mon. She hit me over the head with a rolling pin earlier this week and you might think I'd want to get my revenge and tell on her but..."

"AH! She hit you too did she?"

"Yeah... she did. You goin'a make something of that?"

The reeve drew himself up to his full height. "If I have to. So she has a history of hitting people over the head."

He shouted over his shoulder, "Alfred... get that rolling pin from Mistress Peabody's house... We'll see if it matches the victim's wounds."

"WHAT?" yelled Tom. "She hit me... yes... but I bloody deserved it..." His hand involuntarily went to the back of his head.

'Well done, Thomas,' said the white owl to itself. 'Yes... you did.' It came out as 'ooo ooo.'

"She's never done it before. I'd been goading her. I should'na done it."

"Quite apart from that, she's admitted it. Can't you get that into your thick head?"

'Now', said Mabel to herself, 'why would she do that?'

"I don't know why she's admitted it. But it's a load'a offal, that's what it is. She went nowhere near him."

'Is she confessing to protect someone she thinks *has* done it?' said the white owl.

"She's not in her right mind. She... she... she's..." Thomas was stuttering in his haste and upset..."She's got a head full of water."

"Ah yes... she 'fell' in didn't she?" said the reeve with his tongue in his cheek.

"Other people told you she fell in. Mabel Wetherspring told you. She saw her. Ma's not well. There's something wrong and ma's making it up."

The reeve was beginning to get fed up with the barrage of words.

People who had collected around were nodding and joining in, saying that yes, she wasn't in her right mind. Obviously.

The woman herself said nothing but weakly leaned on the reeve, like the broken and bent stem of a flower, and stared into the night.

"What did she say exactly?" asked a neighbour.

The reeve filled his lungs.

"She came meekly scratching on my door when it got dark. We were all about to go to bed. I opened the door to her. I don't mind saying I was a bit surprised but I let her in. Alys sat her down. She looked very pale... I must say... and in a very weak voice, she said that she needed to tell me that she had killed Master Greathouse."

Mabel was so desperate to ask, 'How did she say she'd done it and where?" but as an owl it wasn't going to be possible."Ooo, ooo, whooo, whoooo?" she said.

"How did she say she'd done it?" asked Master Miller.

"She didn't."

"And you didn't ask?"

"Well no... because she admitted it."

Mabel was puzzled. "And where did she say she'd done it?" she said. "Oooh, oooh whoooo eeerch?" Her question ended in an eerie screech. No one took any notice.

"Did she tell you where they were when she killed him?" asked Mistress Stockman.

"Yes... she did as a matter of fact. I DID ask her that."

"And?"

"They were in his house."

Many people laughed. "Well that's rubbish for a start," said Tom Peabody. "You know full well we searched Edward's house for a weapon and blood and we found NOTHING!"

"Doesn't mean she didn't clean up."

"Oh ma... Stop this nonsense and tell the truth. You're a bit off your noggin, aren't you?"

Mistress Peabody just slumped further and Master Head had to let her fall to the ground gently.

"Tom, I understand... I do. She's your mother, you too Jonetta, and you Mary but... I got my duty to do."

"Look! She's not going anywhere. Give her back to us and we'll make sure she doesn't leave the village and you can make some more inquiries or you can let the constable know... or whatever but, leave her be. It's not goin'ta do her any good lockin' her in the gaol."

This was a tiny lockup in the middle of the village right by the river. It got very damp when the river rose.

Master Head shook his long grey locks. "I can't do that. What if she absconds?"

Mistress Stockman gave the man a severe look. "Does she look like she's able to abscond, you foolish man?"

Now Elinor had come up to the group in her shift, wrapped in a blanket.

"Poor woman. She won't go anywhere," she said, going down onto the ground and putting her arms around Matilda.

"She's shivering."

The reeve saw that slowly his decision was being overturned. He was the most powerful man in the village besides the lord's steward, who hardly ever came out amongst the common men.

But the reeve was rather a weak man. That was why the village had elected him. He was easy to manipulate and manoeuvre.

"Oh by all the holy saints and martyrs, I can see you're all going to go against me." He sighed very loudly. "All right. Take her home and I'll think about it and talk to her tomorrow in the cold light of day."

Jonetta and Mary picked up their mother from the ground.

She rose pliantly.

"But woe betide you all if she isn't there tomorrow for me to question."

Someone gave the reeve a one fingered gesture behind his back and a couple of others giggled.

Master Head spun round. "Find it funny eh? Master Swineherd?"

"No Reeve"

Mabel had heard enough. Tomorrow she'd learn more.

She'd sleep and think... It was often the case that if you went to bed on a problem, the answer would come to you the next day.

Something was bothering her. It was bothering her a lot. She knew without a doubt that Mistress Peabody hadn't killed Master Greathouse. But she did think that perhaps Matilda thought she knew who had. She also knew that Matilda didn't care about her life. If she was hanged for the death of her lover, it wouldn't matter to her at all. Her life was nothing now her love was gone. She wasn't thinking straight, it was true. Mabel could see how awful that would be for her children, Thomas, Jonetta and Mary. But Mabel had a nagging feeling she had missed something. Maybe if she slept, it would come to her and she could present her information to the reeve.

She needed to help poor Matilda Peabody.

Mabel glided on soft and silent wings around the outside of her house and when the coast was clear, she whooshed in through the window.

"I wish to be a woman again."

'Oh how tired I am.' She fell onto her bed, pulled up the covers and fell fast asleep.

WITHERSHYNNES: IN THE DARK

CHAPTER SIX ~ THE LETTER

Mabel woke a little late the next day and rushed around getting dressed, barking her shin on her table.

'Oh Mabel, you never used to be a mass of bruises!' she said to herself. 'It's only since you started becoming animals and investigating Master Greathouse's death.'

The lord was in residence today, moving up from one of his other estates and so everything had to be spic and span and orderly.

She went about her tasks like a whirlwind.

She had all the kitchen, hall and menial staff assembled in a line when the lord clattered into the yard, followed by his lady and children in a coach.

She curtsied. "Welcome home, m'lord."

"Thank you, Mistress Wetherspring," said Sir Robert Stokke, beaming at her. "It's good to be back." He looked round. "I see that you and Henry have everything in good order."

Henry Buttermere, the steward, coughed politely.

"Sir, we have a case for you to look at today, if you will."

"Oh?" The lord seemed a bit put out.

"We have kept the body for you to see and both the coroner and the constable have set their eyes on it. Admittedly at the time that they saw it we had no perpetrator of the crime but now…"

"Ah I see."

"So my lord if you'll follow me? After you have taken refreshment, of course."

"Ah no... I think bodies are best viewed before refreshment, Henry, don't you think?"

"Damn...!" Mabel wanted to see what Sir Robert thought of the body and of the accused and she quickly ran to her cottage, closed the door, twizzled three times and said, "I wish to be a mouse."

Her delicate little shell-like ears twitched and grew large. Her petite snub nose elongated and grew long whiskers. She lifted her little paws to them and stroked the length from root to tip. And out behind her to give her balance, grew a long and sleek tail, twice as long as her tiny body.

She squeezed under her door which had never fitted well and ran full tilt, to the cart full of possessions in the baggage train, which was trundling into the manor yard. Before anyone had seen her, she ran up to the wheel, judging when to scurry safely up its wooden rim and disappeared into the packages and boxes of luggage of the cart bed. It saved her a run through the yard which might otherwise have been dangerous.

As the cart slowed in front of the manor steps, she swiftly ran down and waited in the darkness underneath them until everyone had quitted the courtyard.

On tiny feet she scurried up the incline, through the screens passage and into the hall. She would need to be very vigilant here for the master had brought his lymer dogs with him and they ran freely about the room. A mouse would be a mere morsel for them. Thank goodness cats were not welcome here.

Hiding where she could, she at last found herself clinging to the inside of the pristine white starched napery she herself had lain on the dais trestle earlier that day. Her large ears picked up a voice she knew.

"And you say the woman has confessed?"

"She has, my lord. The man Greathouse and she were lovers and she has admitted that his perpetual inconstancy drove her to murder him."

"She hit him over the head, I hear?"

"Yes," said the steward. "We have the weapon here, we think."

He pointed to the rolling pin lying on the blindingly white tablecloth.

"It is a very sorry tale of a woman driven by her passion to kill the object of her desire." The steward was always a wordy sod, thought Mabel. He really should be a jongleur, reciting the deeds of long dead heroes. He enjoyed embellishing things so much.

"With him gone, her life was meaningless and..."

"Yes Master Steward, I think we have the picture."

"And she has indeed committed this very act since with this very same rolling pin. Her own son has been the recipient of..."

"Yes, Master Steward. I am sure there are many women who are driven to hitting their spouses and adult offspring over the head with rolling pins." There was a titter of laughter, not least from Lady Isabel Stokke. Under his breath Mabel heard her lord say, "And long winded stewards too."

Henry the steward blinked in surprise, though Mabel could not see from the inside of the trestle table.

He bowed. "It is as your lordship says, I suppose."

"Where is the woman?"

"At her home, my lord, being held by her family."

"Have her brought here. Gently mind you. I'd like to converse with her. I'm not going to convene the manor court if the thing turns out to be... a simple misunderstanding."

Trust Sir Robert to get to the bottom of things.

The whole room shifted and Mabel realised that this was how it felt to a mouse's whiskers when people exited and entered a room. A slight draught lifted the hem of the tablecloth and Mabel saw several pairs of shoes, moving about - servitors and people leaving and climbing to the dais.

At last Mistress Peabody was brought in, her eldest daughter holding her arm, her son behind her.

"Damn..." Mabel needed a better view. Casting around quickly from the floor under the trestle, Mabel located the dogs which were lounging by the door, their long pink tongues lolling as they panted in the heat of the day.

Steer clear of them! Mabel scampered along the length of the underside of the table and down the side of the dais.

Holding her breath she made a quick dash across the open floor and disappeared behind a tray which a servitor had left propped up by the door to the servant's room.

If someone were to come and remove it, she'd be exposed with nowhere to run.

Her twitchy little nose poked out from the edge of the wooden tray. Her little black eyes had an excellent view of both Mistress Peabody's party and the lord Robert on his dais.

Today Mistress Peabody looked a little better. She was not so loose limbed, pale and fainting as she had been the previous evening but she stood rather more confidently before her lord. The reeve was three paces behind.

"Mistress Peabody, what have you to say to me about the death of Master Greathouse? It seems you have confessed to hitting him over the head and killing him with an item from your kitchen."

Matilda blinked, and peered up at the dais as if she didn't know who was speaking. Mabel had noticed this behaviour before in Matilda Peabody. When she spoke to you, she often half closed her eyes as if she couldn't quite bring herself to open them fully and see the world as it really was.

Forgetting that she was a mouse, Mabel suddenly had a thought and that caused her to squeak. "Aha!"

Luckily there was quite a bit of clatter and buffet in the hall and her tiny noise went undetected. Her Mabel brain said, "She can't see properly can she? The light has to be really good. She half closes her eyes in order to see more clearly."

Very quietly Matilda curtsied and said. "My lord, I think I must have killed him."

"You... think...?"

"If I might say something m'lord?" Tom Peabody gave a really harsh stare to the reeve. This was all *his* fault.

"My mother has not been in her right mind for some while now. And on the evening when it's said that Master Greathouse met his end, she was at home with my two sisters and myself."

"You are willing to swear to this upon the bible, Peabody? Upon your immortal soul?"

"I... We are... sir."

Sir Robert stood up. "Let me look at the so-called weapon."

The rolling pin was handed to him. "Hmmm." He turned it in his hands.

"There is no evidence of it being used for anything other than... making pastry... Henry."

"It could have been thoroughly washed, m'lord."

"Let's go and see the corpse," said Sir Robert suddenly.

The whole room once again was a bustle of servitors and other people, as those who needed to go with the lord quit the room with him and others disappeared to tasks elsewhere. Mabel scurried back under the table.

Only one young page remained in the room as Mabel hopped from mouse foot to mouse foot wishing that she'd not changed into a rodent. She had no reason to be in the hall at that very moment as a housekeeper but screwing up her courage she turned three times under the table as a mouse and crawled out on hands and knees from under the hem of the tablecloth as a woman.

Unfortunately the young page turned to the dais at the very moment she exited.

He took in a startled breath.

"Ah Johan. Erm... do you think you could get under the table and see if you can find a mouse. I am sure I saw one running under there a moment ago?"

He nodded. "Yes, Mistress Wetherspring."

When his bottom had disappeared under the tablecloth, Mabel ran as fast as she could to follow the party on their way to Master Greathouse's inn.

*****

Half way along the village path, Mabel slowed and began to think things out.

Mistress Peabody's sight is poor. She was at home when the deed was being done, it's said, though could the family be relied upon to tell the truth?

The rolling pin was a very unlikely murder weapon since it was neither large, sharp nor really heavy. Mabel thought back to the wound inflicted on Master Greathouse's head. No. She didn't think it was the weapon used.

She ducked behind a tree and startled a browsing squirrel, feeding on ash flowers by changing into a jackdaw.

She flew in a direct route to the roof of Master Edward's home, jumped down and listened at the door, pecking up a few bits of seed as she walked up and down.

"The head wound is extensive," she heard her lord say. The corpse was now well and truly decomposing, necessitating the lord to put up his sleeve to his nose and mouth. His muffled voice came out to her.

"Which idiot thought that closing the door on a decomposing cadaver in the summer, was a good idea, Henry?"

The reeve shuffled his feet. "Against looting, my lord,"

"Not in my village, I hope," said the lord Stokke sternly.

"Well there's been a murder which is far worse so why not a bit of looting?" said Mabel as she grubbed up a wriggling thing from the path with her beak.

"Pah..." she spat it out. 'Not wormy things... no, no, no. Not wriggly things! Concentrate Mabel!'

The lord was still speaking.

"Come here, Peabody."

All four Peabody's stepped forward.

"Ah no... Mistress."

Sir Robert took the woman's arm.

"Please, place your hand upon the body of the cadaver and swear upon your soul, that you did not kill him."

It was dark in the house and Matilda struggled to see where she should touch the corpse. In the end she touched his thigh and the corpse rolled slightly giving off the most disgusting odour. She swore in a small voice that she had not killed him though of course it's not what she'd firstly intended to say.

The Lord Stokke had sent his young squire to the head of the body and he peered at the head wound with no distaste at all.

"Anything Brockle?"

"No, my lord."

"Ah well, it was worth a try."

"Ah, yes sir, look!" said the young man excitedly after a heartbeat. "There is a little ooze of blood."

"By Jove is there?"

Mabel had seen enough. She knew about the old wives' tale where if a felon touched the body of his or her victim, it began to bleed again. Load of ballocks.

Flying back to her office, really only a small area in the buttery, Mabel turned herself back into herself, snatched up parchment and paper and in the clearest script she could manage she wrote quickly,

MISTRESS PEABODY IS INNOCENT. THE ROLLING PIN DID NOT INFLICT THE LARGE AND DEVASTATING WOUND UPON THE HEAD OF MASTER GREATHOUSE. IT WAS A HEAVY OBJECT WITH AN EDGE WHICH SLICED INTO HIS SKULL. THE WOMAN WAS WITH HER FAMILY WHEN HE WAS KILLED. SHE IS A SLIGHT WOMAN WITH POOR EYESIGHT, WHO COULD NOT HAVE GOT THE BODY FROM THE HOUSE TO THE FOREST.

A WELL WISHER.

She rolled up the parchment tight and sealed it with a blob of wax.

Then it was a matter of a moment to change back into a jackdaw again, fly back to the roof with the missive in her beak, and carefully positioning over the smoke hole, and drop the cylinder into the house interior.

She peered down with her white eye.

Right!

She flew down to the back of the property and as her own self again ambled around the corner of the house and stood in the doorway.

The missive had been discovered by the youthful Brockle who had been startled by it descending from the heavens and landing with a 'poof' in the dead ashes of the fire.

He'd looked at it, peered up, had seen the white eye and glossy back head of the jackdaw, though he did not see it as such.

"Argh! A demon has just..."

"A demon, Brockle?" shouted his lord.

Peter Brockle swallowed. "Something has just dropped this through the smoke hole m'lord." His words were a little wobbly.

"Well let's have it here!"

Brockle handed the parchment over with finger and thumb as if it was plague ridden.

The Lord Stokke looked annoyed.

"Ahem," he said, as he broke the seal.

"I don't think demons will have been dropping letters from roofs, Brockle. Well, not in the daytime."

He flattened it out.

He read it out loud to himself quietly.

No one dared to ask him what it said. Everyone was wondering where it had come from.

Mabel, standing in the doorway, was biting her fingernail. Please let him understand what I mean.

"Ah yes well..." The Lord went to the head end of the cadaver and looked carefully at the wound. There was no doubt that the instrument used to kill Greathouse had been metal. It was not a small wooden rolling pin. *That* might raise a bruise and a lump and incapacitate a man for a moment but kill him? No.

The lord asked Matilda to stand before him and tell him what was in the furthest corner of the room. He pointed.

The woman screwed up her eyes. "I think... I think... it is a barrel... my lord," she said with uncertainty.

"Ah..." In fact the object in the corner was a large chest which had, for some reason, been placed upon its end.

The lord asked Matilda to step outside with him.

Matilda made to squeeze past Mabel but the housekeeper turned aside and they went out into the sun.

"So Mistress Peabody. What do you think that is right *there*?"

Matilda smiled, thinking that, yes she could get this right.

"It's Master Cowman's brown calves, or at least two of them, sir. He always puts them in that field when they are a bit sickly." She knew what they were. Without doubt.

"Ah," said the Lord Stokke.

What Matilda had actually seen were two new chestnut foals which the lord had brought with him from his southern manor, to sell to another local lord in need of good horseflesh.

"I see."

The others had now crowded at their backs and were silent.

"I think that we must find that Mistress Peabody..."

Mabel held her breath.

"Cannot be guilty of the felonious death of Master Greathouse." The lord looked at the letter in his hand and read from it.

"She has poor eyesight and cannot see to find her way around. And the rolling pin belonging to her did not inflict that wound upon that head." He gestured into the house interior at the corpse.

Mabel gave out a contented sigh. The crowd muttered.

"You can now bury the body for Heaven's sake."

He strode off.

"Mistress, follow me."

Matilda meekly followed her lord to stand by a pear tree growing a few yards away.

Mabel scuttled to the back of the house where she wouldn't be observed and then as her jackdaw again, rose up into the branches of the pear tree.

She arrived to hear the lord saying,

"We do not think you guilty so no matter what you say, we will not have you take this sin upon yourself."

Matilda looked frightened.

"I think you are protecting someone."

"No... no, m'lord."

"Then why would you admit to something you obviously did not do?"

"I...I..." Matilda began to snivel.

"Who do *you* believe killed him?"

"I don't know, my lord."

"Need I remind you that I can have you put in the lockup for days... until you tell me. Cold and hunger are not happy bedfellows, woman!"

"No, m'lord, I'm sure they're not."

"Not to mention the damp."

"No, m'lord."

"So come on. Who do you think did it and why do you feel the need to cover for them, at peril of your life?"

"I... I..." Matilda Peabody had now begun to cry in earnest.

"I thought it might be my son, sir."

"Aha!"

"He knew about my love for Master Greathouse and he thought maybe if I married him, his inheritance might be in jeopardy. So I wondered if he'd... got rid of him, sir."

"He thought it might be possible that you'd have other offspring which would inherit the inn and..."

"Yes my lord."

Robert Stokke had rather protuberant eyes and Mabel saw him fix poor Matilda with one of them now.

"And you thought to protect him."

"Yessir. But he won't have done it... oh no he can't have done it."

"Why not?"

"We were all together in the house when Edward was killed... weren't we?"

"Were you?"

"We were sir. Or at least..."

The large round brown eye was employed again.

"I think I saw us all there."

"You can actually see very little, mistress," said Lord Robert with some sensibility.

He sighed. "Right. You go home. I shall take your son into custody and ask him a few questions."

"Oh no!" said Matilda.

"Oh no!" said Mabel.

*****

Everyone was talking about the letter. Very few people in the village were able to write and all eyes were on those people who could.

Mabel just shrugged it off and carried on as normal, saying that she was very unlikely to have climbed the roof of the inn and slid the letter down the smoke hole, now was she? The steward Henry became pompous when asked if he had written the letter, which incidentally, the contents of which no one but the lord had seen. Sir Robert had taken it off to his private apartment with him. Henry had denied writing it in a diatribe which lasted till supper time.

The life of Mistress Peabody had been saved but now her son was in danger. Mabel didn't much like Thomas Peabody but she was sure he hadn't killed the innkeeper either.

She had to find out who *had* killed him.

Mabel needed to search for the murder weapon.

The opportunity came fairly soon.

It was Midsummer's Eve and day. The whole village would take this as a holiday and there would be festivities and feasting for all.

The lord and his family presided after they'd all been to the churchyard for a sort of homily. It was the sort the priest would normally give after mass in church. But of course, they were unable to go into the church building because the Pope had forbidden it and the door had been locked for years.

So Father Ignatius gave them, what Mabel thought, was a warning against fornication and lust - thinly disguised as a story about a virgin and a foolish not-virgin. Lots of drinking featuring in the tale.

They all knew what Father Ignatius thought about their 'fun' on Midsummer's Eve and day and they didn't listen. By dinner time, a percentage of the village was halfway to sozzled and the rest were fully sozzled.

On Midsummer's Eve Mabel drank a couple of beakers of ale with water, ate a little of the communal roast which the lord had provided and disappeared into her cottage, telling everyone she was going to lie down.

No one noticed the jackdaw sneak out of her door and fly up into the apple tree in her garden.

She'd made a mental note of the village's houses and how she was going to achieve her aim of going into every house and workplace.

She started with her neighbour. Peering round carefully to make sure they were all out, she leaned on the door and stumbled into the house. Their door too was ill fitting and it closed behind her with a thump.

Damn... now how was she to get out? Oh, it was alright. The window shutters were open and the bars nicely spaced for her to squeeze through. She really didn't want to keep changing into different animals to escape houses. It was tiring and she needed to accomplish her task today, while everyone was at the celebration.

She started to search for anything which might have made the indentations and slices in Master Greathouse's head.

Naturally there were knives and kitchen implements but nothing really vicious with any weight behind them.

One house down.

She flew onto the next house, which belonged to Master Head the reeve.

His door was closed but the shutters were open and so Mabel landed on the window ledge and walked over the sill.

The reeve was a wealthy man and owned more items. Here there was more to search.

A very nice set of fire tending implements made by the blacksmith, caught her bright white eye.

No blood on anything which might have been used. An axe was standing up against the wall... that too was not bloodied but then, would the murderer have left it in full view, to incriminate himself? Surely he would have cleaned it. Her bird eye scrutinised the blade thoroughly. No. No blood. And her nose could not detect it.

And besides, if he'd been killed with an axe, the wound would look cleaner, one swipe not several.

Out through the window went Mabel.

The next house was Alfred Stockman's. She'd known him all her life and would be surprised if it was him. Still, to be fair she dashed into the partly opened door and began to search.

Alfred was an unfree forester and farmer who owned a few cattle. There were many items in the cottage to do with his job. An axe, a mattock, a billhook. Mabel searched every one for evidence of use on an innkeeper's head.

Nothing.

The kitchen equipment was minimal and almost all wooden. Alfred was not a wealthy man. However she did find something a little odd. Odd for a single man to be hiding in his home. A lady's brooch in silvered metal upon which were depicted two hands clasped was sitting in a wooden box. She left it where it was in the box even though she was very tempted to take it. It was known that jackdaws like shiny things. And at that moment, she did.

Back to her investigation. She knew it couldn't be Alfred.

The next house was that of the Peabody's. Was it worth searching? The lord's men had already done that and found nothing.

'No, don't waste your time,' said Mabel.

Back out into the sunshine of the afternoon and Mabel careered over the trees by Master Hartshorn's home. The door wasn't open and the shutters were closed. Damn! This called for another smoke flue entry.

Mabel wriggled her way down and flew onto the table placed centrally in the two roomed house.

She hopped round the floor. She had been in this house before when she was a girl and remembered it from those days.

Emma's bed was by the back wall with her parents' close by. Her sister's bed was close to the fire and her brother had a special place with walls which were made of white painted wattle and daub to the other end of the house accessed by a ladder and situated over the pen where the animals were kept in the winter.

The jackdaw waddled over to the fire. Nothing here was anything out of the ordinary.

There was a box underneath a bed and Mabel tried to lift the lid but it was locked.

So what was valuable that needed to be locked in a box? This would be Emma's sister's box.

Did Emma have one the same?

She did, underneath her bed, but hers was unlocked.

Mabel got her sharp beak between the lid and the body of the box and using her claws as a steadying tool, she prised it open.

There on a cushion made from a tiny piece of silk, was a brooch.

She'd seen this before.

It was the same as the one she'd found in Alfred's house. The only difference was this one was larger than the one Alfred possessed. Odd. This looked like it was designed for a man and the other a woman's brooch.

Mabel picked it up in her beak, took it out to have a good look at it, when to her bird ears came voices. Drunken whispers. Outside the door.

"Aw c'mon... no one will know." A man's voice.

"No... I can't. If someone finds out then we are both for it." A woman's voice.

Mabel dropped the brooch back into the box and scurried for the door, ready to hide behind it should the people enter the house.

"We'll be off soon and then no one can say anything." The man.

"I know. But I can't, I just can't. Not now. We have it all so well planned it would be stupid to let it all go wrong now." The woman.

"Oh...." Then there was the sound of sloppy kisses and Mabel shuddered.

"I do so love you." The woman.

"And I love you."

"And soon we'll be together forever."

Mabel frowned... or she tried to and then realised that a jackdaw cannot frown.

Was this the lovers Smitan the blacksmith and Emma Hartshorn? She was about to turn to fly out of the smoke hole when the door opened with great force, and the two people fell in embracing and kissing, smashing her against the wall of the cottage and bouncing back again. The two lovers stumbled and righted themselves.

"Oooh," said Mabel. 'Arrkkk!' said the jackdaw as she fell over and landed with her feet in the air.

Dizzied and dazed, Mabel felt herself picked up by the leg.

"How the Hell did this get in here?"

"Ugh... get it out," said Emma's voice. "Is it dead?"

"I think so." The man, who Mabel couldn't see in the dark and also because she was upside down and so dazed she couldn't open her eyes, shook her body. "Yeah! It's dead."

Her Mabel head said "Ow..." Her jackdaw beak was silent.

"Throw it on the midden," said Emma. Both of them sounded much less drunk now.

The man went out into the night. Mabel opened her eyes but the light from a flare blinded her.

She felt herself thrown up and a man's boot rise under her body and lift her up several feet. She flew through the air and not on her own jackdaw wings which she hadn't time to deploy, to land on a soft pile of vegetable peelings on top of the midden.

"Ouch!" she said. "Kark!" said the jackdaw.

CHAPTER SEVEN ~ ELINOR

Mabel came to a moment later, with a cabbage stalk sticking in her ear.

Forgetting that she was a jackdaw, she tried to pull it out with fingers and realised that all she could manage was scratching her head with sharp claws.

She slid and crawled down the midden through many indescribably horrible gobbets of offal and mess, reaching the ground very unsteadily.

Slowly, oh so slowly, she crawled to the back of the cottage and, moaning with every move she turned three times deosil and became a woman again.

Oh how she ached.

Staggering to her cott, she fell in the front door and onto her bed with a moan huge enough to raise the whole village, if they had not all been engaged in noisy Midsummer Eve pursuits.

Quite apart from her black eye, the scratches and bruises on her head and the painful arms, she now had red marks on her lower back and bottom and a throbbing leg and ankle where the man had caught hold of that appendage and shaken her.

The operation of taking off her clothes took her an age. After she had salved her bruises with tumbler's cure all, she donned her clean shift and lay down oh so gently on her bed.

It was a very good job that the Lord Stokke had said that she could have the day off the next day, for there was no way on earth she would have been fit for her work.

He knew that there would be so many sore heads on that next day, there was no point in relying on any work getting done. Besides it was Midsummer's Day... and special.

Mabel slept all evening and night, waking exceptionally thirsty at about the third hour of darkness.

"That is the last time I hide behind any doors," she said to herself as once again, she tended her hurts. Now everything had stiffened up and she could hardly walk or stand.

How was she going to explain her state to the villagers and to her employer, the Lord Stokke?

Rescue came in the form of her friend Elinor Poorgrass upon the next morning.

Just as daylight was peeping through her shutters Elinor came scratching on her door.

"Mabel, are you there? Are you awake? I missed you last night and I was worried." She poked her head around the door. "We always do the last dance together and you weren't there." She located Mabel humped in her bed.

"Are you alright?"

Mabel peeked out of her blankets at her friend who had a basket over her arm.

"Oh... I... erm..."

"Oh no. Have *you* fallen foul of the bad food too?"

"What?"

"We're not sure what it was but some folk have been ill all night. Is that why you aren't up and about?"

"Er no... I had a little accident with a door. I tripped and caught the toe of my shoe in my hem and landed badly."

"And the other day you had a black eye."

"I have two of them now."

"Oh Mabel."

Elinor came into the house and put the basket on the table.

"You really will have to be more careful."

'Yes, yes I will,' thought Mabel as she remembered her escapades of the previous day. 'And I'll have to remember to make sure to have some light and not stumble about in the dark.'

"Is that what happened?"

"I think so." Mabel wriggled.

"Can you do me a favour Ellie and if people ask, say I too have fallen foul of this food tainting?"

Elinor looked a little suspicious.

"I can't go out until I look a bit better, can I?"

"What's really been going on? Has someone attacked you?"

"No... honestly." Mabel hated deceiving her friend but she couldn't possibly tell her that someone had kicked her onto the midden when she was posing as a jackdaw.

"I don't know, lately, I seem to be very accident prone."

"I brought you some of those lovely little white rolls that Master Baker makes. They are a bit old, it's true as he baked them yesterday for the feast in the manor but they're left overs. The steward says we can have them. I thought they'd be nice with a bit of your honey."

Mabel tried to sit up.

"Oh forgive me Elinor... I am about to swear."

Elinor laughed and put her hands over her ears.

"I shan't listen then I don't need to tell Father Ignatius about it."

"Not that you would."

Elinor giggled. "No."

Mabel swung her legs over the edge of her bed and as she'd warned, swore.

Oh, she was a mass of bruises and pains.

She hobbled to a small chest which sat on the top of a shelf by her table.

"I have some remedy here. Willow bark—always good for pain. And I have some tumbler's cure all. That will help my bruises," said Mabel.

"I'll help you," Elinor pulled back her sleeves and began to massage the cure all into Mabel's back.

"Honestly. I don't know how you've done all this damage to yourself. It looks as if someone has taken their foot to you in several places."

'You cannot even guess at the truth,' said Mabel to herself even as she denied it to her friend.

Now they were eating white rolls and honey and chatting about the weather.

"I want to stay in today. I have some jobs to do and I don't think I'll be very good company with all my ailments. You go off and enjoy yourself," said Mabel, "And spread the gossip that I'm indisposed because of what I ate last evening."

"Oh Mabel... you are awful. But alright I'll tell a little white lie for you."

"You know I'll do the same for you someday."

Elinor pecked her friend on the cheek with honey sweetened lips. "I know you would."

"Before you go... just a little question. We spoke about Alfred and Emma."

"Alfred...? Alfred Stockman?"

"Yes. You remember you said that he'd never be allowed to marry Emma."

"Yes I did. Why?"

"Well... do you know if he has passed on to another girl? Has he got another one in tow?"

Elinor shrugged and licked the honey from her lips. "I doubt it. I have a feeling that Alf won't marry... ever... if he can't marry Emma. Just one of those things."

"Things change."

"Yes they do, I suppose. Which reminds me... when are *you* going to marry?"

"Me!" shrieked Mabel with a little too much levity. "Haha! Never. I have no plans at all to marry."

"You're getting old."

"Nonsense. I'm only a year older than you. And anyway you can get married at any age. Mistress Peabody and poor Edward Greathouse, now. They weren't in the first flush of youth but they were going to get married."

Elinor's eyes grew round as cheeses.

"Where did you hear that?"

"Oh... here and there. Why, isn't it true?"

Her friend came close to her. "You know what Edward was like?"

"We have discussed it, yes. In the past he's been involved in affairs with women from Chisbury to Chilton so I'm told. But like I say, things can change."

"You mean that he might have decided to settle with one woman?"

"Well at least marry one. I can't imagine him *settling* for one, no. He'd settle for one who didn't mind his infidelities. He wasn't getting any younger. He had no children, well, not that we know of. He had a business and was a relatively wealthy man. Wouldn't he want to hand everything on to his son... if he could?"

"I see what you mean."

Elinor pulled down her sleeves.

"I'd better be off. Papa will wonder where I am."

She took up her basket. "Perhaps I'll see you later?"

"Maybe this evening?"

"Until later then."

Mabel sighed and lay back down on her bed. She was beginning to feel a little better.

The day was warm and as it was midsummer the hours of daylight were long. She began to formulate a plan. Last evening she'd been thwarted in her desire to visit homes whilst the occupants were out at the village feast. Now maybe she could finish her snooping.

Which animal had she never tried?

Part of her said, 'Oh Mabel... just do what you know, you're in no fit state to try and test something you've never done before.' The other part of her said, 'How difficult can it be? You're getting bored with pigeons and mice and owls.'

Mabel made up her mind.

She dressed in her russet kirtle with her yellow woven belt, turned three times in the middle of the floor and said. "I'd like to be a squirrel."

Why did Mabel want to be a squirrel?

They were fast. No one really took much notice of them in the forest and its villages and they had the most delightful little paws. Little paws which she was certain would come in handy for turning things over and picking things up.

Moments later a little sandy coloured creature leapt from the window of Mabel's house and made for the nearest tree.

*****

Her twitchy little nose wrinkled up. What could she smell? Ah, yes, smoke from the bonfire lit last night. If there was something the village enjoyed, it was a bonfire.

She ran up the trunk of the ash trees which separated her part of the village from the house of the reeve and threw herself over the top of the trees to another set of branches.

Oh that was exhilarating! It was like flying. Even if it hurt.

She reached the gap where Master Reeve's property met that of the Hartshorns'. They had just one tree on their land but owned a cherry orchard a little further on in the village.

Could Mabel manage to jump from this tree to the next?

She decided that with her injuries, it wasn't going to be worth the risk. She scurried down the ash tree and then up the oak, her little claws making light work of the scaly fissured bark.

More leaping from branch to branch and she landed right by the house of Simon Smitan, the blacksmith. His forge was on the outskirts of the village because of the risk of fire and the house was not attached to it.

The shutters were open. In through the window went Mabel as swiftly as she could and stood stock still to make sure that the house was empty.

It was not.

Simon was sitting on his bed, his head in his hands. He hadn't seen or heard her enter.

She froze. And then very quickly ran to a rough curtain which separated one part of the house from another. Mabel seemed to remember that Simon's mother had lived with him for some time before her death and this had been her part of the house.

Mabel peeked out, her whiskers twitching. What was he doing?

He looked very upset.

Then he reached for a piece of cloth and pulled it to his head, burying his face in it.

He took in a long breath as if he was sniffing it for perfume. No one in the village owned perfume. Only the Lady Stokke would be able to afford such luxury.

Eventually Mabel realised that Simon was crying softly.

It seemed very odd for this tall and rather well built man to cry. What had he to cry about?

Suddenly, he threw the piece of material to the floor, rose from his bed, tucked in his shirt and catching up a tunic lying on a chest he thrust his arms into it.

Finding a belt close by, he threw it round his middle as he walked, buckled it and exited the cottage.

Mabel saw him walking out into the morning with long strides to disappear into the trees.

She jumped over to the bed and with her extra sensitive nose, gave the piece of material a sniff.

Did she recognise it? It was only a scrap. It had no pattern or particularly special colour and Mabel couldn't tell what it was from. However the smell was very distinctive. She had smelled it before but she could not put her tiny little finger on it.

She scampered about the house looking into everything she could reach or undo with her surprisingly agile fingers. She found nothing of significance.

Ah well. What did she expect to find?

Out of the window she went again, making sure that no one saw her. It seemed that everyone was on the green, taking their ease with their neighbours. Those that were not laid up with the bout of food taint that was.

Master Hogman, it seemed, *was* laid up in his cott, as was his wife and their six children, though the sixth, aged four, was hale and hearty and was plaguing the rest of them, when Mabel scurried in their open door. She soon realised why the door was open for the smell of vomit and excrement was overpowering. And the sound of groaning.

She wasn't going to stay in there.

Several other homes were like the pits of the privy as folk brought up or evacuated the contents of their stomachs and bowels with this bout of food tainting. Mabel hoped that it wasn't going to be too bad. Things like this for the young and the very old could be serious.

Four more houses and Mabel had had enough. She'd found nothing, learned nothing and had had her squirrel olfactory system well and truly tested. She made for home.

*****

As promised Elinor came to see Mabel that evening.

"Oh that's good, you're looking a bit better," she said.

"My willow bark concoction always works," said Mabel. "My good ol' mam taught me to make it years ago... when I was really quite little."

"You were so lucky to have a mother."

"And you, a father."

"Oh he's alright but he hardly knows what I'm up to."

"He loves you, I know he does."

"He doesn't even know the colour of my eyes."

Mabel laughed. "That's not because he doesn't love you, that's because he's a man!"

Elinor took the proffered beaker of Mabel's elderflower water.

"Have you ever noticed that men don't seem to see as much as we do?" asked Mabel.

She sat down gingerly on the edge of her bed. Elinor had her stool.

Once more her friend laughed. "I have indeed. Ask questions of a woman and you'll get not only the question you asked answered, but five more as well."

"You *have* noticed."

"Have you been asking questions?"

"In a sort of way," said Mabel. "I'd really like to get to the bottom of Master Greathouse's death."

"Why? He was a horrible man."

"Was he? Was he really?"

"Oh Mabel... not you too?"

"No, not me too. He might have been fond of women but he didn't deserve to die because of it."

"Someone thought he did."

"Well, he wasn't popular but I don't think that anyone here would want to kill him for flirting or even for lying with his wife. They'd just have it out with him and probably give him a good hiding. From what I can gather, his affairs were all in the past."

"You can't be sure of that. Maybe a good hiding went too far."

"No I can't be sure, but..." Suddenly Mabel had a thought. Perhaps she had been looking at this the wrong way?

"What's the matter?"

"Oh nothing. I'm tired, that's all."

"Well then, rest and I'll see you tomorrow in the manor."

Mabel accompanied Elinor out of the house and just as they were embracing, a young man came up to them.

"Mistress Wetherspring?"

Mabel looked up. 'Oh my! What a handsome young man. Who was this?'

"Yes?"

The young man nodded very prettily.

"The Lord Stokke begs your pardon but he would like to see you straight away in his office."

"Oh. Alright."

The man nodded again and made off between the trees.

"Who is *that?*" asked Mabel watching his blond curls bounce around his ears as he retreated.

Elinor giggled. "THAT, my dear Mabel, is Sir Gabriel Warrener."

"Oooh," said Mabel as she watched him disappear.

"The Lord's newest knight. He's from Stockley, one of the Lord's other manors... somewhere."

"We haven't seen him here before."

"No, we haven't," smirked Elinor, "And by the look on your face and the blush to your cheek, it's perhaps a good thing we haven't."

*****

Mabel smoothed down her hair and kirtle. 'Whatever can the Lord want with me on my day off?'

The Lord Stokke beckoned her with a bony finger and closed the door of his office.

"Now, Mistress Wetherspring, what about this?"

This was the note which she had written to him explaining why Mistress Peabody couldn't be guilty.

"And before you say you didn't write it, I recognise your handwriting."

"Ah no, my lord... it's written..."

"Mabel, I look through your accounts, I see your work, I know your ways of writing. This is your hand."

Mistress Wetherspring was silent.

"See here. The curl which you add to your 'v'. The long tails on the 'g' and 'y'. It's yours."

Mabel sighed.

"I could not let you make a mistake m'lord, forgive me."

"A mistake?"

"To believe Mistress Peabody guilty without a deal of thought behind the judgement."

'Oh dear,' thought Mabel, 'there goes my mouth again, running away with me.'

"So how is it you know these things, huh?" The lord didn't seem to notice the slight.

"A housekeeper hears many things, sir."

"Eavesdrops you mean?"

"Well... if you like to call it that. She must keep abreast of everything happening in the manor, if she is to know what's going on. It's the undercurrents, sir. Those things which happen and are said which few know about."

"Secrets? You are telling me that there are secrets... on my manor?"

"Well... there are... some." The protuberant brown eye was trained on her now and she quailed before it.

"Hmmm."

He walked around his table.

"For a woman, you have a keen mind. Many would hear the gossip and not understand what it really meant."

"Thank you, sir." Well, she thought it was a compliment.

He was silent for a moment looking at her. She was uncomfortable.

"I always said you had a good mind. I told your mother—get her educated. She'll prove useful one day." He smiled. "Don't worry, I'm not upset. Glory of God, I wish my own girls were half as bright as you."

'Well!' thought Mabel. 'What a dark horse my mother was.'

Mabel could only stand there with her mouth open and say, "Oh."

The Lord sat down.

"So tell me how did you get the missive down into the house?"

"There was a ladder close by m'lord. I..."

"Ah... well next time, don't climb up and put yourself at risk, come straight to me."

"I was just a little worried that... that you..."

"Frightened young Brockle to death, you did," said Robert Stokke with a grin.

Mabel smiled. "I am sorry about that."

The lord laughed. "He thought you were a devil. Swipe me!" The chuckle went on.

"Thank you, sir." She'd just realised he'd seemed to think there'd be a next time.

"And how did you come to these... conclusions?"

Now Mabel had to think cleverly.

"Well, m'lord, as you yourself thought, the wound was not made by the rolling pin."

"You saw the wound?"

"I saw the body when it was brought into the village."

"Ah."

"And Mistress Peabody loved the deceased sir, with all her heart. She is a very mild woman. I know her well. She could never have killed him. She'd use words to hurt but never something as nasty as the instrument which made those wounds."

The Lord Stokke leaned forward.

"And she could never have got a handcart to the forest on her own. As you have seen, she's as blind as a bat..." 'Only of course,' thought Mabel, 'bats aren't blind at all. And I know it.'

Robert Stokke rubbed his nose.

"That was well observed, mistress. I must admit it was something I could never have known."

"But the reeve, who made these accusations, sir, should have known. They have known each other all their lives."

"And by that you mean, mistress?

"That if the man had a brain, he could have worked out that it was impossible for her to do the deed."

"And?"

"Why was he so happy to let her take the blame?"

"Ah..." said the Lord Stokke on a long outbreath.

He leaned even further into her.

"Then Mistress Wetherspring, you must find out."

She grinned. "Yes my lord."

"Well done Mabel."

"Thank you my lord."

"And...?"

"Yessir?"

"Why the blazes have you got two black eyes, mistress?"

"Ah... yes... Erm. I had an accident in my house. I tripped and banged my nose and forehead."

"Oh dear. You need to be more careful."

Mabel gave a weak smile and opened the door and there, behind it was Master Smitan looking up at the rafters of the hall.

"Ah, Master Smitan."

"Mistress Wetherspring."

"Have you come to consult with Lord Stokke?"

"Indeed I have. He's summoned me for some special work he needs doing."

"Then I think he is free now."

And off she skipped.

'Hmmm?' She didn't like the look on Master Smitan's face. She was sure that she wasn't the only one who'd been eavesdropping.

*****

Strangely that evening as the sun went down it became quite chilly. Mabel sought out a blanket which she used as a cloak when the weather was cooler. It was more of a shawl really, was madder dyed and a lovely shade of red.

She had to go out and get her chickens and geese into their shelter and so she threw the shawl over shoulders and tied a knot.

Halfway to the shed, she met Elinor, who had come seeking her to give her yet more food.

"Ellie, you will have me as fat as Goosey Nibbles, there."

"Aw, it's only a small pie." She lifted a cloth from her basket. "It won't make you fat."

"I have to get them inside before it goes much darker. I was called to the manor to speak to the lord and I'm late doing it."

"Ooooh. What did he want?"

Again Mabel hated lying to her friend.

"Oh nothing really. He was just thanking me for organising the feast and getting everything ready."

"We are so lucky in Sir Robert. He's a thoroughly nice man."

"Yes, he is."

"Shooo, shoo go, go Gander," said Mabel with a swishing movement of her hands.

"Wait, let me put this in your house and then I'll help you."

But just then, Elinor gave an obvious shiver.

Mabel stood straight. It was difficult to bend and run about after chickens and geese, with her bad back. She'd be glad of the help.

"Oh you're cold," said Mabel. "You only have your kirtle. These nights you need something more. You should wear a supertunic like me. Here..." She swung the red shawl over Elinor's shoulders.

"Aw thank you. You're right. It might be midsummer but the weather isn't summer is it?"

Elinor disappeared into the gloom with, "you are such a good friend Mabel Wetherspring," as Mabel went on trying to get her animals into safety.

Her shed was a little way from her house and there were a few bushes about it.

"Aw c'mon Tangle," she said, swishing her hands to get the chicken from the base of the bushes. "Do you want M'sieur Reynard to get you?"

In the end Mabel had to pick up the last chicken, Russett; there was always one who was the last into the hen house, and throw her in before bolting the door and pulling the roof tight.

She looked up at the sky. It looked like a cold sky. June and it was cold. Whatever were things coming to?

She made for the house.

"Ellie, will you stay to help me eat the pie?"

There was no answer.

"Ellie?"

Maybe she had realised that Mabel had managed to catch all her fowl and had gone home instead. It wasn't like her though.

Mabel's fingers were cold and she blew on them to bring some warmth to them. Taking one last look around her yard, she shut the door.

The interior of the cottage was dark. Before she closed all the shutters, Mabel went to her shelf by the door and picked up a small oil lamp. Moving towards the fire which, of course, she could gauge perfectly in the dark through years of practice, she bent to uncover the little embers and blew up some flames. She touched a twig to her lamp.

A soft yellow light threw her shadow onto the far wall.

Mabel turned to walk to her larger lamp which was on the table and tripped over something on the floor.

She fell to her knees and lost the little oil lamp.

The flame guttered out.

"What the...?"

Slowly Mabel felt round for the lamp. Into her hand came a soft, warm piece of flesh.

Mabel didn't scream but she did jump.

Despite her bruised knees and the hurts to her palms, Mabel felt further round her.

It was then that she did give a short screech.

The lamp... where was the lamp?

She backed to the fire and took up a taper to light the larger lamp still sitting on the table.

Into her view came her lovely red madder dyed shawl.

It covered the face of a body.

One hand had extended from the shawl and it was this which Mabel had found.

With shaking hands, Mabel picked up the shawl and fell to her knees once more.

"Ellie!!"

Mabel pulled her friend to her and as she did so, Elinor's head flopped back.

"Oh noooo! Noooo!" she screamed.

Elinor had been murdered.

CHAPTER EIGHT ~ SIR GABRIEL

Mabel sat for a while with the cooling body of her friend in her arms. What had happened? Why had Elinor died? Then shock gave way to fear. Was the person who had done this still here in the dark?

Mabel jumped up and as quickly as she could she took the lamp and flashed it into the corners of her small home. There was no one lurking in any part of the house. She didn't really know what she'd have done if there had been someone. It was certain she would have shouted and screamed, struggled and fought, unlike poor Elinor. And anyway, they were long gone.

Ellie must have been taken by surprise. Did Elinor know the person who had put their hands around her throat and squeezed until there was no more breath in her poor body?

Mabel sat on her bed and wept. Wept until there were no more tears for her to cry. Her eyes were puffy; her nose was running; her breath came in short gasps; her head ached. She wrapped her arms around her middle to try to quieten the intense pain which she felt in her heart.

She rose, and taking in a few shuddering breaths, she went around her home lighting every candle and lamp she possessed.

Then she looked at the ruined face of her friend.

Elinor's lovely face was congested with blood, red and puffy. Her lips were swollen and there were tiny red marks in her staring eyes. Her purple tongue protruded as if it was too large for her mouth.

Sniffing back the tears she found it hard to contain, Mabel peered at Elinor's throat. Here she saw the mark of large thumb prints, close together at the little dip in Elinor's neck.

It had definitely been strangulation.

Mabel took up her red blanket and laid it over the head and torso of the only true friend she'd ever had.

As she did this she realised that she should not be asking the question, 'Who would wish to kill Elinor?' But 'who would need to kill Mabel?'

There was no doubt in Mabel's mind that Ellie had been mistaken for her. Everyone knew that Mabel had a red shawl. She was proud of it. She had woven it and dyed it herself.

And as she sat in her cottage alone with the dead body of her friend, she began to be afraid. She started to tremble.

Her friend's basket was on the table and the pie she'd brought sat proudly on the surface.

Mabel would never be able to eat it.

*****

The rest of the night passed by in a jumble of images.

Firstly, Mabel's mad rush to the manor to inform the lord of the death. Then, since she didn't know whom she could trust but knew that Elinor's father was one she could trust, her dash to his quarters in the manor grounds. He must learn of his daughter's death quickly and it was probably best coming from Mabel. An image of the man's shocked face was one which would stay with her for a very long time.

Flares were lit and people were dashing hither and thither. Mabel left them to it. She felt as empty as a spilled bucket.

The lord told her to go and wait in his office and so she climbed the stairs in a daze and sat in the dark with her blue cloak wrapped tightly around her and stared at the wall. Her red shawl she had left with Elinor.

Eventually the young man whom she'd seen earlier that day came in and lit the candles.

"Mistress Wetherspring? The Lord Stokke says that you should not be left alone and so has asked me to keep you company until he has... done... what he has to do."

She smiled at him absently. He was new to the village. She didn't think that this man was a threat to her. And neither did her lord, obviously.

"Sir Gabriel Warrener, isn't it?"

"Yes, mistress."

He hunkered down in front of her. "I am so sorry for the death of your friend. She seemed a ..."

"Nice girl?"

"A nice woman. I only had a very short conversation with her today but she seemed..." His voice tailed off.

"A nice woman whom no one would wish to murder." Her voice was croaky with tears.

He stood up.

"Can I get you a drink?"

"That would be kind."

He poured her wine from his master's jug.

She coughed as it went down. She rarely drank wine.

But it warmed her and she began to feel less like she was a head of hair which had been plaited too tightly.

The young man stood sentinel by the door.

It was awkward and so Mabel said, "She was my best friend."

"Yes. I heard."

"She came to help me round up my chickens."

"That's... kind." What else could he say?

"She went into the house instead of me. Ahead of me. It should have been me!"

"Oh no, don't say such a thing."

"No. No. She died because of me. If I had not lent her my red blanket, she would still be alive."

The man pulled a strange face. "You don't know that."

"And I would be lying in her place."

Except... a little thought came into Mabel's head, 'perhaps... just perhaps I might have been able to spin three times withershynnes and call out and change into something which the murderer would not have expected. Ha! He might not have been so confident if he had had a wolf by the neck!'

He. She had said he. Could a woman have done this?"

Mabel didn't know.

She supposed it must take some strength to push and squeeze so hard, for long enough for a person not to be able to regain their breath. Perhaps not a woman.

Some clarity was returning to Mabel's thoughts now.

"If I had not insisted on investigating the murder of Master Greathouse, then dear Ellie would not have died."

"I beg your pardon?"

"Oh no. I'm sorry. I am thinking aloud."

The young man smiled at her. "I do that all the time."

"You do?"

"I think it helps me put things in perspective."

"Yes, indeed it does."

"And I can always rely on good advice. From myself."

Mabel thought he was trying to make her smile.

She went on thinking aloud. "Who knew that I was looking into the man's death? Who might have something to hide?"

"You have been investigating?"

"Well... I have been asking questions and keeping my ears and eyes open."

"And have you come to any conclusions?" The man pushed off

from the door jamb.

"Several. And I have shared my findings with the Lord Stokke."

'There! That put paid to his ideas,' said Mabel to herself.

At that moment the Lord came in and threw himself down on his chair. Mabel bounced up from the stool and Sir Gabriel stood to attention.

"No. No. Sit, Mistress Wetherspring. You have had a nasty shock. Sit."

The lord rubbed his eyes.

"Appalling. Just appalling," he said quietly. His protuberant brown eyes fixed on Mabel. "We have obviously rattled someone."

"Yes sir."

"And we must be very careful."

"Yes sir."

"You had better stay here tonight. The person who has done this will realise quickly, if he hasn't already that he has killed the wrong woman."

Mabel hung her head. "If I hadn't…"

"Now, now. Life is full of what ifs and if onlys."

"But, sir. If I hadn't lent her my scarlet shawl…"

"Then you, Mabel, would be dead and I would be missing the good brain of someone who I'm sure will help me get to the bottom of all this nonsense."

Mabel saw Sir Gabriel give her a sidelong glance. She thought it looked like a new respect.

"Tomorrow Mabel. Go and sleep. Not at home, here. Maybe in the buttery. There's a good lock there. And we shall review everything tomorrow."

*****

That night Mabel dreamed.

She was a prowling wolf, with slavering jaws, having changed into the beast as the darkest part of the night grew old. She padded on silent paws around the village, sniffing out the houses of the villagers trying to work out who had killed her friend Elinor.

She came to the house of the blacksmith, Master Smitan. Her keen wolf nose lifted and she gave a huge sniff which filled her lungs. The smell of putrefaction came into them and she coughed, as much as a wolf may cough like a human. Then someone had thrown a net over her and she could not move. She thrashed about snarling and whining, until she realised that the net was her bed clothes and that she had fallen to the floor from the palliasse set up in her office, the buttery.

She lay still breathing heavily, wondering what had woken her so abruptly.

Then she could see.

The latch of her door was being lifted and the wood was rattling. She watched in horror. Was she still asleep? Dare she get up and confront the would-be intruder? She had locked the door. Her lord had told her to lock and bar it. And he had been right.

There was just one small window in the buttery. She could just see its stone jamb, grey in the darkness of the night. Quickly she threw off the covers, turned withershynnes and whispered, "I'd like to be a tiny bat."

The bat flew out on confident wings, turning over the courtyard of the manor. Could she see who had been at the door? Had they exited and run across the manor or were they resident in the house and somewhere prowling the rooms?

She quartered the manor yard, watching with her superior senses for any movement, a darker shadow in a lighter area, perhaps, a scurrying sound, maybe.

They can't have got far.

She scooted on her agile wings, across the courtyard again and at last picked up a shadow, bent double running by the wall.

She dipped. It was difficult to see who it was. She dived at the person. He made no noise nor did he seem worried by her presence.

The shadow sprinted along the base of the wall again and was out of the manor running for the trees.

In and out of the trees she followed him. Higher and lower, at what seemed for her, great speed. Once or twice she was even ahead of him and yes, it was a man, and she had to turn and follow him again. He seemed to spin before her eyes.

Where was he going?

She lost him at the oak tree in Master Hartshorn's garden. He had simply melted away.

How could she have lost him? She was fast. An accurate flier. Her senses were twenty times better than his own. But she had lost him. She was so angry with herself.

She flew back to the buttery window, changed and lay down again.

Somehow, she slept.

*****

In the light of a new day, Mabel went over the ground as her human self which she'd covered in the night as a bat. What was she hoping to find? Disappointed that she'd found no clue as to who had tried to enter the buttery that night, she trudged back home. A few neighbours, who would ordinarily ignore her, greeted her, realising that the poor woman had lost a good friend. They were trying to make her feel better in their own way.

But Mabel could not cordially return the greeting for she kept seeing poor Elinor's engorged face and could not help but wonder if these people, any one of them, could be responsible for her death. Everyone was a suspect.

The day passed in a haze. She tried to launch herself into her tasks but Elinor's face kept interrupting her thoughts. Once Mabel and her lord had again been over everything she could remember, she went home and took out some of her anger on her garden.

Eventually she gave up the work and retired to her house, locking and bolting the door and securing the shutters. This was not something she usually did. No one in the village locked their doors but there was now a presence of evil as tangible as the few raindrops which had begun to fall on the dusty earth.

By the light of the fire and the one candle she'd allowed herself, she darned some hose whilst the sounds of everyday life went on around her. Someone whistled their dog to them. Another was brushing the dust from their doorstep. There was the sound of someone knocking nails into a piece of wood. And then two children passed close by, happily laughing. A fat tear trickled down Mabel's cheek. She remembered the carefree days when she and Elinor had run about the village laughing. Both Elinor's and Mabel's mothers had been alive then and life was good. And only a year later, they'd grown up. Ellie had lost a mother and then Mabel too.

Mabel thought that she would dine in the hall that evening as was her right as a member of the manor staff. She had prepared no food for herself at home, and frankly didn't have the energy to do so but she was hungry. She had eaten nothing since all this horror began.

In a moment of abstraction she searched for her red blanket.

And then it all came back to her and she stood in the middle of her floor feeling totally lost.

Someone scratched on her door and Mabel jumped.

"Who's that?"

"Mistress Mabel, it's Sir Gabriel, Sir Gabriel Warrener. The master has sent me to bring you to the hall for safety."

She opened the door. How much longer did she think she'd have to hide away from this mystery enemy?

"That's most kind of you."

"He believes that until the murderer is caught, your life is in danger and so he would like you to sleep in the manor at night."

Mabel doused the candle and covered her fire and went with him.

As they walked she appraised him with sidelong glances. He was very handsome in a sort of girlish way with soft features and good skin. How old was he? Twenty three, twenty four? He was clean shaven as many men were not in those days. His hair was the colour of new straw, wavy and shiny. His eyes were a speedwell blue. He was tall, though not too slender and he walked very gracefully, his hand on the pommel of his sword, as if he would leap to her defence at any moment. She felt an unusual frisson pass through her, realising that she liked the look of him. For the first time in her life, she liked the look of a man. The feeling made her a little uncomfortable.

"You are from Stockley, I believe, Sir Gabriel?"

"Near Calne, mistress. My father was the Lord Stokke's master at arms. It is his caput as you probably know."

"I do. My father was the bailiff of this village until his untimely death. He came with his lord from Stockley when he was young and married my mother here."

The man seemed to take that in, savouring it like a sweet taste.

'That just tells him that I am a free woman and from a good background,' said Mabel to herself.

They walked on in silence.

Sir Gabriel politely helped her up the steps, a hand on her elbow.

"I will be in the hall tonight. If you have any worry, just call for me."

"Thank you," said Mabel, not quite knowing how to deal with the surge of feeling rushing up on her.

He took her to her place on the second table and once she was seated, walked around it to sit at the very end of the table on the dais.

The meal went on, Mabel stealing glances at Sir Gabriel whenever she could. He laughed and joked with his compatriots but she noticed he managed the odd peek at her whenever he was able.

Mabel finished her meal early. She was not fond of pork or yellow pepper sauce, the main dish on the servants table and so ate sparingly. She found it always gave her indigestion. She slipped out of the hall and once the room was vacated by the servants, she went into the buttery.

Her palliasse was laid up against the wall, her blankets and pillow folded up on a stool where she had left them. Mabel sat and pondered her situation. She hadn't been able to do any further investigating and it was eating at her. That Ellie's killer was running free about the village hurt her enormously. The fact the person had probably murdered Master Greathouse too, she no longer considered. Yes, the person had claimed two lives but it was Elinor's which had really hurt her.

Noise in the hall began to die down as people vacated the room or spread out their beds in preparation to sleep. Good nights were spoken and she heard the lord and his family retire to their solar.

A few people started a hum of conversation but it was quiet and disturbed no one. Eventually even that died and Mabel got up to lock and bolt the door. She had already closed and bolted the shutters.

She was tired but even though she tried, she could not relax enough for sleep.

She lay on her bed, staring up at the ceiling until her eyes began to see little pinpricks of light dancing before them. She took her knuckles to her eye sockets. The lights intensified.

The tawny owls, which had begun their courting ritual behind her house, hooted at each other from the roof of the manor hall.

A small animal no doubt meeting a grisly death on the talons of the barn owl resident in the manor grain barn, screamed in terror.

Mabel listened.

And then she heard it. First a surreptitious footstep coming as if from nowhere. Then silence as the feet ceased their tread right outside her door. Mabel blew out her candle. The door latch was once again tried and found locked and bolted.

A whispered voice swore. She could not recognise it.

Then strangely she heard the voice whispering to itself. It sounded so much like someone had said the word 'mouse,' but she knew that couldn't be true.

She held her breath for a few heartbeats.

The night was dark but Mabel had acquired her night sight, as she watched the door carefully.

Her eye was quickly drawn down to the bottom of the door by the hinge where wear and tear had made it ill fitting. Something had scurried underneath. Something very small and quick.

Foolish girl. It was a mouse. A little grey house mouse. Someone must have passed her door, seen it and commented on it before frightening the creature into scurrying under the door.

She let out a relieved breath.

In the next instant she wished that she hadn't, for the next thing she knew, a large black shadow was outlined on the surface of the door.

Without any hesitation, Mabel threw open the nearest shutter, turned withershynnes with the shadow's hands grasping for her, and whispered to herself.

"I wish to be a..."

"Arghh!" Whoever it had been was surprised by the fact that Mabel was now in possession of sharp claws and vicious teeth. She used them, leaping onto the shadow and digging in both. There was a noisy screech and a tussle as Mabel scratched again.

Then she leapt for the sill and was gone into the night.

*****

As a cat, the leap from the first floor window caused her no ill and she lunged for the darkness of the wall of the manor. There she waited to see if she was followed. Lights began to be lit in the hall and one or two folk came out onto the steps.

"Damned cats! Why do they have to be so noisy about their business?" said one man.

Another man laughed and made a rude joke and they closed the manor door again.

She noticed that one light left the rest, joggled through the hall as if someone was running and she heard a voice quietly call out,

"Mistress Mabel?"

She thought it was Gabriel but she couldn't be sure. Not until she saw him with her own eyes would she acknowledge that it was indeed him and it was safe.

She heard him banging on the door of the buttery, now with worry in his voice.

"Mistress Wetherspring? Please... it's Sir Gabriel. Open the door."

Should she go back in?

Was her attacker still there?

"Shut up you idiot!" shouted an interrupted sleeper.

Mabel decided to try to lure Sir Gabriel out into the courtyard. That way she'd be safe.

Turning quickly back into herself, she shouted as loudly as she could, "I am here, Sir Gabriel."

It took the man a while to realise that she was no longer in the buttery.

More groans and shouts of, "Oh for the love of Christ shut up!" echoed from the manor hall as folk took being disturbed from their slumbers with ill humour.

Sir Gabriel crashed open the outer door, just as Mabel called to him again.

"Oh do be quiet!" Mabel recognised the voice of one of the undercooks who did not sleep in the kitchen.

Sir Gabriel came down the manor steps.

"Mistress Mabel?"

"Here."

The knight lifted a candle to catch her in its glow. He jumped in surprise when he saw her for she was as white as a ghost in her shift, barefooted with a face as pale as the barn owl she had heard earlier.

"What? What...?"

"Someone managed to get into my room."

"No... They cannot..."

"I tell you they did."

"But I have tried the door. It's locked."

"Then they are still there."

"Mistress... why would they have locked themselves in?"

"I don't know... I..."

Sir Gabriel looked her up and down.

"Did you lock them in?"

"No. I... I... jumped through the window."

Quickly Gabriel looked up at the wall of the manor.

"The window?"

"I wasn't asleep and heard them enter, however they did."

"Who did you see?"

"No one but a dark shadow."

"You were dreaming."

"No. I tell you. Someone was there. They tried to lay hands on me." Mabel was now shaking with shock and cold.

The knight put his arms around her and she noticed he was dressed only in his braies and shirt.

Mabel limped a little as he led her back up the steps. 'Let him think that the jump from the window gave me some damage.'

"Oh... you are hurt?"

'Success.'

"How on earth did you manage to get to the ground without much more hurt than you seem to have sustained?"

"Ah... I have hurt my wrist too where I landed and..." She showed him her palms, hurt the other day. "Grazed my palms too."

"We shall get you to the still room... if we can find the key, and tend your hurts."

Mabel sighed. "Alas all the keys are at my home." She smiled sweetly at him.

"The Lady Stokke has keys as does Master Steward but I do not want to disturb them."

"Then perhaps we shall turn about and walk to your home? Can you walk that far?"

"With help, no doubt."

He wound his arm around her and gently, so that she did not bruise her delicate feet, he steered her to her cottage.

At the very last, he picked her up and pushed open the door.

"There are spills by the fire and I have left it lit for tomorrow. We need only to blow on the embers."

He set her down and on his knees blew on the fire until it was a good blaze, feeding it with twigs and pine cones which she had set to the side.

She sought out her shoes and her blue cloak.

"Thank you so much for your help."

"I am fulfilling a promise to the Lord Stokke to help and protect you."

Mabel's heart sank and her stomach lurched. Not for himself then.

"Well, I thank you anyway."

"Now, let me find you something to drink to warm you and you must tell me everything that happened. The lord will wish to know tomorrow."

Mabel sought out an unguent for her palms and then, with some warmed ale in a pot and her fingers curled around it, she sat on the edge of her bed and told her tale again.

Sir Gabriel leaned forward attentively and listened, a cup clutched in his hand.

"I retired before everyone had gone from the hall."

"I saw you."

"Oh…" He had noticed her then?

"And I locked the door and bolted it. Then I did the same with the shutters. I lay down to sleep but I could not. After a while I heard footsteps approaching."

"Do you know where they came from?"

Mabel thought hard.

"The manor door was locked from the inside so they must have come from the hall or the pantry."

"There are about twenty people sleeping in the hall tonight. No one would take any notice if someone got up from their place and went, for example, to relieve themselves."

"I thought I heard the person say that they'd seen a mouse."

"A mouse?"

"Yes and next I knew, there was a little mouse crawling under my door."

"Mistress Wetherspring, have you made all this fuss over a little mouse?"

Mabel grew hot and cross. "Of course I haven't! What is a little mouse to me? I'm not afraid of mice. But I am afraid of men who'd like to strangle me like they did my best friend."

She'd managed to get a sob into her voice; it wasn't difficult. She did feel very vulnerable and teary.

"If you don't believe me, you had better leave and go back to your bed by the fire."

The man ran his fingers through his wavy hair.

"Forgive me. I can see this has rattled you." He licked his lips and held them with his teeth for a moment.

"But I still do not understand how this man got into your room, through a locked door, managed to attack you, perhaps get out again and lock the door from the inside and bolt it, for there's no doubt the bolts are still employed and then..." He shook his head. "Disappear completely before anyone who was awakened, noticed them."

Mabel shrugged. "Perhaps he came out of the window after me?"

"Did you see him?"

She had to admit she had not.

"I can only tell you what I saw and felt. Do you think that I would propel myself out of a window if I was just frightened by a dream... or a mouse?"

"Well... no... you don't strike me as the sort of woman..."

"Well then!" said Mabel petulantly.

"Then tomorrow we shall have a look at the room and see what we can see. But I still cannot understand how anyone could have got in there and locked the door... and got out again without being seen."

Mabel turned away from him and in the tiniest voice possible she said. 'No. You can't. But I can.'

CHAPTER NINE ~ CLUES

Mabel was afraid.

She was afraid that there was another shapeshifter in the village and that they were using that power for evil. She'd never do that.

For eight years, the ability to make herself any animal she cared to change into, was achieved solely for her own fun. Then with Master Greathouse's death she'd tried to use her skill to help. She'd tried to use it for good.

Now she felt she was in danger.

And there was no one she could tell.

That was the most terrifying thing.

She could not tell *anyone*.

Sir Gabriel decided that he would stay with Mabel in her house that night, even though she did not think it was a wise idea. She'd rather protect herself by changing into something which would evade her enemy and she didn't want Sir Gabriel there when she did so.

But he wouldn't be influenced.

"I'll sleep here by the door. No one will get in without I hear or feel them," he said.

Mabel nodded. "If you must," and under her breath muttered, 'you have no idea what you're dealing with.'

"I beg your pardon?"

"Nothing."

The man looked at her with a look of disbelief. "I am only doing my job."

"Yes. I'm sorry. It's just I don't want anyone else to be in danger because of me."

He opened the door and looked back at her.

"I'll just go and fetch my things and then..."

"I have a spare mattress, some blankets and a pillow. There's no need to drag yours from the hall in the dark."

Mabel sought out the mattress which had been her mother's and Sir Gabriel laid it by the door.

"Right... well then..."

"Shall I leave a candle lit?"

"That might be a good idea."

"I'll leave it in a dish of water... just in case."

Mabel had never slept in the same room with a man before and it felt odd. A little embarrassing. She turned away from him and lay on her bed wriggling to get her poor hurts comfortable. It was going to be a long night.

"Goodnight."

Mabel's brain was too active for sleep. She heard Sir Gabriel tossing and turning.

After a while she rolled over onto her back and took a look at him. He was lying with his eyes open, staring at the roof, his hands clasped on his chest.

"Sir Gabriel?"

"Hmm?"

"When it's light, in addition to the buttery, might we go and look in a few cottages in the village. I have an idea which I'd like to try out."

"What do you want to try out?" He rose up on his elbow.

"Well... I think that whoever killed Master Greathouse also killed my friend Elinor. And that they think that I am a danger to them because I know something."

"Yes. I think we are both in agreement there."

"And yet we are still not absolutely certain *why* Master Edward was killed."

"You're saying if we can discover that, then we have the murderer of Mistress Elinor?"

"I think we need to look in his house again and in the houses of any of the people with whom he had a... shall we say, disagreement."

"You know who those people were?"

"Well most of them, I think."

Suddenly there was a rolling grumble.

"Oh I beg your pardon, if I am up in the middle of the night, my stomach tends to grumble."

"Oh... are you hungry?"

"Well..."

"I have a pie. It's a rabbit pie. It was made by my friend Elinor. She left it for me the night she... was ... died."

"Well, I don't want to put you to any trouble."

"I don't want to eat it."

"Then it won't go to waste."

Mabel padded over to her table and took out the pie from the metal box where she stored food to keep it from vermin and flies.

"The pastry may be a little stale and hard but the contents will be alright."

Mabel cut Sir Gabriel a piece of pie.

He set to with relish.

She watched him, her chin on her hands. She had never been given to flights of fancy. Oh, dear me no. But in that instant the possibilities of a life with Sir Gabriel Warrener, scored themselves across her mind like a stylus on a waxed tablet.

'Could this be how it might be?'

She sighed. And the wax tablet was suddenly erased with a hot flame.

He was a knight and she merely the daughter of a bailiff. 'Don't be daft, Mabel.'

"This is very good. Your friend was a good cook."

"She was."

"Did she often bring you food?"

"When she had time, yes."

"Is this because you are not a very good cook, Mistress Mabel?" he chuckled.

The dream was shattered. The wax tablet disintegrated.

"I..."

"Oh I'm sorry. I didn't mean to imply..."

"I can cook. When I have to," said Mabel with just a little irritation.

'Poor, hungry wifeless so and so,' she said to herself. 'Look at him, tucking in with delight to a two day old pie!'

"I eat sometimes in hall and sometimes when I want to be alone, here at home," she said.

"You don't have any family?"

"None. And Ellie was my only friend."

"So no young man?"

The church bell began to ring in Mabel's brain. Like it did when there was a marriage in the village. Now what did *that* mean?

"No... I have no young man."

"Oh. I thought that a lovely young lady like you would be in demand... in the village."

"How so?" said Mabel, fluttering her eyelashes even though he couldn't see them.

"Well. You have a good position. Your own home..."

"No. No one."

"And Elinor...? She was a very pretty lady. Did she have anyone?"

The wedding bell suddenly sounded cracked in her brain. And then the clapper fell out.

"No... No one for her either." She stared at him. "But you're right. She was a very pretty lady."

Sir Gabriel realised by the cold tone of her voice that she was displeased with him.

He sought to make amends.

"If I were to put the two of you together side by side... well. I would find it difficult to choose between you."

Mabel got up and lurched over to her bed.

"I am tired. If you have finished... your pie." she said with further irritation.

"I'll have another piece if you don't mind."

"Certainly. Help yourself."

She swung her legs up.

Then... she stopped.

"What did you say?"

"I said that I'd have another pi...."

"No. Before that."

"Oh I..."

"That you'd have difficulty telling us apart?"

"Yes. You are both pretty ladies. Both the same height, similar hair. If I came upon you from the back, I'd find it difficult to..."

Mabel hugged her knees. "Do you know, I think you have just said something very clever?"

Gabriel Warrener paused mid bite.

"I have?"

"You have."

He chewed and swallowed.

"Like what?

"What if Master Greathouse was *not* the person whom the killer wished to die?"

"You mean like mistress Elinor was mistaken for you because she was wearing your blanket?"

"Yes. Was Master Greathouse in the wrong place at the wrong time? What if he looked like someone else? What if the murderer mistook Master Greathouse for his target and made a mistake?"

Sir Gabriel swallowed and coughed as a large piece of pie went down the wrong way.

"I thought a while back that I was looking at this from the wrong end," Mabel said.

"You mean that you have been looking for clues about Edward Greathouse and why folk would want *him* dead but all the time..." said Sir Gabriel, "he's had nothing to do with it?"

"It's not impossible... is it?"

Sir Gabriel's gaze withdrew from her and she could see him turning things over in his mind.

He lay down slowly.

"Then we must start again."

"We?"

"We must start again and look at who Edward might be mistaken for and what might be the motive for *their* death."

"We?"

He turned his head and smiled at her and her heart gave a huge lurch.

"You'll need help," he said.

*****

Mabel did not want help.

How could she use her shapeshifting powers if she was always having to be on her guard because Sir Gabriel was with her?

She knew it was a reliable method of hearing and seeing things which in her human shape she would never be able to ascertain.

She wanted to argue with him but was too tired.

Upon the next morning, a dull and overcast day, she went to the manor to oversee those jobs which she had set aside for that day and those which were done every day.

There were many people staying at the manor at that moment and Mabel had to make sure that all chamber pots were emptied, all washing basins of water replenished, floors swept, laundry done and jugs of wine and ale ready for consumption.

She stood the scullions in a row and gave them their instructions.

"And Adera, make sure this time that the Lord Stokke's brass is polished to a gleam. Remember how I taught you to do it so you leave no fingerprints?"

"Yes, Mistress Wetherspring."

"And Amys, leave the buttery. I will do that room."

Amys gave a bob of a curtsey.

Sir Gabriel followed her around like a loyal dog, his eyes watching everything and at last when they came to the buttery, he wandered in after her and closed the door. They'd had to break in and it would need repairing.

"So, show me here, what happened."

"There's the little hole through which the mouse crept," she pointed.

He bent to look. "Doesn't look big enough does it?"

"They are really tiny and can squeeze themselves in the smallest of spaces." She didn't like to tell him that she knew from personal experience.

Sir Gabriel went over to the window. He looked back at Mabel and then looked at the window again.

"Show me how you got out of the window."

She had been dreading this question.

"I squeezed myself through the bars and jumped."

"There's not a lot of room."

"Sir Gabriel, are you saying I'm fat?"

He looked horrified.

"No. No of course not." He looked her up and down. "You're a petite, well made woman."

She did not thank him.

He stood by the window and looked into the room.

"How did you manage to get away?"

"As he lunged for me, I scratched him."

"Scratched him... that is interesting."

"And I bit him."

"Bit him eh?"

He smirked and scraped his cheek with his fingernail.

"A veritable cat, Mistress Wetherspring."

Mabel took in an involuntary breath. No, he didn't know. He didn't. He couldn't.

"This means of course that our culprit may be easier to spot."

"You mean he will be marked."

"If there are suspects, we must examine them not only by speaking to them but by looking for scratches and bite marks."

"Well I never. I'd never have thought of that!"

He gave her a snide look but did not reply.

Gabriel began to search the floor; he quartered the flagstones thoroughly.

"He's left us no clue here." Then a thought came to him.

"He cannot have got through the window after you. He must have been able to lock the door with the key and somehow get the bolts drawn. How might you do that?"

Down on one knee, the man began to fiddle with the lock, the latch and the broken bolts.

"Who has a key?"

"I told you last night. The Lord, Lady Stokke, the steward and me but it's not often locked. Only at night when all are finished with supplies."

"Anyone might come in during the day and tamper with the locks."

"Difficult because you'd be seen by anyone in the great hall, if you were here for any length of time and were not supposed to be."

"There are times when there's no one about."

"It's rare. The passageway is a thoroughfare."

Mabel was getting cross. Here they were discussing things she knew *hadn't* happened and they were wasting time.

"You cannot have locked and barred the door as you thought you had."

"I *did*. And may I remind you, that you found it locked and barred when you answered my call."

His lip lifted in disdain. He was getting annoyed with this awkward woman.

Mabel turned her back to him and looked out of the window. "I think it would be a good idea if you were to distract the people whose houses I wish to search and…"

"Why's that?"

"Because you have authority. You are a knight. The village people will obey you."

He chuckled. "*You* don't."

She ignored that. "You think you will be better at examining them? You who don't know them at all?"

"I think I can ask questions just as well as you."

Mabel sighed. "Someone has to get the folk out of their houses, if they are at home."

Sir Gabriel opened the buttery door.

"Then let us go and see who *is* at home. Where to first?"

As they walked down the steps together, Mabel said, "Alfred Stockman."

"Why?"

Mabel almost betrayed herself then, but at the last moment drew back from telling him about the brooch. "I have seen him acting suspiciously. I need to see what he's been up to."

Luckily Alfred Stockman was not at home. It seemed he was busy out in the fields tending to the lord's cattle.

"You stay here and I'll go in and look. If I find anything then…"

"What are you looking for?" asked Gabriel.

"I won't know until I find it."

He tutted. "Meanwhile, what do I do?"

"Keep watch. I'll need to know if he comes home."

Whilst Sir Gabriel walked up and down outside the cottage, not trying to look conspicuous at all, Mabel searched for the brooch which she'd found the time she'd entered Alfred's house as a jackdaw.

It was missing. But in its place was the larger version of the same brooch which Mabel had found in the Hartshorn house.

'So now where's it gone?'

"Anything?" asked Warrener.

"A puzzle that's all," said Mabel, worrying her lip.

Gabriel tapped his foot. "Going to tell me, are you?"

"Not quite at the moment."

"So when will be the moment?"

"If I find the thing I'm looking for elsewhere, then I'll tell you."

"I might be able to help."

"I could tell you and you'd have no idea what I was talking about."

"How do you know that, Mistress-know-all?"

"I know this village. I know the people. You have been here... what... a week? What do you know?"

Gabriel stared at her. He wanted to slap her with some witty rejoinder but he couldn't think of anything quickly enough.

They had been so busy arguing that they hadn't seen Alfred approaching his house.

"Good day, Sir, Mistress." He cast a glance inside his open door. "Did you want me?"

"Alfred," said Mabel, a little surprised.

"That's my name. Every day. Since I was..."

"Don't be flippant," said an irritated Sir Gabriel.

Alfred's face lost its grin.

"I want to ask you a question Alf and I want a truthful answer," said Mabel.

"Always the truth for you, Mistress Mabel," said a smiling Alfred, pointedly looking at Sir Gabriel.

"You have a brooch... in your house..."

"Have you been snooping?"

"I've been asking around."

"What for?"

"How did you get that brooch, Alf?"

"None of your business."

"The Lord Stokke has made it my business," said Mabel. "He wants to find the killer of Master Greathouse and I want to find Elinor's killer."

Alfred's face blanched. "You can't think that I had anything to do with either of those..."

"The brooch is valuable, Alf," said Mabel. "You're a humble farmer... how did you get it?"

"It's mine. It was my mother's." Alfred jutted his chin in defiance.

"There's another one, isn't there?"

"I don't know what you mean."

"Alfred, please don't lie to me or I really will have to think that you have something to do with these deaths," said Mabel.

"Just answer the question," said Sir Gabriel, coming closer.

Mabel towed Alfred into the darkness of his house.

"Come with me."

She fished the brooch out of the box.

"Now... this one was last seen in the Hartshorn house..." Mabel held it out on her palm.

"How do you know that?" shrieked Alfred, now visibly worried.

"Will I find the smaller one which *you* had, in the Hartshorn house now?"

Alfred was perspiring. "How do *you* know?"

"I just do."

"Mistress," he glanced towards Warrener lounging outside. "Mabel. You don't understand."

"Oh but I think I do, Alf."

"I can't tell you. It would ruin everything."

Mabel took hold of the man's sleeve and towed him to the back wall of the cott.

She whispered. "You and Emma Hartshorn?" Mabel realised that the two lovers she'd heard were Emma and Alfred.

Alfred closed his eyes and groaned. "Ohh nooo."

"Still in love with her aren't you?"

He tossed his head back and forth.

"And she with you."

"Ah no... We..."

"An exchange of gifts?"

Alfred tried to deny it but he could see it was futile.

"She's set to marry Smitan next Friday," said Mabel.

Alfred looked sad. "I know. We know."

"Then why all this... underhand...?"

"Mabel. Her da won't let me marry her," he said at a loud whisper.

"So she'll marry Simon Smitan and carry on a clandestine affair with you?"

Alfred's head ducked to his chest. "If Simon gets wind of this..."

"He hasn't, he won't."

"It won't be pretty, Alf."

"Listen Mabel... please. You are the only one who knows. Please... just leave it be."

"Leave what be?"

Alfred threw a concerned glance at Sir Gabriel but he was watching a pair of squirrels high up in the branches of an oak tree.

"We're eloping."

"You idiots! You're a tied villein and so is Emma. Tied by law to Sir Robert Stokke. They'll come and find you. And then that will be that. You'll never be together again. He'll probably transfer one of you to another village. And your punishments won't be pleasant."

"They won't find us..."

"You leave the village before the wedding and everyone is going to think that you are the killer. Stands to reason. Flee and you're guilty. They'll come after you."

"But I'm *not*."

"No. I don't think you are."

"Please Mabel, don't say anything."

Mabel looked up at the heavens and swore in her head.

"You have no idea what it's like. I love Emma... have done for a long time. She loves me. It's agony being apart."

"Yes, I suppose it is." She did feel sorry for them.

He grabbed her sleeve.

"Let us at least try to have a chance at happiness."

She sighed. "I know nothing," she said baldly into the air and walked away.

"Well?" asked Sir Gabriel.

"He's not our killer."

"How do you know?"

"I just do."

He scuffed up the stones of the road. "I thought we were going to work together?"

"I never said that."

He fixed his blue eyes on her with reproach in the look and sighed. "Do you know, I could get angry? But I won't because I am such an amenable man. Sometimes I think I am my own worst enemy!"

"Not when I'm around," said Mabel testily and instantly regretted it.

*****

To cover her embarrassment she strode off in the direction of the forge house.

Sir Gabriel was forced to catch up.

"So where are you going now?"

"Just to the next house where I think we might find a clue."

"I take it you didn't find a clue at the last one?"

"Actually, I did but it served to clear the occupant of all guilt."

"And this one? What are we looking for here?"

Mabel really didn't want to tell Sir Gabriel that she had remembered something important from one of her little investigations when she had been passing as a squirrel.

"I thought I saw Simon Smitan with something interesting earlier on."

"You thought that about the last man, I suppose."

"This is what investigating is all about, Sir Gabriel. You have an idea. You test the idea and on many occasions you are wrong and have to think again."

"And upon what do you base this amazing theory? Your one investigation?"

"If you are getting bored, sir, you may leave me." 'Oh yes please,' she said to herself. 'Then I can get on with doing things properly.'

Warrener shrugged. "Whatever I think, I promised the lord I'd stay with you and make sure you are safe. So that's what I shall do."

She gave him an exasperated look.

"Well then let's just 'happen' to pass the smithy and see whether Master Smitan is there. That will give us an idea of how long we might have to search his house."

They passed the forge at an amble, trying to look for all the world as if they were simply out for a nice walk together.

Simon Smitan was looking at a horse's hoof, his back to them and didn't even notice their passage. But Mabel saw that he had scratches to the bare arm with which he held the hoof.

Quickly they skirted the back of the smithy and sped to his house a few yards away.

Mabel took a deep breath.

The interior, like all cottages, was dark, for the windows were small and little light came in through the door. Mabel noticed that the windows both had horn panels inserted into them. She couldn't remember if they had been in place before. She stared at them. No, she was certain she'd entered the house as a squirrel and had dropped in through the right hand window. These were new. Now why had

Simon decided he needed to have horn in his windows?

Mabel stood by the table. Gabriel peered into the interior from the door.

"What are you looking for?"

Mabel was searching quickly and didn't feel like answering him.

"Aha!"

She had found the piece of material which she'd first seen Master Smitan pulling up to his face. She did the same.

"Ugh!" Yes, the same smell she had noticed as a squirrel and as a jackdaw.

"What? You alright?"

"Yes... perfectly."

Mabel stuffed the material into the neck of her kirtle and trotted out of the cottage. Not until she reached the tree behind the Hartshorn house did she stop and take it out.

Gabriel, looking behind him all the time, as if they were being followed, came up quickly.

"What's that?"

"This is a piece of the sheet which covered the dead Master Edward," said Mabel with meaning.

"How do you know?"

"I saw the body brought in," she half lied. "And shortly after, I saw Smitan with it."

"What does that mean?"

"I'm not sure. But why would you want to keep a piece of what is effectively a shroud of a man who has been dead four days?"

"There are some strange people around, Mabel, you know."

Mabel looked him up and down.

"Yes, I know," she said.

CHAPTER TEN ~ BAITING THE TRAP

Mabel felt brave.

"Let's go and ask Simon Smitan about this. See what he says."

"If you're sure."

Once again they ambled along the lane to the forge.

The controller of the horse which had been shod was completing the transaction. No money was changing hands, just a little barter. This often happened in the village where food or goods were just as important as coin.

Mabel hid the scrap of fabric behind her back as the horse was led away.

"Simon, have you a moment?"

"Mistress Wetherspring."

Not sure if Gabriel had met the village blacksmith before, Mabel introduced them.

Simon bowed. "Good day sir. You are from Stockley, I believe."

"Yes, here with the Lord Robert on his progress through his manors."

Simon nodded. "What might I do for you?"

Mabel noticed that the man spoke to Sir Gabriel, not to her.

"How long have you had the horn panels in your windows,

Simon?" said Mabel quickly.

The blacksmith laughed. "Ah yes. I got them recently for when Emma comes to live with me."

"When you marry?"

"You know that she is used to fine things. I promised to try to mend my bachelor ways and make the house a little more..."

"Secure?"

His eyes crinkled in mirth.

"Warm, for one thing and private for another. Emma insisted."

"And... What are you doing with this?"

The man's eyes screwed up. She saw him swallow.

"Ah... yes... I know it's awful... but... it was a moment of... sentimentality." He didn't ask her where she'd got it. Interesting.

"You Simon, sentimental?"

Sir Gabriel was out of his depth. He didn't see the inner workings of the conversation.

Mabel turned to enlighten him. "The dead man, Edward Greathouse, was Simon's childhood friend. They were very close. You were very close weren't you Simon?"

"Aye, aye we were."

"And this is why you felt that you had to have a piece of what amounts to his cerecloth?"

"I know it seems odd but it was his. It smelled of him. It was something to remember him by. For a short while."

"Not the sort of thing you'll want your new wife to see in your house, eh?" said Mabel.

"No. It's quite unsavoury and I'd decided to get rid of it."

"A piece of material which wrapped a dripping corpse of... How many days?"

Again she saw his Adam's apple bob up and down. "I know. It was stupid of me. I have been so shattered by his death."

Mabel took the cloth by the finger and thumb and gave it back to him. "Here we are. I think you should burn it, Simon."

He took it. "Yes. Yes I shall."

Mabel walked into the forge and ran her eyes around the place.

"How long have we known each other, Simon?" said Mabel.

The smith stared at the sky and widened his stance, folding his arms over his chest. "Oh it must be almost twenty years?"

"Really so long?"

"Well I knew your mother so..."

"You have been at Bedwyn all your life?" asked Sir Gabriel.

"Ah no. I came from one of the lord's other manors."

"Rutishall, I believe?" said Mabel.

"Yes that's correct." His brow furrowed in puzzlement.

"Your father was the blacksmith there and transferred here, didn't he?"

"The lord had no blacksmith farrier here in Bedwyn. He decided that we should come here."

"And that is when you struck up the friendship with the young Edward?"

"That is why we have been friends for so long. Yes."

"You must miss him," said Gabriel.

"I do. I do... greatly."

"Oh dear. I see that you have a nasty scratch on your arm. I hope you're looking after it. You know how these things can turn nasty," said Mabel, suddenly changing the subject.

"Indeed I do know. A blacksmith is in danger of all sorts of injuries. Mistress."

"How did you get that?"

He stretched out his forearm. "This? Would you believe, I was helping Mistress Houndstooth with her new puppies? Have you seen them?"

The Houndstooths were the Lord Stokke's huntsmen. They bred the dogs which the lord used to hunt. Not here in the forest, for of course, it was forbidden, but at his other manors.

"They are lively little beasts. They have very sharp claws and teeth."

"I'm sure they do." Mabel smiled. "I'll go and have a look at them. I love puppies."

The blacksmith smiled back. "They're in the south barn."

"Ah well we shall leave you... you must have a lot of work to do."

"Yes indeed."

They ambled nonchalantly away from the forge.

Gabriel looked back once.

"You know Mistress Mabel, the blacksmith's forge has so many implements which can do harm, in the wrong hands."

"I know it, Sir Gabriel," she said, picking up speed.

"Where are we going?"

"Well, I don't know about you... but I love puppies. I am going to the south barn."

*****

Sir Gabriel scratched his head.

"Well... there they are. Puppies."

Five little brown dogs were tumbling about in straw with their mother looking on. She seemed quite happy for visitors.

"So now you know what they look like," said Warrener, leaning on the wattle fence which kept them in the pen.

Mabel squeezed through a panel of the wattle and went down on her hands and knees.

"Do you notice anything Sir Gabriel?"

The puppies squirmed and clambered over each other to reach her, squeaking and yelping.

Suddenly she was crawling with mewling, writhing creatures and she laughed and laughed and laughed and fell onto her back, one of them sitting on her face.

"Don't they make you happy?" She picked one and held it up in front of her. It loved being singled out.

Sir Gabriel smiled.

"Well they obviously make *you* happy."

Mabel could not help it; she giggled and squirmed with the puppies whilst Warrener looked on.

Eventually even he had a huge grin on his face. Sadly he wouldn't come and play with them.

Mabel wiped her eyes of happy, laughing tears and sat up in the straw. Picking out the bits from her hair and clothes, she said, "Notice anything?"

Gabriel stared and cocked his head to one side. "There are five of them. They're brown."

"They are about six weeks old now. And my, how they've grown since I saw them last."

"Ah... you've seen them before? You knew about them?"

"Frankly, any puppies born in the village... I have to go and see them."

He shrugged. She supposed he meant, 'And?'

"Their eyes open at two weeks and at three they're clambering around tussling with their littermates. They get their baby teeth at two weeks."

"They're much more confident now."

"And at six weeks, their tails are constantly wagging and they are already seeking the approbation of their human companions."

Mabel held out her hands and the little creatures began to play with her fingers, biting and pulling.

She lifted her sleeve, offering up an arm for the puppies to clamber over.

Mabel was in her element. She adored puppies.

Finally she stood and squeezed back out of the compound.

"So I ask you again. Notice anything?" She held out her arms.

Sir Gabriel frowned. Then slowly light dawned.

"Ah," he said, "I see."

The puppies had damaged Mabel's arm but the scratches were superficial. No blood had been drawn and they were merely red or white marks.

*****

They wandered back over the green and out from the house by the river came Thomas Peabody.

He sported a face as black as a thunder cloud.

"Ah Thomas. Just the person," said Mabel. "Oh dear, are you in a bad mood?"

Sir Gabriel gave her a strange look for hadn't she just told him that they were off to speak to Master Hogman.

"How is your mother now?"

"Better now that Master Greathouse is in the earth."

They'd buried Edward Greathouse, at last, the previous day.

"She's come to terms with the fact he's gone?"

"Well if you mean by that there's no more moping about. Yes."

He was walking away from them when Mabel said. "You too will be glad when things are over."

He turned..."Over?"

"I mean of course the marriage of Simon and Emma."

Tom's face reddened.

"Why should I care?"

"Oh I think you do."

Tom put his hands to his waist. "I can't stand about chatting... I've work to do."

"Oh Tom. Is your work a little difficult today? Does that account for your bad mood? What are you doing?"

"What?"

"Your forearms—you're scratched."

Tom looked at his arms.

"Pah. I didn't even know I'd done it."

"And yet blood has flowed."

Sir Gabriel narrowed his eyes and took a good look. "How *did* you do it?"

"If you must know, we are assarting the wood at the back of Master Hogman's. There's many brambles there. It must have been those which got me."

Mabel nodded.

"It must be something which happens to you often."

"Yes, Mistress Wetherspring it does. Now if you don't mind."

"Take care Tom," said Mabel. "Keep that temper of yours in check."

Tom eyed her strangely, then nodded. It was a look which said, 'what does she know, eh?'

They followed him at a distance to Master Hogman's property.

The little pigs were squealing and snorting at the back of the house, happy in their mud and grime, their mucky little snouts grubbing in the earth for roots, worms and insects.

Mabel remembered her time as a pig and watched them for a while, revelling in the memories. She'd really enjoyed being a hog.

Master Hogman was supervising the lads grubbing up the bushes at the back of his house.

He caught sight of Sir Gabriel and hurried over.

"Before you say anythin'. I got permission for this from the lord."

"I'm sure you do," said Warrener. "You know too well the penalties for illegal assarting, don't you?"

"I'll go and get my warrant... thing."

"Ah no, Master Hogman. That isn't why we've come to talk to you," said Mabel.

"It's not?"

He seemed really puzzled. What could the housekeeper of the manor and a trusted knight of the lord's mesnie want with him?

"I just have some questions," said Mabel. "I hope you and your family are better now, after the awful food tainting."

Hogman rubbed his belly.

"No real lastin' effects but it wasn't pleasant."

"You were laid up for some days I hear."

"Aye. Me and the missus, several days. The childer got better quick. Young Harold managed to miss it completely. Dunno how."

"Was it one of your porkers which was roasted at Midsummer, Master Hogman?"

"Aye it was. Did it meself." He puffed out his chest.

"Perhaps... you hadn't quite cooked the beast properly?" said Mabel wide eyed.

"What? Corse I 'ad. What a thing to say. I bin' cooking hogs since you were a glint in yer father's eye."

Mabel had only eaten a piece of the crackling at the edge of the roasted pig. And then only a little. She wasn't fond of pork. Perhaps it was a good job.

"Did you let Mistress Hartshorn have some, Arthur?"

"Now why would I do that? It's up to 'er to get 'er own from the roast on the green."

"Because I think you are rather fond of Mistress Hartshorn aren't you?"

"Fond?" The man looked at her with one eye.

"As in you enjoy her company, now and again when her husband is away in the forest. And your wife is at her work in the manor."

"Well...?"

"Be careful Master Hogman. Husbands, lovers and husbands-to-be around here have a habit of becoming quite dead." Gabriel gave Mabel a strange look. He desperately needed to know why she was going round insulting and making accusations against village men.

"And I'd get that bite tended to. They can fester nastily."

Hogman clutched his neck where he sported a very red bite mark.

As they walked away Gabriel stood in front of her. "What's all this about?"

"Just one more man."

Gabriel stopped her. "Haha no. Not until you let me in on what you're doing?"

Mabel chewed the inside of her lip. "Alright. What have you noticed about all the men that I've spoken to so far?

Now Gabriel felt just a little clever. "Ah yes. They all of them have bites or scratches on them."

"They do... yes... It's true. But there is also something else."

"There is?"

"They are all the same height and build as Master Greathouse."

She walked on.

*****

"So what was all that for?"

"I have been sowing seeds of doubt amongst some of the village men."

"Only those who have wounds which you may have inflicted when they attacked you and who are the same size and shape as this Greatman fellow."

"Greathouse. Correct."

"Why?"

Mabel sat on the edge of her bed and took off her shoes. Wriggling her toes and massaging her soles she said, "One of them may have been the man who tried to kill me last night."

"Yeah."

"Master Edward was mistaken by the murderer for one of them."

"Why's that?"

"Because he was allegedly seen kissing a woman with whom quite a few men in the village have had an affair or are having a relationship."

"Emma?"

"That's right. But Emma now only has eyes for one man and wouldn't be seen kissing anyone but him. Truly. I know her, she's a good girl really."

Gabriel clapped his hands, "I see it. Someone thought that Greathouse had kissed Emma."

"Er... no."

"No?"

"You remember this is all about the similarities between people?"

"Ah yes."

Mabel jumped up from her stool. "It's dinner time. We'll go to the hall and then I really must do some work."

"And I have to stay with you."

"I shall be polishing silver in the buttery."

"A boring job."

"Yes. I'm sure I'll be quite safe there during the day."

Gabriel laughed. "If anyone approaches you, you can swipe them over the head with a silver ewer...or something."

"I could... yes."

'Or I could do something else entirely,' thought Mabel.

They walked on in that dull morning, to the manor and climbed the steps.

"You go to your accustomed table and I will go to mine," said Mabel, "and if you insist we shall meet afterwards."

Mabel went to the steward Henry Buttermere who was supervising the drink for dinner.

"Master Buttermere, after dinner I shall be in the buttery and wish to clean some of the silver. Can you have someone leave it for me there?"

"Certainly Mabel."

She never trusted anyone but herself to clean the silver. Sometimes, Master Buttermere beat her to it but more often than not he left the job to her. She enjoyed seeing the tarnish disappear as she rubbed the metal with grinding paste and buffed it to a shine.

The steward lined up a few jugs for the servitors to collect.

"Oh, Henry. What have you done to your hand?"

"I'm glad you are doing the cleaning, Mabel. I don't think I could. That blasted hound of the master's!"

"I think I know the one."

"He's a bad tempered sod... forgive me." The steward never swore. "I lean out to pick up a piece of meat with my knife. Up rises the blasted dog to the table and before I knew what was going on, he'd nabbed it."

"Oh you didn't fight him for it?" She truly would have liked to have seen that.

"I did... and he bit me."

"Oh dear. He really did. That will scar, I think." The steward had a crescent shaped wound on the back of his hand inflicted by an eye tooth piercing and then grazing.

"Take care of it, Henry." She picked up his hand. "Do you know, if I didn't know that it was a dog bite, I'd think it was a cat? An angry cat."

"Oh no mistress... it was definitely Thor. Bad tempered God and bad tempered dog!"

"Haha! Master Steward, you've made a joke."

'Well... swipe me... so I have."

Mabel mentally measured the steward. Yes, he too was similar to Master Greathouse but it was hard to see what motive he might have for his murder. Or Elinor's. He had been very fond of Ellie.

After dinner, taken at the fourth hour of the day, the servitors began to bring in the silver.

"Smidget?"

"Yes Mistress Wetherspring?"

"Can you tell me if any of you saw the master's big dog, Thor, attack Master Steward? When was it?"

"Oh yes... There was a great to do."

"There was?"

"Oh aye! It was when the mouse was seen under the dais table and one of the dogs got under there and it was kicked out and..."

Mabel cleared her throat. "Ah I see."

"It had come in at dinner and that was when..."

"Hmmm."

'Lucky escape then,' she said to herself.

She applied herself to the cleaning and washing and was finished by late afternoon when the silver was once more needed for the high table.

The servitors came back in and trooped off with it to set it all upon the pristine white linen tablecloth again for supper.

Mabel's back and neck hurt. She washed her hand of the mixture used to clean the silver and the tarnish which would inevitably stain her hands black.

Where was Sir Gabriel?

She decided to go and look for him. Might he be at her house, waiting for her?

Taking off her apron and tidying her hair, she left the buttery to the servants and slipped down the manor steps.

She looked up at the trees towards Ramsbury. A little breeze had blown up with the incoming dusk and she saw the top leaves riffling and swaying.

Oh how she'd love to be up there. In the free air. One last fly about before supper and bed.

She hadn't changed into anything which could fly for quite a while.

Well, it seemed like a while to her. The urge to fill her wings with soft summer air was overpowering and she took a swift look round.

No one was about.

She turned withershynnes three times.

"I'd like to be a swallow."

It was glorious to feel the air ripple over her. She skimmed the top of the trees and headed for the open field where she knew she'd be able to get up some speed. She wasn't alone. Many other swallows were diving and swooping, catching insects which were low to the ground in the dull and not too warm weather.

Mabel didn't need to catch insects.

She would go to her repast in the hall once she'd located Sir Gabriel.

She landed for a moment on a branch of a large wild pear, conscious of the cover this tree afforded. Other birds were there with her—a sparrow or two, a chaffinch singing his last song of the day 'wheet... wheet,' and a diminutive wren pouring his heart out, proclaiming this his tree.

One by one, the birds left, the wren chasing off a competitor.

Mabel lifted off and soared back to the village, swooping over the river as many other swallows, martins and swifts were doing. She felt safe amongst them. There were so many of them.

She followed them, mimicking their flight patterns and learning how they twisted and turned to catch flies.

Then she heard the alarmed shouts of the blackbird and the wren.

He had been on Mistress Hartshorn's roof singing his beautiful evening melody when suddenly he vacated his spot with a 'chuck, chuck, chuck,' followed by a shriek, dashing into the holly bush by the wall.

The swifts and swallows scattered making for the barns and their nests.

The sparrows ceased their chatter and hid in the hawthorn.

Mabel looked up. High above her silhouetted upon a pale grey cloud was the unmistakable shape of a sparrowhawk.

It stooped.

It had seen her and it singled her out.

She dived and as she plunged for cover into the tree in her garden and made for the dense growth by the trunk—the sparrowhawk would never find her there—she saw the feet of a man sticking out of a hazel bush.

"Jesus!" she cried, "No!" as she recognised the mailed feet of a knight. "It's Sir Gabriel!"

WITHERSHYNNES: IN THE DARK

CHAPTER ELEVEN ~ CONFESSION

She watched carefully from her safe perch to see if Sir Gabriel moved. Oh no! He wasn't moving at all.

Mabel turned deosil despite the fact she was still sitting in the tree and she set herself on a sturdy branch in order to clamber out of the foliage as a woman.

With difficulty she jumped down. The sparrows came out of their hiding places and began to cheep furiously above her. The blackbird continued his evening serenade from the roof of her house.

Quickly glancing at the heavens to see if she could spot the sparrowhawk, she ran full tilt to the bare earth under the hazel. "Sir Gabriel... Sir Gabriel!"

She pushed her way into the base of the bush and heard the man groan. He was alive... oh, thank the heavens.

Grabbing Sir Gabriel by his clothes she realised that he was wearing his maille as he always did, under his pale blue surcoat.

As his face came out of the bush, Mabel gave a short scream.

It was a mass of blood. It had trickled down onto his surcoat; it was coating his hair; it dribbled down his neck.

His eyes were closed; Mabel wiped her hand across them to clear them. He moaned again.

"Come, we must get you up."

"Argh..." the man staggered as Mabel tried to lift him and fell down to his knees. It was then she saw his hands. They too were bloodied and torn.

"Come... you must help me... Sir Gabriel... HELP ME!"

She looked round for his sword. His belt was missing entirely. He had no weapons.

Tiny though she was, Mabel somehow dug out some strength from deep inside her and managed to get Sir Gabriel's arm over her shoulder. Then slowly—agonisingly slowly—she staggered and dragged the poor man across the grass.

They fell through the cottage door.

Gabriel was moaning and tossing his head as if dreaming.

"Teeth... such... huge... couldn't... no... no... claws!" None of what he was saying was making sense.

"Just rest. Do not worry. I am here. We have got you to safety. You are now in my house. I will look after you."

She lit several lamps and set to work.

These words had seemed to calm him and his head flopped back. Where his maille coif had been folded down over his shoulders, she saw that his neck was a mass of bites and scratches.

Gently, Mabel laid the man on the floor and lifted the very heavy coif and ventail over his head.

'How do they wear these things all day?' she said to herself.

Next she pulled his arms up above his head and wriggled off the surcoat. His maille hauberk was very difficult to pull off and had to be done in stages. Under this he wore a gambeson, a padded jacket which also had to be pulled over his head. She undid the ties to the maille chausses and pulled them from his feet. Mabel was exhausted by the time she had him down to his braies and shirt.

Leaving the armour on the floor, Mabel got the man up and dragged him to the table, where she sat him on a bench. He fell forward and his head hit the wood of the table with a thunk.

'Oh dear.' Well, one more bruise was not going to be fatal.

Then she heated some water.

First she bathed his hands. He had obviously defended himself with them because they were torn and scratched. One finger was so badly bitten, Mabel wondered if she would have to take it off. She stared at it for a while. She even took out her knife and laid it on the table. No, she needed to make it good; as well as she could. He was a knight. He would be no good without fingers. How would he hold his sword?

She took some of her needle and thread made from gut and sewed it as neatly as she could. It was a good thing the poor man was out of his body.

Then she turned his head to the side.

There was a bite mark to one cheek which wasn't too bad but the worst thing, and the thing which had bled most copiously, was the deep gouge to his left cheek from the edge of his eye, almost to the crease in his mouth. Gone were his girlish good looks. That was for sure. This would scar.

Mabel bathed it gently, almost fearing to touch it. There was nothing for it. She took up her needle and thread again and in the tiniest stitches she could perform, she sewed the edges together. Sir Gabriel's face and forehead was a mass of bruises and smaller scratches; those would heal on their own. The puffiness would recede, she knew. Mabel's mind was working furiously as she performed all these tasks.

She fetched some of her special ointment, a recipe of her mother's, which she knew to be good for wounds. And then she cleaned his throat and neck of blood. Here too was a bite mark but this one had not been so grievous. She guessed this was because the maille coif and ventail had protected him in this area.

She examined the bite and was sure that if he had not been wearing that coif, his throat would have been torn out.

In a daze she went to her chest and fetched out some of her willow bark remedy. She poured it into a pot of ale and tried to get the poor man to take it. He could hardly swallow but some of it went into his mouth. That should help with the pain, if only a little. It was growing very dark now and Mabel lit more candles.

Then she staggered with Sir Gabriel to the bed and almost threw him onto it. Exhausted, she sat on the floor and put her head onto her arm, alongside the man's body and rested.

She had not intended to sleep but sleep she did and in the deep of the night, she awoke with her heart thumping.

She listened.

Could she hear footsteps?

Could she hear tortuous breathing?

A growl perhaps?

Mabel stood and taking her courage in both hands, she threw open the door.

By the tree in her garden she saw a humped grey shadow.

It turned and for a moment Mabel saw an unholy pair of evil, red amber eyes staring at her.

"You do not frighten me!" she cried out. "I will hunt you down. I know what you are."

The eyes dimmed. The shadow disappeared.

Shaking like an aspen leaf, Mabel closed the door on the wolf and bolted and barred it.

*****

It was dawn before Sir Gabriel awoke.

Mabel was looking at him when he opened his eyes. The immediate fear in them; the horrendous memory, the anguish and the pain made her gasp.

"I am here." She took his shoulder in her hand and squeezed gently.

Gabriel swallowed.

"Would you like something to drink?"

She lifted his shoulder and wriggled underneath him so that she could prop him up.

"Now take this slowly. It is ale with a pain relief potion in it."

He tried his best but a lot of the liquid went onto his bloodied shirt.

"Have you spare clothes in the manor?"

"I do," he managed to say.

"Then I'll go and fetch them in a while."

Gabriel looked up at her. She could see that he did not know how to explain what had happened to him.

"I will listen to your story before I go, so that I can tell Lord Stokke what has happened." Perhaps Gabriel would tell her something she *could* tell the lord.

"Ah... no... He will think I am bewitched," said Gabriel with difficulty.

"No... I ... I understand. I do. And so will he." Mabel wasn't really sure but she needed to keep him calm.

Gabriel shook his head violently. It obviously pained him

"No... he will... *not*."

"Just tell *me* what happened."

More drink later and Gabriel was ready to explain to her how he'd ended up in the hazel hedge.

"I swear to you, I was not drunk."

"No, I know you were not," she said. "There was no odour of drink on you."

"I was waiting for you to come back to the cottage. I knew that if you didn't come, you'd finish your work and then I would meet you in the hall for supper."

"It's a good job I did come home."

"I'd come to the house and had taken off my sword belt in order to wash."

Mabel knew how difficult it was for Gabriel to speak. His mouth was surrounded by scratches and gouges. He kept his teeth together and tried to speak through narrowed lips. It wasn't easy to understand him.

"I had just begun to search for a bowl into which to put some water when..."

Gabriel sobbed, "I swear to you..." and the rest was an incoherent mumble.

"You were about to take off your clothes, for you had no belts. No weapons."

"No... I'd thrown them down over there when I heard what sounded like someone calling my name from the yard outside."

"And perhaps you thought it was me?"

His eyes were full of tears. She didn't know if it was because of his tale or his hurts.

"I opened the door and looked out."

Gabriel closed his sore eyes.

"And there in the yard was..." Mabel took hold of him and gave him a reassuring hug.

"The biggest wolf you ever did see?"

Gabriel's eyes slowly moved up to her face.

"How... how can you possibly know?"

"I do know. I have seen it too."

Now tears were falling from his eyes, running down his scarred cheek.

"Shush... it's all right." said Mabel.

"I went out into the yard because I couldn't believe my eyes. It sprung and attacked me."

"You saw it clearly? In the growing dusk?"

"But there are no wolves... no wolves. Are there? Not here. Not anymore."

"I know... I know."

"So it... wasn't a wolf..."

"Sir Gabriel, it *was* a wolf. It was a wolf that made these nasty wounds on you."

Poor Gabriel was slipping into a pained sleep. A sleep borne of anxiety and the effort of fighting the demons in his brain and Mabel's remedy.

"You sleep and I'll stay here. And in a while I will go and get you some clean clothes and fetch the lord."

"Take care... take care..." he said as his eyes closed.

*****

The lord had gone to visit one of his neighbours and so she could not speak to him.

Sir Gabriel wasn't going to die of his wounds, she knew that, but she was worried the beast would return to finish what it had started so she did not want to leave him alone too long.

She tidied the house and set about making it absolutely animal proof.

She bolted the shutters and filled the gaps with mud. Not even a cockroach would get through now. As a swallow she flew up to the smoke hole and filled that too with mud, in the way in which that bird makes its nest.

The gap underneath the door she stuffed with rolled materials; old clothes which she was going to give to the poor. She wetted some rags and jammed them into the uprights to make sure that there could be no ingress for even a louse or an earwig.

A heavy animal might break down the door but she would have her bow ready. She would sit up all night if she had to.

Then she did sit and took some of her elderflower drink, watching for the rise and fall of Sir Gabriel's chest. The best remedy for him was sleep. At least for a while.

She began to think about the problem. Why was Sir Gabriel singled out?

It was a dangerous thing to do, take on a fully armoured knight. Mabel realised that if Gabriel had *not* been wearing his hauberk and maille coif, he would now be dead. The shapeshifter had not known how difficult it would be to attack and kill him.

Why did the shapeshifter not take *her* on again?

Perhaps he was firstly disposing of her aid and support and then he would come for her. She sat all morning in a cold sweat thinking about how she would deal with that moment.

*****

The sun was high in the heavens when she at last decided to go and fetch some clothes for Sir Gabriel.

How to do it?

With a quick glance at the knight sleeping on his bed, she rapidly changed into a spider.

Her body shrank. Her arms and legs multiplied. She became acutely aware of her surroundings and once again had to conquer a fear of being preyed upon. It was only for a few moments then her Mabel brain took over again.

On eight quick legs, she scurried up the wall to the thatch, wriggled into it and threaded her way through it at the gable end. Here she carefully made her way to the edge of the thatch and out into the air through the stalks of reed. Down, down she fell, suspended on a soft silken thread, pulled by a slight breeze.

She landed gently on the grass at the side of her house.

"Phew." That had taken it out of her and she rested a moment all eyes out for predators. All eight of them.

Whilst she rested, she glanced at her legs. How pretty they were; banded black and white. She realised that spiders could see only in muted colours. The green of the trees was a dark grey, the sky a whitish grey, Master Farmer's house a pale grey. Distance was blurred but her near sight was marvellous. How clear it all was.

She ran along the base of her wall, large sarsen stones one placed on another, and scurried to the back of her property where she couldn't be overlooked.

As a woman again, she peered around the edge of the house. Master Farmer was in his garden hoeing.

Mistress Mosspath was traipsing across the lane with her daughter; both had large jars on their shoulders. They were off to the river.

Mabel sauntered out and watched John Swineherd, driving his pigs from one enclosure to another. He would be there some time and her cottage would be in his view. She felt happier about that. No one was going to force their way in immediately.

She ran full tilt to the manor and located Sir Gabriel's pack. She found a clean shirt and some braies and pulled them out. Stuffing them into the neck of her kirtle, she ran speedily back.

Ah... a problem. "How am I going to get it into the house?"

There was nothing for it. "I wish to be a spider."

The same journey was executed again in reverse; this time Mabel scuttled up the gable end of her house and through the tangle of reeds to the inside. Then she dropped on a thread to the floor.

She turned and became a woman again hoping with every shred of her, that the clothes she'd thrust into her kirtle was still there. They were.

She looked over to the bed.

Sir Gabriel was not there. A terrible surge went through her. A surge of fear. Where was he?

She turned.

With his back to her, he sat at the table looking disconsolately at his hands.

"Oh!" In an instant he had her little knife, which still lay on the table, clasped in his good fist. "You startled me."

"I'm sorry."

"I woke and... you'd gone."

"Here, a clean shirt. Give me that one and I'll soak it."

Later, the shirt dumped into a bucket of cold water and lye,

Gabriel in a clean shirt, and both of them sitting by the fire; he looked round her house.

"I tried to open the door to see if you were in the garden, but saw that you'd stuffed it with rags. What's that about?"

"I have sealed the house as best I can."

He frowned. "Then how did *you* get in and out?"

Mabel sighed, "It's... it's a secret."

"What kind of a secret?"

"The sort of secret I can't share with you."

"Why do you want to seal it? Why do you need to seal the house?"

Mabel stammered..."I can't tell you."

"Suddenly there's a lot of things you can't tell me. Why's that?"

Mabel gave him a searching stare. Could she confide in him? What would he think? Would he be able to keep her secret? His poor ravaged face looked over at her through the smoke of the fire.

Would he even believe her? Well, *that* was one thing she *could* remedy.

She could see that his hands and facial wounds were paining him. Talking was difficult; even sitting on a stool caused him anguish; he wavered and held himself awkwardly. She decided he deserved the truth.

"I bet you never thought that as a knight of the realm, you'd have to fight an unseen enemy, as you did yesterday. Without weapons."

"Unseen? I can assure you..."

"I meant unknown."

"Pah! You don't believe me then?"

"An enemy, the likes of which you've never seen before?"

"A wolf?"

Mabel settled her feet nearer to the fire.

"Wolves *were* a common pest here in the forest in the days of my grandfather. I remember my mother telling me stories. They were, even then, poor specimens driven only to come near man through fear of starvation. Ribs starting from their hides, eyes dull with diseases."

"The wolf I saw was a fine specimen," he said through clenched teeth.

"The wolf you saw was *not* a wolf."

"The wolf I saw was a large male in the prime of life with..."

"There have been no wolves in this forest for years. The last one in the Chute Forest, that is the next tract of forest over towards Andover and Ludgershall, was killed a few years ago."

Gabriel's face registered puzzlement. What was she trying to tell him?

"Does someone own a wolf? Someone around here? A wolf which has slipped its master's leash."

"In a way, though it is owned by no man. Not in the sense that the *wolf* is owned."

"I don't follow you..."

Mabel took hold of her courage. She went on her knees in front of him; she did not want to speak to him through the smoke of the fire.

"What I am about to tell you must never ever be revealed to anyone, Gabriel."

Mabel had never called him by his first name before. It felt strange to her tongue not to address him with his full title. He didn't seem to mind.

"Not to a living soul."

He stared deep into her eyes.

She took in the devastated face, the dull blue eyes; dulled with pain and the remedy for it.

"You were very lucky yesterday."

He lifted his hands. "This doesn't look like lucky, to me."

She grasped the least damaged hand gently and smiled.

"You have your life."

"For which I thank you, greatly."

"Ah no, you were never in great danger. Not while you were wearing your maille. If you had not... then you would be dead now. I came upon you by accident. I was not intended to see you, I'm sure.

To find you. I only saw you because... because I was somewhere... someplace from whence I *could* spot you."

"Oh and where was that?"

"Erm..." she nearly chuckled. "Sitting in a tree."

His tired eyes blinked. "A tree."

She nodded. "I was in a tree and saw you from my perch. If I'd been on the ground, I am sure I would not have found you."

Gabriel could not take it all in.

"And what were you doing... in a tree?"

"Oh just sitting, watching."

"You often climb trees, do you, Mistress Wetherspring?"

"Climb them, sit in them, fly to them."

The words passed him by.

He took back his good hand and wiped his brow, grimacing with pain. "I am afraid, I must have lost some wits in the fight with this wolf, I can't quite understand what you're trying to say."

"That's probably because I am not telling the story very well."

"No. I don't think you can be."

Mabel licked her lips. "Listen carefully Gabriel. I am not like ordinary women."

He stared at her then with a different look. She could not quite understand what it meant. 'Oh no. I too am confused,' she said to herself.

"No, you're not," he said eventually. "You are... not like most women. You're quite..."

"Yes?"

"Different."

"Well, I suppose I am quite different from the women with whom *you* have experience. They are all probably noble with fancy ways and fancy speech. I am an ordinary girl with no airs or graces."

"They don't climb trees."

She chuckled. "No, I don't suppose they do."

"I would rather have a girl with no airs or graces," he said. "Even if she does climb trees."

The corner of Mabel's mouth lifted in a smile.

"Well, I'd wait until I tell you *how* different I am, if I were you, before you make up your mind that you prefer a girl with no airs or graces."

He took hold of her hand. "You are... infuriating, wayward, argumentative..."

"Oh I am, am I?"

"But also very pretty, kind, clever and... and... capable."

No one had ever called Mabel pretty. She heard *all* the words he'd said, but the word 'pretty' resonated in her head.

"And I find that... I like you. I like you a lot."

She smiled widely at him. "And I like you too."

His face tried a smile but it was very lopsided.

"Gabriel..."

"Yes?"

"The wolf which you saw was a man. A man who is able to change himself into an animal."

The smile left his face.

"No!"

"I am sure that you have heard of it. Some people have this special skill. Very few... it's rare. I have no idea where it comes from, nor how it's able to be done, all I can say is that it happens."

"It's a story. A legend."

"Every story or legend has to begin somewhere. In some truth."

He looked incredibly shocked.

"How do you know this for sure? It's just... just a myth."

"I know that you are a modern man and as such may not believe..."

"Oh I believe in magic, don't we all?"

"There are things in life of which we have no understanding. I sometimes think that we understand less in life than we are certain of. We watch things happen but we have no idea how it *does* happen. We let it happen and never question."

"Like the magic of growing things... or how the sun warms the earth? Night and day?"

"Yes... things like that. And stranger things. We believe, do we not, that the wine and bread at mass is changed to the blood and body of Christ?"

"Well, yes we do... we must."

"That Christ died upon the cross, was buried, and was resurrected on the third day."

"Yes of course."

"So why should we not believe in other miracles?"

"That a man can change himself into a wolf?"

"That a man who is a shapeshifter who wishes to do evil can change himself into a wolf to kill or injure another who is causing him worry."

Sir Gabriel was immediately with her thoughts.

"One of the men we have spoken to? The murderer."

"Who else? Why else? He has already had a go at me."

"But you escaped."

"Yes... I did and I only escaped because..." Somehow Mabel did not want to actually say the words.

"You jumped from the buttery window."

"Yes... I did. As a cat. I scratched him and bit him—as a cat."

Gabriel stared at her.

"You had a cat with you?"

"No, Gabriel. I can be a cat if I wish. I *was* the cat."

He simply stared at her again and blinked in shock.

"I told you I was different. I am a shapeshifter, like our enemy. The man who is a wolf. But there is no way on earth I would change my appearance simply to do evil, as this man has."

Gabriel seemed to wake up from a stupor. He laughed.

"Ah no... not you? It's not possible!"

"It was on my thirteenth birthday that I realised I could do it. I have been changing into this or that for years. But when Master

Greathouse was killed, I thought I would use my skill to try to find out who had killed him."

"That is how you know as much as you know?"

Poor Gabriel had gone deathly white despite the redness of his wounds. She could see the pale skin of his face had blenched behind the scarring.

"I have been investigating for a while. Only recently has our murderer realised that I can do what he can do."

"And he is trying to stop you."

"He is trying to stop *us*."

"God's teeth, Mabel, is this true, all of it? Is it true?"

"I can see that you will not believe me unless I give you a demonstration."

Gabriel swallowed. "A demonstration?"

"I will change into something."

"You want me to sit here and... watch? What will you become?"

She smiled sweetly at him.

"I will become the thing I love most. I enjoy being a bird. I love to fly. That is why I was up in the tree when I saw you under the hedge. I had flown there because I saw a sparrowhawk."

"A sparrowhawk?"

"I am not even sure that this was our enemy, whoever he is. He certainly singled me out from other birds, quickly."

"Oh Mabel... you must take care."

"I have been doing just that for some time."

She moved backwards away from him and, turning withershynnes she said, "I wish to be a swallow."

Her nose and mouth turned to a beak; her back became a glossy blue. Just before her gaze was diverted from Gabriel by an old spider's web high in the rafters of her house, (oh why must the animal brain always try to take over from her own Mabel brain?) she saw his face take on a look of incredulity.

He started up from the bench.

"Good Lord!"

Mabel flew up to the main beam, sat for a heartbeat and then flew down once more.

In a further heartbeat, she was a woman again.

Gabriel was still standing with his mouth open. How that must have pained him but it seemed he had no control over his reaction.

"Good Lord!"

She bowed, as if this had been a mummer's play put on for his delectation.

He sat down with a thump and as his face rose up to hers, he said. "My God Mabel... you *are* different! *Very* different!"

CHAPTER TWELVE ~ THE ENEMY

If Sir Gabriel had been able to rub his eyes he would most certainly have done it. But though he lifted his knuckles to them, he made no contact.

"No... It can't be true."

"It is true Gabriel. Do you need a further demonstration to convince you?"

He jumped up again in confusion. "Another animal?"

"This time, you may choose whatever you wish for me to become."

He thought. She could almost see the deliberations going across his face.

"Might you be the cat which you said you changed into upon the night our enemy, as you call him, attacked you in the buttery?"

"Certainly I can." Once again she backed away from him and in an instant she was a silver and black striped cat with a distinctive 'M' upon her forehead.

"Good lord, a tabby cat!" said Gabriel, chuckling but with a straight face, for the first time that day.

Mabel jumped up onto the table and came close to him. Tentatively he stretched out his good hand and carefully stroked her arched back.

"Can you speak when you become these things?" he asked.

Mabel mewed assent but all he heard was "Meeeeow. Prrrrr."

"Ah yes, that is too much to ask, I suppose."

He rubbed the place between her eyes.

"Well mistress cat, I can well see how you evaded our enemy. And no... you are not fat."

Mabel rubbed herself alongside him and he laughed.

She jumped from the table and the next thing he knew, she was Mabel Wetherspring again.

She poured two beakers of ale and pushed one to him.

"How did you get in and out of the house? You were suddenly just... well... there."

"I became a spider and tunnelled through the thatch."

"That was clever." Then as he looked up to the thatch she saw his eyes register something.

"You have proofed the house against the enemy?"

"I have, as far as I'm able. He will perhaps not think, as I did, to become something which can penetrate the thatch."

"Ah no. But he might become a mouse again and squeeze under the door—as I suppose he did the night he attacked you."

"The only way into the house is for a very small creature to get in and then he must change himself back into a man or into a larger beast. Now in my experience it's very difficult to change quickly into a large animal from a small one. I have done it. And it's very tiring. He won't wish to make himself vulnerable in this way. This is why I have blocked all holes and gaps."

"You are so clever, Mabel."

"No, not really. I just think ahead."

"And if he becomes a large animal... then you have a bow ready and waiting for him."

"And I *will* use it."

Mabel yawned. "We must eat something. I will see what I can find."

She bustled about the cottage, gathering food together and Gabriel watched her with what seemed to her was a newfound admiration.

"When is the Lord Stokke back?"

"Tomorrow I believe."

"Then tomorrow, I must go and tell him what has happened."

She turned in the action of cutting chunks of stale bread with which to make a pottage.

"Gabriel... you may tell the lord anything you like but you must never divulge that I am a shapeshifter. You realise that it could be very dangerous for me."

"Ahhh," he nodded.

"We must tell the lord what happened to *you* but... I think we must bend the truth a little."

"How so?"

"How do you think the village would react if it knew that you'd been attacked by a man-wolf? There would be absolute panic. Neighbours would suspect neighbours... friendships would be severely tested. People would be afraid to go out... no we can't. Upon reflection, we can't tell the lord the truth."

"Then we tell him... that... I was attacked by a large dog. That's isn't too far from the truth."

"We must say it's a dog which no one recognises or the Lord Stokke's large dogs would be suspect and it would be unfair to make people distrustful of them."

Gabriel chuckled. "That great brute Thor would get the blame!"

Mabel smiled. "Thor's an ugly, bad tempered so and so but, even so, we can't get him into trouble. He has a reputation. He bit the steward Henry the other day."

Gabriel laughed through a mouth which would not open wide.

"There are times when *I'd* like to bite Henry," he said.

*****

The pottage consumed, Mabel went out to shut away her hens and geese. She had a goat but Mistress Houndstooth was looking to her for the day and would milk her and keep the proceeds. Mabel had lost her cow to heriot when her mother died and frankly, she didn't want to acquire another.

With the day turning to dusk, Mabel removed a rag from the base of the door and asked Gabriel to replace it when she'd gone. She'd knock on the door and call out when she'd finished her jobs and he could take it out again.

"I'll see if I can find us some eggs for our dinner tomorrow."

A moment later, those who cared to see, might have discovered a little mouse scurrying along the base plate of her cottage and dashing for the woodpile by the henhouse.

Mabel squeezed through a gap in the paling and inside the little hut, turned to herself again. Out from the small door she came and with flailing arms and shoo - shooing noises, she chivvied her animals along.

"Come on Brownwenge!" she cried as a hen ran past her. "Where are you off to? Home is this way."

She clapped her hands at a couple of geese. "This way Elfie, Cassie. Let's get in before it gets dark."

Most of the hens would happily go into the hut but Brownwenge was not to be intimidated. She flew up onto the lowest branch of the oak tree and pouted. Mabel could tell it was a pout by her angry brown eye.

"Now Brownie, you know that you can't stay there." Mabel lifted her hands to lay hold of the hen who cackled and chuckled and screeched, flapping her wings. Mabel threw her into the hut. Now only two geese remained. Mabel knew all her animals by name. Many needed no encouragement to go home.

"Hira, Ella, come on now." She ran behind them and shuffled her feet to urge them on.

They waddled with the odd complaint, as they always did and disappeared into the hut. Mabel took hold of the wattled door panel and pushed it shut, tying it with a piece of string which was wrapped around a peg and pushing home a bolt.

She turned and looked round the yard.

Something she hadn't done recently was look for eggs. If she didn't do it, she knew that other animals and birds would soon find them and she'd lose them to *their* dinners.

Mabel knew all the places that her hens, ducks and geese laid. She lifted her kirtle and made a pouch to contain her finds and, searching under leaves and in the roots of her oak tree, she gathered several newly laid eggs. She and Gabriel would eat well tomorrow.

Then she noticed that she had failed to capture one of her geese. It lurked silently and shyly in the shadow of the oak's canopy.

"Hermia, is that you?" Ah no... It was a gander, large and pale grey with white tail feathers. How could she have missed him?

As she neared the bird, her heart began to beat faster.

No! This was not Hector. Mabel realised this was a swan.

She turned just as the swan took off with a terrible flap of its wings. Neck outstretched it made for her.

Mabel knew that a swan was not the most fearful of animals but they were still powerful and could, with a peck of its sturdy beak, a swipe of its muscular wing or an equally strong neck, break a bone and bruise. On the water they could drown a human.

Mabel dropped the eggs and fled back to the house. She banged on the door and yelled, "Let me in!" just as the bird hit her with powerful wings.

Three times withershynnes she turned and became a snarling fox.

She could hear Gabriel behind the door shouting her name but was too busy trying to get hold of the swan with her sharp teeth.

She thought she had it by the wing but eventually it flew free and disappeared into the night. Mabel was left with nothing but a mouthful of feathers. Taking a quick look round, Mabel spun, became a tiny shrew and ducked under the door.

Immediately Gabriel saw her, he stuffed the rags back under the gap. He'd no sooner completed his task than Mabel was back in her human body if a little out of breath.

She fell onto a bench. "Why? Why a swan... Why?"

Gabriel handed her a pot of ale and she took it gratefully.

"Tell me what happened."

"I had just got all the animals in when I saw what I supposed was my grey gander, Hector. I realised it wasn't right for I had got him into the hut... I know I had. He is one of the first to retire at night. He leads most of his girls in."

"And then this swan attacked you?"

Mabel rubbed a sore arm.

"Before I knew what was happening, he was flying at me." She shook her head in puzzlement. "Why not a wolf? Why not something more powerful? If he wants to kill, then why not..."

"Because he wants it to look as if you have been dispatched accidentally. He doesn't wish to arouse suspicions. One attack by a wolf and people might be taken in. Two would be more than coincidence."

"But a swan?"

"It would no doubt be an accident. What if... what if..."

But Mabel was there before him. "You mean what if our felon had managed to hit me hard enough to disable me? All he would need to do was pick me up in his human form and drag me to the river where I would drown."

"The swan would be blamed."

Mabel then explained to Gabriel how she had rescued Mistress Peabody.

"Let's face it, if I was found tomorrow in the river and there was a swan paddling around somewhere close... conclusions would be drawn.

"Wrong conclusions," said Gabriel.

They did not speak for a while and then Gabriel said,

"Pity. I was quite looking forward to an omelette tomorrow."

*****

They were very careful how they approached Lord Stokke when he arrived home the next day.

"You say it was a large dog?"

"Yes m'lord. Though I can assure you none of your gentle beasts would ever be so vicious. The creature came out of nowhere at me. I have no idea who it belongs to."

"The beast was not lawed?"

"Oh no sir," said Mabel, "the damage done to Sir Gabriel's face, throat and hands testifies to that."

"Hmm. We must make inquiries. We cannot have unlawed beasts running around the forest. The Warden would take a very dim view of it."

All dogs who lived in the forest had to have two of their front claws amputated so that they could not damage the deer. Failure to comply with this rule meant a hefty fine for the owner and the death of the dog.

Robert Stokke peered at Gabriel's face.

"Tsooo. That's made a mess. You can say goodbye to your good looks, Gabriel!"

"It's thanks to Mistress Wetherspring that it's not worse, sir," said Sir Gabriel. "She was quick on the tail of the dog and managed to patch me up wonderfully."

"Well done mistress," said Sir Robert Stokke. "Are we any nearer knowing anything about the rogue who murdered my villager, Greathouse?"

"We have a few ideas, sir," said Mabel confidently. They proceeded to tell the lord about their suspicions that Edward had been killed in error.

A cup half way to his lips, the lord's face took on a worried look. "Does this mean that we have another who is in danger of his life being taken, when the murderer realises that he has killed the wrong man?"

"I'm afraid so, sir," said Gabriel.

"He didn't like it one bit. Did he?" said Gabriel later as they walked back to the cottage that Sunday morning.

"He's worried there'll be a spate of killings…"

"Random killings of men who looked like Edward Greatman?"

"Greathouse."

"Hmm. Meanwhile we have to take care that the murderer doesn't come for us too."

"Mabel!. Hoooee Mabel!"

They both turned quickly, catching in each other's eyes, the expression which said, 'If we are to be murdered it's unlikely to be by a person who calls out our name in broad daylight.'

"Stephen?"

Stephen Meadow caught up with them and bowed low to Sir Gabriel. "My Lord."

"Erm… not a lord, Stephen… just a Sir."

Upon rising he caught sight of poor Gabriel's spoiled looks.

His chin dangling in surprise, Stephen took in the nasty slicing of Gabriel's face. "Jesus… what's done that to you?"

"A large dog which we were unable to recognise, Stephen," said Mabel quickly. "We don't know who owns it. It's obviously not lawed. It attacked Sir Gabriel on Friday."

"Holy Saints. What's wrong with animals in this part of the forest lately?"

"I beg your pardon?"

"I was going to ask you how *you* are this morning."

"Me..?" Mabel gave him a wily look.

"Well, if I saw right and I think I did, I reckon I spotted you last night in your yard being attacked by a swan!"

"If you saw right?"

"Well it was going dark. But I was sure that it was a big swan. Why he was so angry I can't imagine. And so far from the river."

Mabel closed her eyes. "Didn't think to help then?"

"Ah no. I was too far away," squirmed Stephen.

"Skulking around surreptitiously, were you Stephen?"

"Eh?"

"What were you doing passing Mistress Wetherspring's cott at dusk? It's nowhere near your own," said Sir Gabriel harshly.

"Ah... I er..."

"Been poaching, have we Stephen?" said Mabel at a whisper.

"I was going out to..."

"Look to your traps in the forest?"

Stephen fidgeted, he was obviously very nervous. "I don't have..."

"Stephen. I've seen you."

He tried to deny it again but saw he wasn't going to be believed. "Oh... no you won't say anything... will you... please?" He threw a very worried look at Gabriel.

"It's only a very few teeny traps."

"Take them all up and we'll say no more," said Mabel remembering the time she'd come up against one of his home made traps when she'd changed into a squirrel and nearly come a cropper.

"Ah... right..." said Stephen blushing. Trying quickly to change the subject, his words ran on.

"And you know what? I know it was dark but just after, I suppose, you got back in your house, a fox came along and took on the swan and there was a terrible hullabaloo. I'm surprised you didn't hear it."

"We heard it," said Gabriel. "Both of us from inside the cottage."

"Inside the cottage... the two of you?"

"Yes. That's right. Mistress Mabel had been... bringing me to... seeing to me... patching me up... erm to my wounds."

Stephen gave an inane grin. He was good at inane grins. "Ah I seee."

"And we are about to go back there now so that Mistress Mabel can give me some relief..."

"Oh?"

"From the pain."

"Aye... that must be... very nasty... nasty," he grinned, inspecting the wounds closely. "I once did myself damage... see here, you can see the scar."

He pointed to the edge of his eye. "I couldn't see for a week and I had to get Adam in order to satisfy my wife."

Gabriel's expression remained blank. Mabel raised her eyebrows.

"To do a few jobs around the house."

"What did you want, Stephen?"

"Aw nuffin really. Just to tell you I saw the swan."

"Ah..."

"You reckon it was the one which rescued Mistress Peabody?"

"No... I shouldn't think so. That one was intent on good. The one who attacked me last night was full of evil."

"Ah well. Just thought I'd let you know."

As he was walking away he turned. "Mind you...I wasn't the only one who saw it."

"No?" Mabel's ears pricked up.

"Yeah. Ol' Peabody was out and about."

"Mistress?"

"Nope. Tom."

"Was he now?"

"Where was he exactly, Stephen?" asked Mabel.

"Oh, walking off in the direction of the river."

"Not the forest?"

"Nope..." Mabel and Gabriel exchanged glances.

"He met Simon Smitan. I heard 'em havin' a laugh. Know his voice anywhere."

"Seems the whole village was out last night."

"Aw no... Doesn't do to be out at night. You know how dangerous it is."

Gabriel looked puzzled, despite his face not quite yet registering expressions fully.

"Devils and demons eh, Stephen?" said Mabel.

"You know how it is." Stephen looked round with wild eyes.

"Then you'd better not go into the forest poaching at night had you?"

"I don't..."

"They'll get you, you know," said Mabel. "The demons and devils."

"Ah... mistress, you will have your bit of fun."

"Yes, she will," said Gabriel.

They left Stephen with an ugly smirk on his face.

*****

"Was what we just heard significant, do you think?" asked Gabriel as they closed the door of the house and stuffed the rags under the door again.

Mabel sighed, "I think I shall have to do some more spying."

"Do you think it might be that Stephen fellow?"

"Stephen!" Mabel roared with laughter. "He's much too much of an idiot. Always has been."

"Maybe that's just how he wants you to see him."

"You forget I have known Stephen all his life. He's always been an idiot. He had a thing for me when we were younger. Hung around me a lot. I know him of old. And I know a lot about him. Our villain is not Stephen."

"Then these other two."

"Hmmm. Like I say, I need to do some more spying."

"You can't go alone. I won't let you go alone."

"That, Sir Gabriel, is very chivalrous but, without seeming ungrateful, what might you do?"

"Er... Keep watch."

She looked at his red and scarred face. She couldn't forbid him.

"Alright then. Keep watch." She hastened her footsteps and was out of the cottage before he'd realised she'd gone. He suddenly had to hurry to catch her up.

"I am going to infiltrate a house or two to see what I can discover."

"Don't tell me that you are going to be a spider again and crawl into someone's thatch!"

Mabel listened carefully to the little voice in her head and was silent for a heartbeat.

"Alright," she said. "I won't tell you."

Gabriel shook his blond locks.

"No... That's too dangerous."

"I said that I would not tell you that I was going to change myself into a spider again and crawl into someone's home. So I shall not tell you that I..."

"And I say it's too dangerous. What if they know you are there?"

"How will they know that?"

Gabriel grabbed her sleeve, "Perhaps because they are doing the same to us as you are going to do to them."

"Spying?"

"We have left the house open. Anyone could be there... in any form."

"Then we do our planning out here."

"Mabel, I'm worried. He looked up. "That kite circling up there, that bird..."

"You mean the blackbird on my roof?"

"That yellow butterfly; any of them could be him."

"Sir Gabriel. Shall I tell you something which is an absolute fact? An omnipresent truth?"

"You always do," he said with a loud sigh.

"Men. A man—like our shapeshifter—would never change himself into a butterfly. His pride would not allow it. He would never become a common blackbird. His masculinity would never allow it. The kite—perhaps." She shaded her eyes. "But I have noticed this bird flying here all week, with its mate. Have you ever seen the mating dance of the kite, Sir Gabriel?"

"Er... No I don't suppose I have."

"Well look up and watch. It's quite astonishing."

Gabriel too shielded his eyes.

The kite wheeled overhead at great speed and then dropped, as if it would fall from the sky and the knight had to spin to keep in touch with it. When he looked down, Mabel had gone.

*****

Ten heartbeats, ten steps, ten feet, and ten inches from Sir Gabriel Warrener, Mabel became a swift. Her nose and mouth formed a stubby brown beak which grew hairs to the side. Her plumage became dull brown. Her eyes grew large, black and round and her arms curved to form bow-like wings which were very long. Her legs were stumpy and her feet consisted of long pointed and segmented toes, two forward and two back.

Mabel gained height quickly and flew to the highest point in the village. The church tower.

Sitting on a stone shelf high above Bedwyn, accompanied by two paired doves from the Lord Stokke's dovecote, and a cheeky raven who seemed, with a look of his glassy eye, to be making improper overtures, Mabel surveyed the village below her.

"Kark," said the raven.

Mabel moved off to the other end of the ledge and turned her back.

There was Master Tom Peabody with his back to his cottage wall, a large rush hat over his nose, no doubt snoring and roaring like the furnaces Mabel had heard at the smithy. Taking his post Sunday dinner snooze. His snoring was legendary.

Mabel could see his sister Mary walking out with one of her friends by the river and her little sister, Jonetta was laid out on the green plaiting daisies into a crown.

Of their mother there was no sight.

'I'll take my chance with her,' said Mabel as she lifted off and soared down with one soft sweep and several jerky movements of her wings.

Into the house she went and landed on the cob wall, where she'd noticed on her previous visit, the plaster had fallen off leaving a rough but flattish surface. Her long toes with their sharp claws, dug into the wall. She stayed perfectly still in the body and turned her head.

Sitting at the table with a pot of ale was Mistress Peabody. She seemed to be staring into space.

Opposite her was Simon Smitan, the blacksmith. He too had a pot of ale.

It appeared he'd been there a while, for their conversation seemed well developed.

"I just can't imagine it Simon," said Matilda. "Why... why would he be killed for that?"

Simon sat forward on his stool. "Matty, you know what he was like." Now and again Simon rubbed his arm as if he'd got a cramp.

"But he'd changed, I promise you."

"Well maybe he had. But... how long would the change have lasted? He would probably have been playing you false within the year. How would you have felt then?"

"I could have borne it... I could."

"Well I suppose it would have mattered who he was playing with."

"I suppose so. But not Emma. Never Emma."

"No... Not Emma," said Simon and there was a strange tone to his voice.

Matilda Peabody shifted restlessly on her seat. "Emma and *Tom* did have a thing... many years ago but, well Tom has had to accept rejection."

"I know."

"You know?"

"Emma told me everything."

"You know about the Peabodys and the Hartshorns? Their feud?"

"I do."

'Pah... Emma hasn't told you everything, you great black bearded lummox,' said Mabel to herself. 'Three days... just less than three days and she'll be off.'

"Matty, do you know anyone else who held or still holds a candle for Emma?"

"Ah no..." said Mistress Peabody, "I don't. I can't tell you."

"Can't? Or won't?"

She shook her head. "I don't know. Tom might though."

Simon got up. "I'm not asking Tom."

Suddenly Matilda had a thought. "Did Edward know anything, do you think?"

"What do you mean?"

"Who might be involved with Emma."

"I had it out with him. He knew nothing."

Suddenly the plaster to which Mabel was attached began to crumble. She scrabbled to keep a hold.

Two heads whipped round to see her.

She had no wish to be slapped with a broom again, so she took off at speed and dashed through the open door.

On she flew, not gaining much height, swerving through the buildings until she came to the tenting ground. She slowed. There were no pieces of cloth being stretched at the moment and so the frames were empty.

She perched with a wobble on one of the uprights, her long tail out behind her giving her balance.

A friendly spotted flycatcher, who lived in the stone wall surrounding the tenting ground, bobbed in front of her with his haul of flies and vanished into the ivy.

Mabel's little heart was pounding.

Off she went again but failed to see high above her, the rapid flight of a sparrowhawk, arrow-like making straight for her.

At the last moment, she saw him.

WITHERSHYNNES: IN THE DARK

Twisting like a thread on a distaff, she propelled herself forward. She had to reach a safe perch which she could manage. Unlike a sparrow or other small bird, a perch in a friendly bush was not going to work with such long wings and tail.

Mabel spun on. A crafty look over her shoulder made her swerve left to avoid the talons extended by the raptor.

On, over the village they flew. Mabel was panicking now. She saw the dyeing ground underneath her and dropped to fly onto a support for one of the thread driers; a forest of beams and uprights where the dyed thread and wool was dried. She might hide there.

Someone had left a green thread in the rank and she could not see it, for it blended into the background. Mabel flew right into it and stopped abruptly upside down, entangled in the woollen filaments. She struggled for a moment.

Her Mabel brain said, 'Goodbye world,' as the talons of the falcon hit her.

CHAPTER THIRTEEN ~ UNMASKED

The sparrowhawk hit her and the air was knocked from her lungs. But the power of the creature had also been reduced as he too became tangled in the woollen threads a little way off from her.

Mabel wasn't able to struggle; she felt terrible. Neither could she turn deosil to undo herself and become a woman again. The talons had not managed to pierce her little body but he had injured her.

She would have to stay where she was and hope that someone would rescue her. Someone friendly. Soon.

The sparrowhawk struggled to be free of the tangle of woollen threads. His lethal talons were twisted into them. He was also caught in the dangling filaments and he just succeeded in enmeshing them further. He dangled by his feet and looked fiercely at her. Mabel stayed still.

Suddenly the sky turned dark.

A hand came out of nowhere and stroked her head.

"Wait little one. Let's get him out first."

She knew that voice.

The hands untangled the sparrowhawk who was most ungrateful and pecked and jabbed at his rescuer. As one claw came out of the now ruined wool, it made for the hands of the man rescuing him. Already damaged hands.

'How ungracious,' said Mabel to herself. 'It seems this sort of behaviour is cross species. He's a man... a male sparrowhawk'. She was sure a female would be more amenable.

"Yes... yes, I know you have missed your supper but go and find another victim."

The rescuing hands grasped the body of the small falcon and threw it up in the air. With a slight hover, it flew up and was soon a speck in the clouds.

"Mabel?"

"Squeak?"

"Is it you?"

"Gabriel," she yelled but it came out as a 'whee, whee, whee'.

"It IS you."

Sir Gabriel looked round quickly and freed Mabel from the web of wool.

He threw her in the air knowing she would land somewhere she could perch and change into a woman.

"Aw!"

"What's the matter?"

"I am a mass of bruises again."

"I told you!"

"Help me back to the cott. I shan't be going out again today." Mabel limped over the grass. "Oh..."

"What?

"Poor Mistress Dyer's wool. I've ruined it."

"She's not to know it was you."

"How did you find me?"

"I followed you."

"How?"

"Well you were I admit at one point just a speck in the sky but I did see you land on the church tower. And lift off again. And that was not kind to try and distract me with the kite."

"Ah yes. I'm sorry. The courtship of kites is carried on in April.

You'll see them now paired up but not the clever dance they do."

"Cruel... Mabel."

"Sorry."

Gabriel folded his arms and grimaced at the pain of it. "Thank you Gabriel for saving my life," he said.

Mabel sighed. "Thank you Gabriel for saving my life."

The door closed behind them and stuffed again with rags, they made for the comfort of the fire and blew up the flames.

"Did you learn anything?"

"I did but my little accident has driven it from my brain. I'll think about it again. Tomorrow."

"I'll take the first watch."

"I am so tired."

Mabel fell onto her bed fully clothed and fell asleep instantly.

*****

When she woke, Gabriel had removed her hose and shoes and covered her with a blanket.

She lay quietly watching him as he toyed with a wax tablet in his hands.

She watched him write something in tiny script.

"What are you writing?"

He jumped in surprise and quickly put the tablet into the breast of his shirt.

"Oh nothing."

"I didn't know you could read and write."

He scratched his hairline. "I like to write... now and again, little things which come to me."

"What sort of little things?"

"Oh nothing important... sort of poetry."

She sat up..."Poetry? Oh I don't know anyone who can make up poetry. I know there's a blacksmith in Kennett who makes up songs but no one around here is a poet."

"Like I say... it's nothing really."

"What were you writing?"

She swung her legs off the bed and took up her comb to tidy her hair.

"It was just that..." He seemed rather embarrassed. "I was thinking..."

"Yes."

"That I know very little about the animals around us. You have shown me..."

"You have a horse, don't you?"

"Well of course I have a horse. A knight must have a horse. He is at the stable in the manor being looked after by the grooms there."

"You must know a lot about *him.*"

"Yes... yes I do... but you... you have shown me..." He suddenly went very red. "Shown me that there are so many animals in the world and...'"

"I only know so much about them because I have *been* these creatures, Gabriel. I have an insight into their lives."

"And that is marvellous."

Now it was Mabel's turn to blush. "What did you write then?"

"Oh no... It's nothing."

"I won't be satisfied until I have heard what you have written."

"It's just that, when you were a bird..."

"A swift?"

"I thought that it was wonderful to be so close to both the prey and the preyed upon."

"Ah... our friend the sparrowhawk."

"I had the chance to be kind to both."

She stood and walked over to him. "Why would you not be kind to both?"

"It's never really occurred to me before to be kind to wild animals. I would never have thought to rescue... a... a rabbit from a trap or a bird from a net. But now..."

"Oh... I see."

"And since you tell me that you have been a deer, I am now wondering if I could ever go hunting again."

"Oh my... we must eat, Gabriel. As long as we kill to eat and not for the sheer pleasure of killing..."

"We are told that animals have no souls."

Mabel smiled. "I have been so many animals over the years and I will tell you that they *all* have souls. Even the tiniest ant. I can feel them."

Now Gabriel took out his waxed tablet.

"That is what I thought... and so I wrote this.

'A man of kindness to a beast is kind.
A brutal action shows a brutal mind.
Remember he who made you made the brute,
Who gave you speech and reason, formed him mute.
He can't complain, but God's all seeing eye,
Beholds the cruelty and he hears the cry.
He was designed a servant not a drudge,
Remember he who made you is your judge.'"

He folded the wooden covers over the words with deliberateness and would not look up.

"Oh, Gabriel, that is so beautiful."

"Nah..." He cleared his throat. "Are we going to eat today? Shall we go to the hall for supper?"

"And when they serve us meat, will you eat it?"

Then he looked up and smiled.

"If an animal has given its life for us to eat, it would be ungrateful for us not to eat it... don't you think. It would be a waste of life."

Mabel felt a small tug at her heartstrings. Oh, this knight, this young man, this relative stranger was so lovely. His face was ugly now but his soul was beautiful.

It was then she realised that she was beginning to fall in love with him.

*****

He took her to see his horse on the way. She learned his name was Bertran, after some long dead hero.

He was a beautiful Flemish stallion with a golden coat and a pale mane of rough hair.

"My father gave him to me on my twenty-first birthday. He's taken a lot of training but now, he's as reliable as a donkey."

"He must be, mustn't he? You have to entrust your life to him, in battle." As Mabel said those words, a fearful constriction overtook her heart. He was a knight. He had to go into battle and fight. He could be killed.

Gabriel stroked the horse's neck and he threw up his head at the familiar hand.

"He's a good friend."

"You must ride him out into the forest sometime. I'd like to see that."

"Well yes... I could do that."

Bertran brought his head down to Mabel's level and nuzzled her neck.

"He likes you."

"And I like him. He recognises a horse lover when he sees one."

"Have you ever... you know... been a horse?"

"I have but as I said it takes a lot of energy to be an animal larger than I am as a human. I have only done it once."

"I'd like to see it if you were to do it again."

"I'll think about it."

They walked up to the manor and took supper sitting at two separate tables. They would never be able to sit together, of course. Sir

Gabriel was noble and Mabel was a bailiff's daughter, an employee at the manor. Their relationship was going nowhere.

The mental waxed tablet, upon which she had once scribbled her hopes and dreams with Gabriel, rose up again in her consciousness. Yes there it was again, only this time the notes had been scribbled with charcoal upon a piece of parchment. A life as the wife of Sir Gabriel Warrener.

She turned to the high table to see Gabriel sharing a cup with one of Lord and Lady Stokke's daughters—Emmeline, she believed. The parchment burst into flames and turned to ashes and the food turned to ashes in her mouth.

"Are you alright Mistress Wetherspring?" said one of the servitors.

"Yes, thank you. Quite alright." She slipped from the bench and went out into the yard. The stars were just beginning to come out.

"Ah my fowl!" she cried and ran swiftly back to her house where she shut up all her chickens and geese, keeping an eye out for strange shadows.

It was too early to retire and she'd slept the afternoon away. Why not have an evening's flying in the cool air? And if she happened to fly near to a house of one of her suspects, then why not do a bit of spying?

Four furlongs, four feet and almost four inches away, Sir Gabriel was busily scanning the hall in search of Mabel.

"That infuriating woman!" he spoke aloud. "Where has she gone?"

He made apologies to his supper partner and slid away into the body of the hall.

Did she not remember that he had been tasked with keeping her alive by his master? If anything were to happen to her and he knew from experience that things DID happen to her, then he'd never be forgiven. He'd also never forgive himself. He began to realise that Mabel Wetherspring had got under his skin without him letting her in. Oh yes! It was fascinating that she was a shapeshifter but even if she hadn't been so... special... she would be special ... to him.

He realised of course that they could never be together but...

Gabriel was an optimist and a great believer in fate. 'Let's see what happens', he'd said to himself. But first he had to find her.

At that precise moment, Mabel was wheeling over the trees surrounding the churchyard, spinning along the edge of the lane with a few other bats. She had chosen that night to become a tiny pipistrelle bat—the bird of evening—whose erratic flight made it hard to follow... or catch. What caught bats? She had once seen a roosting bat caught by an owl and thought that if she managed to keep going, and then hide carefully nothing would be able to touch her. But spying required her to stay still. Then so be it.

She landed on the thatch of the house belonging to the Hartshorns. How were the wedding plans coming along, Mabel wondered?

The night was very warm and the door was open. She scurried towards the opening and fluttered down to hang upside down from the eaves. She would be well hidden in the shadows. And she was so very small.

She heard several voices. My! Simon Smitan, the bridegroom; he was getting about the village a lot. Firstly at Mistress Peabody's and now here at the house of his intended.

A joke had just been shared, for they were all laughing; the Hartshorns senior, Emma and her siblings. It seemed Simon was in a good mood tonight. And why should he not be, he was marrying the girl of his dreams in two days' time.

"So you should be very pleased with what I have done to the house Emma," he was saying.

"Horn in the windows I believe," said Master Hartshorn. "Hmmm daughter, you will be the envy of all the women of Bedwyn."

"And I am going to lay a proper floor. No beaten earth for my darling," said Simon.

"No expense will be spared to make a house fit for my queen."

"You can't manage on your own surely, Simon," said Mistress Hartshorn. "It's hard work laying stones. I know. I remember when this floor was laid—goodness the air was blue and Master Hartshorn here said he'd never do it again alone."

"Oh I shall have help. Alfred has agreed to help me."

"Good man," said Wilfrid Hartshorn.

There was no utterance from Emma. 'Hmmm what was she thinking about this?' asked Mabel of herself. She knew and Emma knew that Alfred had no intention of helping Simon with his floor. For the very next day, they were off to... wherever they were off to.

Mabel swivelled her huge bat ears.

"I spoke to him about it yesterday. It's the first time I've spoken to him for months, I have been so busy at one thing or another. He's more than happy to help. Oh yes, he'll help me... if he knows what's good for him."

Everyone laughed.

Something in her bat memory set a little bell ringing.

"Oh no! It can't be."

The thing she had forgotten in all the fuss of the afternoon came back to her. It was something which Elinor had said.

Something which had not agreed with what someone else had said. And it should have agreed.

Elinor had not been telling tales so... someone else was lying.

She suddenly became uncomfortable and wriggled on her perch.

"What's that?" said Mistress Hartshorn.

"Something in the thatch that's all."

"Oh Master Hartshorn; (his wife always referred to him by his proper name), I've told you about those rats."

"For the last time Emmy, we have no rats!"

Master Smitan got up and came to the doorhole.

"Ah no... just a bat. A hunting bat. A little one. It's gone scooting off over the river."

Indeed the little bat had gone scooting off. But she did not go over the river. She wove a path straight to her own door.

She'd half expected to see Gabriel waiting for her but the sense of disappointment that he was not there was overcome by the elation of what she'd discovered.

She sat behind the cottage and turned deosil on stumpy feet to become Mabel Wetherspring again.

'Now Mabel, hold onto the thoughts you had as a bat. Remember what you worked out. Recall too, what you discovered the other day and put the two together.'

She carefully entered her house and lit both the fire and her lamps.

Then she sat with a jar of ale and cogitated.

The pair of screech owls who lived in the barn came roaring and hissing over her thatch. She was not deflected from her deliberations.

How was she going to prove it... oh how?

She knew why and who... but how was she going to make them come out into the open?

She stared into her ale pot. She was getting low on supplies. She needed to go to Mistress Brewster who lived at the other end of the village, for fresh ale. In fact she realised how she had neglected her home and her job these past few days. That must be remedied. No one must suspect that she had been investigating, except the Lord Stokke and Gabriel and no one must know she'd come to a conclusion.

She felt elated.

She'd done it. She had found the killer.

*****

A shrill whistle broke her reverie and she hid behind the door of the cottage with a little trepidation. As a human it was unlikely she'd be hurt by the door opening. Anyway it was locked and barred.

She listened with night tuned ears. Oh how she wished she'd still been a bat; she would have heard the person approaching and known exactly who it was.

Suddenly she heard the chink of his maille as he neared the door. Only one person sounded like that. He must be feeling better, he'd donned his armour again.

"Sir Gabriel!"

"Let me in, Mabel."

Before she'd even closed the door he was berating her for leaving supper in the hall.

"How could you put yourself in such danger?"

"Listen. I heard something tonight and I want…"

"No… Listen to me for a change."

"It's important."

"It's important for you not to get killed."

"Only so you don't get into trouble with the Lord Robert."

"Yes… there's no doubt… No… I… that's not…"

"Oh shut up and listen to me. I found something out and I remembered…"

"Mabel, you are infuriating. I have only just found you… I don't want to lose you now."

But Mabel was not listening.

"I went out tonight as a bat."

"Oh you did, did you?"

"And I…"

"Well that was foolish."

"Foolish it may have been but I am trying to tell you…"

"You are always trying to tell me. Have you never thought to yourself that you are a bossy woman?"

"Bossy?"

"Bossy… you always have something to say."

"Well, yes of course I do."

"But you also need to listen."

"Well you need to listen to me now because I know…" began Mabel.

"You always know, Mabel. You are always so damn certain."

"Well, I am not certain of this… but I am certain if you see what I mean."

"No… no. I don't see what you mean. Oh woman! You bother me.

Really bother me."

"Well if I bother you so much you can go away and I won't tell you what I have discovered."

"I don't want to go away."

"What?"

"I don't ever want to go away... you... bothersome woman."

"But..."

"I know. But."

"You'll have to. You will have to follow your lord."

His voice was now almost a whisper. "I know I will and I don't want to."

It all went very quiet.

"Oh Gabriel. I don't want you to go either. But we must both know..."

He smiled his lopsided smile again.

"Let me look at your face."

He sat down and allowed her to wash the wounds and dress them again.

"Another day... just one more day and the stitches will come out."

He nodded absently.

"Then it will be a matter for the healing to do its work. I can continue to use the unguent I make. That will help to minimise the scarring but... you will always be interesting to the girls with your scars."

"I don't want to be interesting to the girls... well only to one girl," he said quickly.

"The Lady Emmeline?"

"What? Certainly not. She's going to marry my cousin John!"

"Oh."

"John from Frome."

"Ah right."

In the silence that followed, they heard the screech owls on their return journey.

"Where's Frome?"

"Somerset."

"Ah."

Then the night was very quiet.

"So, are you ready now to hear what it was I thought?"

He leaned back on the wall.

"You will tell me anyway, I know you will."

"We think we know that Edward Greathouse was killed because he was mistaken for another man."

"We narrowed that down to a few."

"Yes. We needed to know why he was killed, didn't we?"

"Because it was thought that he'd been carrying on with Emma?"

"Or someone who looked like him had been carrying on with Emma," she said more emphatically.

"I suppose it could have been night time. No light."

"But. But... and this is the really important thing. Simon Smitan told the Hartshorn's tonight that he had had it out with Alfred Stockman. That he'd caught him kissing Emma. Elinor too saw them and he told her that they'd made up."

"So?"

"He was lying."

There was silence.

"And there's only one reason why he's lying."

They looked at each other in the gloom.

"And what's more, Smitan said tonight that he'd not spoken to Alfred for a while when he'd admitted that he had confronted him about Emma," said Mabel. "Fairly recently."

"Another lie?"

"How are we going to get him to confess?"

"He won't confess," said Gabriel, getting up and walking about in agitation.

"Men like him don't confess."

"Then we have to catch him and we'll have to be careful. He's our shapeshifter," said Mabel.

She took in a quick breath. "And I think that the blacksmith has it in for Alfred Stockman. He is the man whom Edward was mistaken for. They are the same build, same height. I heard the tone of Simon's voice. I think he's going to kill him!"

CHAPTER FOURTEEN
~ THE CHASE BEGINS ~

"We need to somehow let him know we know," said Gabriel. "We do that and he's going to cause *real* trouble for us. We have to catch him in the act."

"What? You think he's going to make an attempt on Alfred Stockman's life..."

Mabel made a strange grimace. "Ah yeees. There's something I haven't told you."

Gabriel raised his eyes to Heaven.

"Oh for goodness sake. I thought we were sharing everything? All information."

"Well... I needed to keep quiet about this."

"Don't tell me... you made a promise?"

Mabel walked about rubbing her hands against her kirtle in anxiety.

"Alfred Stockman and Emma Hartshorn are..." She looked round the cottage and then whispered, "Running away together... tonight, I think."

"But they're villeins. They belong to the Lord Stokke. They can't."

"I know."

"We must tell him and stop them."

"No... we can't. If Alfred's life is in danger we have to let them go."

"But..."

"No buts, Gabriel. We have to let them try."

He searched her face. "They'll be punished if they're found."

"We can maybe speak for them... the Lord will listen to us. *If* they are brought back."

"You want us to give them time to get away."

"I want us to let them go... If they can live somewhere for a year and a day without discovery then, they'll become free and can't be brought back. It's the law."

"It's because you've known these folk all your life isn't it?"

"Yes, I have. But that's not why I want them to go. They are unfree. I'm free and within reason, may do as I wish. What must it be like not to have that freedom? To do as you wish, to live as you like and to marry whom you love?"

Gabriel looked down at his maille-clad feet. Marry whom you love! Ah that struck a chord. "If they run away... tonight you say... then Alfred will be safe."

"Not if Smitan has wind of what they're doing."

"I still say we need to confront him," said Gabriel.

They sat down in the light of the flickering fire and considered the problem.

"That is why Smitan was so upset after Greathouse's death. He killed his best friend *in mistake* for someone he thought had been kissing his love."

"That's why he had a piece of his winding sheet. I saw him that day, crying over it and he was beside himself. And then he got angry and stormed off," said Mabel.

"Angry with himself?"

"That's why I never really considered him. He and Edward were such friends it seemed inconceivable that he could kill him."

"And he killed Elinor... mistaking her for you?"

"Perhaps he has a problem with his sight... like Mistress Peabody. Some people do and manage to conceal it for a long time."

Gabriel laughed. "Ah yes... my father pretends he can see perfectly, as well as he did when he was young, but he's always asking my sister to see things for him."

"Ah... you have a sister?" Mabel realised she knew very little about the life of Sir Gabriel Warrener.

"I have three sisters."

"And brothers?

"One."

"Ah."

"Felicite, Isabella and Mariotta."

"Oh…"

"And my brother is John."

"Ah."

"And before you ask, he's younger than me by ten years. Mistress nosy."

"So you are the eldest child?"

"I am the second son. My elder brother Thomas died when he was fourteen."

Her mind went off to a field of corn glowing yellow in the sunshine and five children playing happily there, in the summer warmth.

His next words broke her reverie.

"Felicite is married to a neighbour's son. Isabella is affianced to a son of the Hungerford's of Farleigh Castle, Somerset and Mariotta... well Mariotta is…"

"Is…?"

"Is not a well girl."

Mabel did not dare ask what was the matter.

Gabriel chuckled. "She is... not quite right in her head... before you ask. I can see you are dying to know. Our mother laboured long to bring her into the world and she suffered damage as a result."

"Oh that's sad. Is your mother still alive?"

"Yes... yes she is. Mariotta will never go from home. She's my mother's little lap dog."

"How old is she now?"

"Ten." Gabriel chuckled, "Though to look at her you'd swear she was as old as Isabella, though Issy is fourteen."

"Oh?"

"They're very alike. She's almost as tall as Issy and has the same hair. With her back to me I mistake her all the time."

Mabel chuckled. "It must be…" She stopped.

"Gabriel… That's it…"

"What?"

"Aw come on Gabriel… Think!"

"I am thinking."

"Well not hard enough."

"You're being bossy again."

"Listen. Bossy or not, this is what we are going to do…"

*****

They could not wait until daylight. If the plan was going to succeed, then they had to act quickly.

Mabel approached the steward, Master Buttermere.

"I need to speak to his Lordship."

"Oh it's nice to *see* you at last. I thought you'd run away like…"

"What?" Mabel's brow puckered in worry. Did Henry Buttermere know something? Something about the lovers Alfred and Emma?

"Like a frisky colt…"

"Ah… no… I've been looking after Sir Gabriel Warrener. He's been attacked by a large dog."

"Hmm. I heard about that. Blasted Thor… that dog should be… He bit *me*, you know…"

"It wasn't Thor who attacked Sir Gabriel. Please Master Steward, can you go and ask the Lord Stokke…?"

"See, here on the thumb."

"Yes, how awful… Please…"

"He has retired for the night, Mistress Wetherspring."

"Well, it's very important that I speak to him."

"I couldn't possibly."

"It's a matter of manor security."

Master Buttermere always took manor security seriously.

"Security you say?"

"Yes. Something into which he has asked me to inquire."

"You?"

"Er... yes."

"Well... why you?"

"Please, it's most urgent."

The man looked down his nose at her.

"Why the lord thinks we need a housekeeper *and* a steward here, I do not know."

'Perhaps because you are a pompous, inefficient idiot,' said Mabel to herself as she smiled sweetly at him.

'Actually we only need a housekeeper,' she said in her head. Oh how she would have liked to tell him.

"I'm sure the lord knows how well you work when he is not here at the manor to see it," she said pointedly.

Many times Mabel had had to undo something of which the steward had made a mess. He was a lazy so and so, when no one was there to watch him. And when watched he was busy as a bumbling bee.

Buttermere sniffed.

"No guarantee. I will go and see if he is... available."

"Manor security," Master Steward," said Mabel importantly. "Manor security."

Eventually the lord came down hastily dressed and with his hair all awry.

"Mabel... what's the matter? Buttermere said it was important."

"It is, my lord," said Mabel curtseying. "Sir Gabriel and I have managed to unmask the killer."

Sir Robert pulled his hands through his hair. "Ahhh. Well done. So what must we do now?"

"We have as yet, no actual evidence..."

"And you have woken me from my slumber to tell me this...?"

"Ah no m'lord. We do have some sort of evidence but if we are very clever we can catch him at his next attempt at murder."

"Next you say? Next, oh dear!"

"Yessir. And we must act quickly."

"Tell me all about it."

*****

Mabel approached the cottage with faltering feet. Did she know what she was doing? The man knew she was a shapeshifter but of course he was unaware *she* knew that he was *also* able to change his appearance. At least she fervently hoped he didn't. Yet.

She scratched on the door.

A voice said, "A moment."

"It's Mabel Wetherspring, Master Smitan."

"Ah Mabel. Out so late?" He towered over her and she felt decidedly uncomfortable. "Are you a night owl eh?"

"Haha, Master Simon. You will have your little joke."

"What can I do for you?" he said looking round in the gloom surrounding his home. "You don't have that knight following you around eh?"

"He is in hall tonight; he's not feeling too well."

"Aw that's sad. I suppose it's the nasty wounds he has suffered?"

"Yes. I suppose so." 'Come on Mabel... you have to be convincing. Stop sparring with him.'

"I just wanted to say that I hope you and Emma will be very happy. You are marrying tomorrow, are you not?"

Simon spread his feet and folded his arms. He rarely wore anything upon his forearms. Blacksmithing was an unpredictable job and sleeves could catch fire easily. He always wore them rolled up to his elbows, even out of the forge.

Mabel caught sight of many small burn marks, products of the hazards of his trade but also the scratches she had seen upon him the day after she'd fought as a cat.

"That's very kind of you."

His eyes were still scanning the dark. He did not trust her. She knew it.

"Do come in and take a pot of ale with me. My last night as a bachelor."

"Ah no... No thank you. I have things to do. I just wanted to say that... Oh I hope you don't mind me saying this..."

"Saying what, Mabel?"

"Well... it's what you said to Elinor. Dear Elinor, just before she was killed."

He turned an ear to her as if he was unable to hear correctly.

"What did I say to Elinor?"

"Oh that you had talked to Alfred about kissing Emma."

He shrugged.

"It's magnificent how you managed to forgive him. I think if my loved one had been, well you know... messing about with another..."

"She hasn't been messing about with another."

"Well... I wouldn't be able to forgive Alfred for kissing Emma if I were you... and I think it's amazing that you are a big enough fellow to ignore it."

"Ignore it?"

"What's been going on..."

Simon sniffed. "What *has* been going on, Mistress Wetherspring?"

"Emma and Alfred..."

"Nothing has been going on with them."

"Oh... no... no... of course not. If you say so. She's marrying you and... that's that." She grinned.

"Are you sure you won't come in?"

"Ah no... I must get back. I have to bathe Sir Gabriel's wounds."

"Ah... your over friendly little knight."

"But anyway... I just wanted to say that I think it's the measure of a man to forgive and..."

"Alfred and I grew up together. Like I said, he can be a fool when he's drunk. He assured me there was nothing in it."

"Ah no... I'm sure. Like you were best friends with Edward. All friends together eh?"

There was a moment's hesitation as Simon Smitan scratched an itch at the corner of his right eye.

"Yes indeed."

"Well... I'll leave you now. Good luck for tomorrow. And take care."

"And you too Mistress Wetherspring. You take *great* care."

That was a threat if ever she heard one.

Mabel backed away from the door and took a few steps. Then she ran into the darkness.

A moment later, Gabriel popped his head over a hedge.

"Psst."

"Gabriel."

"What do you think? Did you manage to get him interested?"

"Oh he was interested all right. Not sure if he'll act tonight, but I think he might."

"Then I'll be off."

"Right."

She tripped after him into the dark.

"Oh Gabriel, be careful," she whispered into the night.

*****

The village was dark and quiet.

Inside the cottage it was pitch black. No light was lit, no fire visible under its protecting turves for the fire had not been lit that day.

No food had been cooked; there was no lingering smell. The house was totally empty. Alfred and Emma had already gone.

No sound came from anywhere, but outside the nightjar, intent on his supper of insects, sped on his way across the garden. He settled somewhere close and after a couple of 'chuck chuck chucks', he began his unearthly warble. Mabel listened, her ears sharpened by the silence. "Prrrrrrrrrrr." A loud prolonged purring on a single note, over and over.

'I must find out how they can sing so long without taking a breath,' said Mabel to herself. 'It's amazing.'

A shadow detached itself from the trees at the back of the cottage. Mabel slunk back into her own shadow. The nightjar, surprised by the visitor, rose up and moved a few feet away with another series of 'chuck chuck chucks'.

"Ah... in human form are we?" said Mabel under her breath. If the murderer had been a nocturnal animal then the nightjar would not have worried.

The tall shadow moved surreptitiously along the wall.

Mabel's heart began to pound. 'Oh please. Let it be him and let him not resist. And let Sir Gabriel come out of this unscathed.'

She knew that Gabriel was used to danger, to fighting, but nevertheless she was fearful and nervous for him. He was alone in the house. What if the killer was quicker than he was? What if Gabriel was taken by surprise? If it came to hand to hand fighting, Gabriel had power and control and training in the use of weapons but the killer was a shapeshifter and was dangerously unpredictable.

She moved a little closer.

The shadow was now at the door.

At that moment the cloud which had blotted the moon, lifted and a silvery glow suffused the yard in front of the cottage. It was *him*. She could see it was *him*.

Again she prayed and this time crossed herself for good measure.

She desperately hoped that Alfred and Emma were miles away now—many miles—which kept them from being pursued. The longer the hue and cry for them was put off the safer they'd be.

And this little story playing out before her, was helping to put off that moment.

She heard the door open. It always creaked a little in the summer. Alfred kept his home in good repair but, yes the door would creak a little. It had been a dry season, despite the recent storm. Everything was dried and dusty, tight and rasping.

The door closed and Mabel could see no more.

She held her breath.

No... There was nothing for it. She was too worried.

She spun withershynnes and whispered to herself.

"I wish to be a rat."

A rat, she thought, would be better than a mouse for it was not likely to be picked up by a passing hungry owl.

But she'd still have to be careful.

On small pink feet, she crossed the yard and insinuated herself under the door.

Her rat eyes could see quite well but only for a few feet. After this it became blurry. She saw few colours, even if there was colour to see. But her whiskers, oh her long sensitive whiskers allowed her to feel everything.

They were able to judge distance and proximity. They could pick up movement and her little pink nose could detect an odour ten times more powerfully than her human one.

She sniffed. 'Ah yes. There he was. The enemy.' She knew him by the smell. The smell of the burning of charcoal and the tang of iron; sweat and a musky smell of masculinity.

She scurried forward and now had him in her sights.

He was searching the cottage, ranging his eyes around the four walls.

He located the bed and its humped occupant.

Mabel heard him whisper quietly, "There you are, you corrupt bastard."

Well, that was something coming from his mouth!

The killer moved on silent feet nearer to the bed situated by the far wall.

Mabel held her breath.

This was going to be so difficult.

The killer stood above the bed. "Wake up you thieving bastard."

There was no movement of the body on the mattress.

"Alfred! I want you to know who it is before I kill you."

Still no movement.

"Come on you coward. I killed Edward in mistake for you. My best friend. I'm going to make you suffer for that."

The killer stuck out a hand and made a grab for the blanket covering what he thought was a body.

The blanket fell away. It was merely a sack of grain.

In anger he took the large knife he'd been holding, to the bag and ripped it.

It was then he noticed that two legs were sticking from underneath the bottom of the bed.

"Ah you coward. Knew I was coming did you? Trying to hide? To fool me?"

Mabel scurried nearer. Oh why did Gabriel have to do it this way?

She watched as the murderer bent to pull out the person from under the bed.

'Ah yes... at a disadvantage... clever,' her rat brain said. 'Gabriel has him at a disadvantage.'

"You... you were kissing my wife to be... *you*...Thieving kisses. It was you, wasn't it?" said the blacksmith.

Suddenly the body under the bed was out, on his back and in full view.

"Drop that knife. Drop it now," Gabriel's voice was confident and calm.

The outer door opened and Lord Stokke stepped in with two of his burly soldiers.

WITHERSHYNNES: IN THE DARK

"I would advise you to drop it, Smitan," he said. "Sir Gabriel is a very good shot."

Mabel stared. Pressed to his chest, Gabriel had a small bow nocked and ready to loose.

"And at this range he's unlikely to miss."

Mabel let out her rat breath.

Simon Smitan dropped the knife and it clattered on the beaten earth of the floor. He backed away into the darkness of the corner, his hands above his head.

No one but Mabel expected him to do anything but concede defeat. But he did not.

As they watched, Simon Smitan, the blacksmith, thrust his hands high in the air and yelled, "I will be a raven."

It was still dark in the cottage, and though the guards with Sir Robert had brought lamps, not every corner nor part of the room was lit. Most were in darkness.

With eyes starting out on stalks, the guards ducked as a large bird flew out of the open door.

"Oh no!" Mabel yelled in her ratty voice.

Rats were quick, she knew, but not quick enough. She sped out of the door between the two guards and after Smitan, and once she had managed to work out where he'd gone, she spun withershynnes and cried, "I wish to be a barn owl."

CHAPTER FIFTEEN
~ TRANSFORMATIONS ~

The next few moments were a blur. Gabriel had wanted to loose the arrow but the raven had been too small a target in the dark. Poor Gabriel had been fearful of hitting his lord or the two soldiers.

Mabel lifted off as a barn owl and as quickly as she could she gained height. The glossy black of the raven disappeared into the night and was lost to the sight of the humans in the cottage.

But the pursuing barn owl could see wonderfully well in the dark. In addition, her dished face funnelled the sound into her extra sensitive ears and she could hear a blade of grass rustle with a tiny mouse, at nine hundred feet.

She would know where Smitan was, even if she could not see him.

He was heading for his cottage.

How foolish was that? Surely he would know that would be the first place they'd look for him.

She left the humans behind and sped under and over tree branches as if they were made of gossamer. Not once did she even touch them, so great was her sense of direction. Her main problem was that she was quite a slow flier and Smitan, as a raven was much faster.

However, his senses were designed for the day; for flying and foraging in the daylight. He would be at a disadvantage at night.

Mabel's barn owl eyes funnelled every bit of available light, no matter how small and she could see everything as clearly as if in daylight.

She saw the fences around Master Hartshorn's garth with its cherry trees and the moths resting on the leaves; she saw the tiny sparrows roosting there. She saw a fox patrolling the ground around Master Farmer's hen house. Out into the field to the edge of the village where lay the forge, she could see the tiny voles and mice at their scurrying in the long grasses. But they were not of interest to her.

She let out an unearthly scream.

She heard what she thought was Gabriel following, his heavy tread loud in her ears and his maille clinking with every step; his breath hard fought for.

She knew he'd heard her cry when he shouted. "I hear you!"

'Well done Gabriel.' He had not tossed her name out into the night for anyone listening or following to hear. That was the last thing she needed. He was keeping her secret.

She heard his breath as he ran and the mutterings he made and they caused her to chuckle in her barn owl brain.

The raven had slowed, thinking that he was alone and not followed.

Mabel circled and made sure that he had gone inside his forge.

She knew when he had changed back into a man for he too started to mutter.

"Stupid... stupid. You should have changed. It was idiotic to do the work as a man."

He was berating himself for trying to kill Alfred as a man. But it was hard to think what animal he might have become to thrust a knife into a man's chest.

Simon Smitan did not have much imagination. Had she been him, Mabel would have thought out her strategy long ago.

Mabel peered through the one window as she passed the forge again. The man had a bag and he was stuffing things into it. He was panicking, that was sure. How did he think he would get away as Simon Smitan? It made much more sense to just fly away or run at speed, incognito. Mabel knew what she would do if she were placed in this situation. They'd never catch her as a speedy horse or a fast bat or bird.

Smitan realised that he was pursued and eventually he heard Gabriel's approach.

He grabbed a large piece of iron from his stock in the forge and waited.

Mabel was worried and she let out another evil shriek.

It brought Gabriel to a halt outside the forge. He had heard her warning.

She heard his sword scrape as he drew it from his scabbard. So did Smitan. He lowered his iron bar.

"Warrener!"

"Smitan?"

"Are you alone?"

"The others will be here in a moment. With reinforcements."

"Pah! They'll never catch me. They don't know what I am."

"No. And *I* will not tell them. If they knew, you know what your chances would be."

The blacksmith chuckled. "You take me down in that way and I take your girlfriend down with me."

Sir Gabriel laughed. "Oh I'd like to see you try. She'll make ten of you."

Smitan did not like having his masculine prowess called into question.

'Mabel was right,' said Gabriel to himself. 'He is proud and arrogant and too full of his mastery as a masculine shapeshifter; he will eventually make a mistake.'

"Come out and take your punishment. I will say nothing."

"Come in and fetch me."

Gabriel was about to take a step forward when a barn owl landed by his feet.

"Mabel?"

Mabel stepped up to the window, and looked in, as white as any milk.

Simon looked out of the window, as black as any silk.

"Simon, you know that I will not let you escape."

"Then Mistress Mabel Wetherspring, it will be a duel to the death."

"We are already weary with our transformations, Simon. How do you think that will end?"

"One of us will survive."

"I have no wish to fight you."

"Who is talking about actually fighting? This will be a battle of wits. A battle of strengths. You are merely a weak woman."

She must admit at that moment that made her blood boil.

"It has nothing to do with strength, or the fact I am a woman. It is a matter of who is the cleverer." As he laughed she said. "And I think we all know who that is."

"Mabel... no," said Gabriel from outside the cottage.

"Oh he knows, does he?" said Smitan.

"He knows. Yes."

"Well then... let's see."

He disappeared from the window.

In the next instant a large white bird came wheeling from the forge.

The last thing Gabriel heard was, "Keep your eye on me. He will use every trick to evade us," in Mabel's voice.

A large bat flew up into the night and followed the bird.

Gabriel was worried. They would no doubt rapidly change from one animal to another and how was he to keep track of what was who?

Mabel on the other hand was streaming through the night after the slow barn owl. In fact she was so fast she had to slow down so as not to overtake him. She needed to think out her strategy before she confronted him.

She knew that she could not knock him to the ground as a bat but she had a better chance of staying on the wing than he did. Bats rarely landed except to roost. Barn owls would lose impetus, tire and have to land to rest.

The owl made a huge loop around the village and was making for the church tower.

'Ah,' thought Mabel. 'He does not know it but we have another barn owl who lives here and he has a mate and young. And he is very territorial and aggressive.'

As Smitan came up to the ledge where the owl was feeding its young, there was a screeching and flapping of wings as the parents saw off the intruder. This, thought Mabel, was their second clutch. She had met their first offspring when she'd been a bat one day in the late spring.

Smitan slowed and dived for the ground.

Next Mabel knew he had become a robin. He could easily become lost in the dense foliage of the forest under canopy.

Mabel darted lower and touching the ground she became a peregrine. She did not wish to kill Simon Smitan but if she could wound him enough for him to fall to the ground perhaps she could obtain help to subdue him.

Gabriel was now, way behind her though. She was on her own.

*****

Just to taunt her, Simon Smitan, as a robin, began to sing. It was well known that robins sang at night. They were one of the only day flying birds that did.

Ah... there he was at the top of a holly tree in the churchyard.

Mabel made a few passes and located him.

She swooped lower. Bats by nature were gentle animals. It went against her natural instincts to hurt or attack another creature as a bat, but peregrines were raptors, used to killing.

Then she'd begun to wonder why he was just sitting there singing. Why was he a tiny robin? Time was passing. Dawn was early at this time of year and there would soon be tinges of pink and yellow in the sky. Perhaps he was uncomfortable in the dark? Perhaps he needed the daylight to feel powerful? Maybe his sight *was* poor?

Mabel could wait.

She found a branch of a yew in the churchyard which had been almost stripped of its leaves, and sat down to wait. Peregrines were good at waiting and watching.

Simon Smitan as a robin, grew restless. It was one thing for his human brain to decide that he would bide his time; another of his robin brain to keep him still. He dotted about the tree restlessly. She could see him but she did not pounce. Let him tire.

At last, after some time, the blacksmith grew reckless and sat at the very top of the tree preening his feathers. The longer you remained a particular animal the harder it was to ignore their behaviour. Smitan was letting his robin brain have mastery.

She supposed he thought she was still a bat and that he was safe.

Mabel made her move.

On noiseless wings, she left her perch and stooped at speed towards the top of the tree. She had no wish to kill him, as she'd said and so, although her claws were out, she did not penetrate his body but at the last moment, she pulled back letting the inertia of her speed knock him from his perch.

There was a flurry of feathers and the robin bounced from the small holly tree in two tumbling falls, and landed on the ground winded and stunned.

Mabel flew once overhead and then stooped again to land close by him and cover her foe with outstretched wings. There were some animal behaviours it was not possible to immediately override as a shapeshifter, even if you tried.

No sooner had Mabel done this than her human brain overturned her bird brain and she stepped back. No one was going to take him from her. She did not need to mantle to keep him safe from thieves.

It was a mistake.

The robin, now recovered, threw up its wings and shakily leapt into the air. It landed changing to a golden eagle.

Now Mabel was in serious trouble. The golden eagle was one of the only animals feared by the peregrine. It was twice her size and, although it was not as speedy, it was a great danger with its superior wingspan and power.

Mabel flew up quickly. The eagle sped after her. Mabel gained as much height as she could panting heavily, her sharp yellow beak open, her little tongue trembling. At least she was faster and more manoeuvrable.

Then as she made a stoop for the ground, an idea came into Mabel's brain.

She turned withershynnes in a spiral as she dropped and a few feet from the ground became a beetle.

She landed with a bounce and scurried for safety into the leaf litter and buried herself there for a moment.

The eagle did not know where she had gone.

He landed and looked around furiously.

Mabel could not see him, buried as she was but her beetle antenna could smell him. And she smelled the fear on him.

She trundled through the leaf litter to give herself a little time to distance herself from him.

Climbing onto the root of one of Master Hartshorn's cherry trees, she sat and made sure her body blended into her background. She knew if he used all his senses Smitan would smell where she was. This was merely a temporary respite.

Now, the blacksmith was back in his own body and was searching the ground carefully for what he thought she might have become.

It was then that a little hedgepig came trundling around the tree trunk upon which Mabel lay.

Its beady black eye spotted her. Out stretched its long snout. Out came the pink tongue. Oh a crunchy beetle!

In a flash Mabel turned and became a fox. If the hedgehog could have raised an eyebrow, it would have done so. As it was, it backed off with an almost human expression of shock and would have scurried away had not Master Smitan seen it.

"Ah... Mistress Mabel, you think you're fooling me." He bent to pick up the poor animal. Mabel came out from the tree trunk where she had hidden and made a feint for the blacksmith, catching him by the hose with her sharp vixen teeth. The hedgehog fell from his hands as he yelled, and it rolled away into the leaf litter, a tight curled ball of spines.

With a turn of her bright russet brush, Mabel fled across the orchard and towards the open field by the river.

Now Smitan became a hunting dog and pursued her.

Mabel knew the fear an animal felt when chased by hounds. But they were not well matched in speed; the hound was lumbering and slow, reliant on his nose and Mabel was getting away. She was getting away until she met the barrier of the river. A sheet of water twenty feet wide suddenly lay before her.

In she plunged fearlessly. It wasn't too deep at the edge and turning three times she whispered, 'I want to be a fish.'

Her body thinned. She lost her bright russet colour and the lovely brush of her tail. Scales grew where moments before there had been harsh hair. Her mouth elongated and grew large. She gulped. Ah! She was drowning. Roughly where her ears used to be gills had appeared and she found she could breathe perfectly well but in a different manner to her normal breathing or that of a land animal. Her eyes became used to the murky water, made more murky by the feet of the hunting dog stirring up the mud as it searched for its prey.

Mabel swam into the clearer water and found other fish just like her.

Small minnows, swimming in the weeds, floating with the flow of the water, asleep in the dark of the night.

She nestled amongst them. They didn't seem to mind. Mabel found she could sit quite still in the water with very little movement of her fins and tail. The stream flowed on around her.

Let Simon Smitan find her here!

She scouted round for the feet and legs of the dog. It had gone.

But where had it gone?

She swam up the length of a dark waving frond of river weed and peered out.

She could see nothing. She was so tired. Might it be good to just stay here and recover for a little while?

No, that was not going to be possible. She had to apprehend the villain somehow. Lying in weed in the river was not going to help her to do that.

She turned against the river's flow to make her way back to the little shoal of minnows when a huge mouth full of teeth, ploughed up the water close by. The little fish scattered but many were gobbled up and disappeared into the dark maw of this new beast.

Mabel realised that Simon Smitan had become a pike.

The pike was the most feared freshwater fish. It ate anything it could find. Spry, other grown fish, frogs, insects, tadpoles, anything. It would even rise up to the surface and pull down unsuspecting ducklings to a watery grave.

Mabel had to change and change quickly if she was not to be scooped up in those evil teeth!

She turned withershynnes.

And was suddenly an otter.

She scampered up the bank and looking back once, located Smitan in the weed.

Could she sink her teeth into him and drag him from the river?

She plunged into the depths again and circled the pike who seemed unaware of her presence. Suddenly he'd realised who she was and began to snap with pin-like teeth. She felt a bite on her leg.

How dare he?

She opened her mouth and her white teeth glistened as she drew back her lip.

Her webbed feet paddled expertly around the pike and launched her towards him, the small fingers and claws of her paws ready to grab him.

He thrashed in the water, desperately trying to turn himself into something more effective, in order to avoid this otter.

Before he changed, Mabel received another bite, not too injurious, but it smarted and it made her very angry.

She bit at him in her anger, and her teeth crunched together onto nothing as he evaded her once more and became a small diving kingfisher.

Smitan rose up out of the water in a flash of blue, droplets cascading from his glossy plumage and made for a low lying branch of an alder tree just above the stream.

He shook himself and more droplets caught what little light there was in the night and fell into the water.

She watched as he lifted off and darted into the trees at the river's edge.

Damn!

She would have to follow him.

Swimming to the bank Mabel shook her waterproof fur and looked quickly at her injury. It wasn't going to prevent her trailing him.

In an instant she had transformed herself into a squirrel and she plunged into the trees after him..

The light was now better. Better for Smitan, if his eyes were not good and better for her. Dawn was suffusing the ground with a greyish tinge.

Mabel dashed up a tall tree and surveyed the coppice by the river. There was Smitan flying from branch to branch.

Mabel followed all the while thinking out what her next move would be. Why was the silly man going back towards the village?

Had he lost his sense of direction? If folk were up at dawn, and many were, if they spotted him they would wonder what a kingfisher was doing so far from the river. Few people would notice, it was true, but Sir Gabriel might. Where was he?

Now sitting in the bush in the Peabody garth, Mabel chattered away wondering if Gabriel might hear her.

He had done his best to follow her but it would have been impossible for him to have understood that she'd gone into the river. And come out again.

She saw the two soldiers outside the forge. The Lord Stokke was walking up and down in agitation, calling for Sir Gabriel.

Mabel realised a little time had elapsed since Smitan had tried to kill Gabriel. There were a few villagers out now who were collecting around their lord.

"Call the hue and cry," said Robert Stokke. "You are looking for Simon Smitan the blacksmith. He is wanted in connection with the killing of Edward Greathouse." Mabel noticed he did not mention the death of her friend, Elinor.

People nodded their heads but were wary also. Smitan was a large, well-built fellow. It would take a few of them to subdue him.

"He has a pet bird it seems. It's a vicious thing. Look for a raven and you'll no doubt find Smitan."

So that was how the lord saw it. Smitan was just a man and the bird they had all seen was nothing more than a pet. If only they knew the truth.

Mabel scurried down to the ground and searched for Gabriel. It was no good; she needed to be airborne again. She needed to find him if she was to put the plan she had formulated in her head, into action.

She was getting far too tired for many further transformations. She realised that she was getting slow. Slow changing into what she wished and slow moving.

Mabel was happier on the wing as a bat and as she wheeled over the village, she found her bat voice and started to chunner for all she was worth. Would Sir Gabriel hear her? And if he did would he recognise it as Mabel? Would Smitan hear her?

She was quite surprised how loud she could cry. To her ears it sounded like a squeak but to Sir Gabriel running back from the field where he had last spotted Mabel as a fox, the sound was a loud but short ticking sound.

He shouted out into the dawn "I hear you."

Things were a little more difficult now, for there were many people running hither and thither and it would be hard for Mabel to change and not be overlooked.

Then Gabriel spotted the bat above him. It whirled around him, screeched, dived and flew around him in circles. No real bat would ever do that.

"Mabel?" he whispered loudly.

"Eek."

"Where is he? Where's he gone?"

Mabel landed behind him and he screened her as she changed into a woman again. He saw how bedraggled she was and how tired she looked.

"Last I saw him he was a kingfisher though I doubt he will stay one so far from the river. I think he is somewhere in the centre of the village," said Mabel out of breath.

"Then come on." He turned, holding his sword as he pivoted and made for the path to the green.

"Wait... I have an idea."

"Quickly then. Tell me as we run."

"I *can't* run Gabriel, I am exhausted. Stay a moment and listen. I will change back to my bat in a moment and you can follow me. I will still see better than you in this light. I can find him."

He took her arms in his two hands. "You are a brave woman, Mabel."

She swallowed. "You remember Alfred's cottage?"

"Of course."

"You remember what he had on the table?"

"I think so ... yes."

"Then find it and bring it to my house. I will attempt to lead Simon to my house and see if I can catch him. Open it and drive him in."

Gabriel kissed her full on the lips.

"Are you absolutely sure?"

Oh my! He had kissed her. All thought of chasing felons was driven from her brain.

"Mabel!?"

"Oh yes... *yes...*"

"In a moment then," he said, as he ran off.

Mabel stood for a time, totally spent and totally elated. He had kissed her!

*****

Smitan had decided that it was best to stay small. Though he preferred them, large animals were not only tiring but more conspicuous. That much he'd learned from Mabel. He too was growing tired with transforming. He had never done so much changing and had not realised how very exhausting it would be.

The starling he had become, bounded and flew through the trees searching for mates with which to join up and a murmuration into which to disappear.

A few were now coming out of their night time roosts.

Then he spotted Mabel, standing by his house, talking to her knight.

Oh how he'd love, just one more time to be an animal of power and danger. He could kill Mabel with one toss of a tusk.

He became a boar.

Mabel was taking deep breaths prior to lifting off as a bat again. She closed her eyes.

'Sir Gabriel has kissed me.' A warm glow grew around her heart.

'He cares for me. He really does,'

Suddenly she became aware of the thundering of a creature coming out of the trees to her left.

A huge boar, with tusks glowing white in the dawn light, escaped the green darkness of the forest and was almost upon her before she realised it was Smitan.

"I wish to be a bat!"

Mabel lifted off just as the pig lowered its head to strike.

Mabel circled a little and then made off in the direction of her house. Was he following?

He was.

She saw him change into a bird. A starling she thought. There were many of those in the forest and the village. She would have to be careful and make sure she kept this particular bird in sight. It was going to be nearly impossible.

On they travelled, the starling pursuing the bat. Did he realise she was slow flying in order that he would follow?

Oh she hoped her ruse would work.

She dropped as she saw her own house.

'Please let Gabriel be there in a moment.'

Sure enough, he came jogging across the grass with something under his arm.

'Eeek. Eek'

He looked up.

There was the large bat and it was pursued by a starling.

Gabriel darted into the cottage leaving the door open.

No one could see him standing in the open doorway, in the darkness of the interior. In this spot there was little light and it did not penetrate Mabel's house fully. The cott faced west.

Mabel slowed, dropped and made one last change.

Gabriel could no longer see her.

And neither could the blacksmith.

He flew on into the house, looking neither right nor left. He was sure she was in here and he would have her. She could not escape now. No matter what she had changed into.

Smitan flew at starling speed into the darkness of the house, not knowing what was waiting for him.

SNAP.

The blacksmith tried desperately to change direction. He tried to slow his flight. He screeched in a starling voice as he hit a wall of something hard.

The air was knocked from his lungs.

He fell into the bottom of a metal cage and the small door swung behind him.

He was trapped.

*****

Gabriel lit a couple of lamps sitting on the table and placed them close to the cage. The starling shook its head, snapped its bill a few times and sat hunched in the bottom of the cage. The light was blinding it for a moment and it had been knocked senseless.

Then around the cage, coming into the golden glow of the lamp, Gabriel saw a small insect.

It was difficult to ascertain exactly what the animal was but, to Gabriel's ears, it sounded like a bee. A bumble bee.

It hovered over the cage, between the lamps and then sat right at the top of the cage.

The starling shook its head again as if to clear its sight... or maybe its hearing.

Gabriel bowed his head over the cage.

"Master Simon Smitan, I presume?"

The starling blinked. And in that blink, Gabriel was certain there was malice and evil intent.

He searched the form of the little bee now sitting on the cage top stretching and rubbing its head over and over with its legs.

"Mabel...? Is that you?"

Mabel lifted off from the cage and flew up in front of his eyes. Side to side she hovered.

"Ah it is you."

His brow puckered. "Why a bee Mabel?"

He waited for her to spin withershynnes and change but she did not.

"Ah... maybe you're too tired eh? Just rest and I'll keep my eye on Smitan here."

Mabel, however, was keeping her eye on Smitan. All five of her eyes in fact. The three small eyes on top of her head told her what was happening above her and so they saw Gabriel secure the cage door with string.

The larger eyes either side of her head saw the room as the dawn began to fill the world with sunlight. Her eyes were also very good at picking up light, even if it was subdued or filtered through clouds. Her senses could detect movement of the tiniest form. Gabriel only saw the starling as it tried to undo the string with his beak, for a fraction after it had attempted it.

Mabel saw Smitan move a few feathers, long before he actually physically moved.

She was up in an instant and buzzing around the cage.

Smitan starling hunched down again and stared malevolently at Mabel, as much as a starling may stare in such a wicked way.

Gabriel scratched his chin. "Is he afraid of you?"

Mabel buzzed around his head.

"I think that probably means he is."

Sir Gabriel Warrener knew very little about the natural world, over and above that which he had learned as a knight; of horses, falcons and other useful animals. But he thought that he knew that starlings were not usually afraid of bees. In fact he was sure that he had actually seen a starling eat a bee before now.

They didn't catch them on the wing but he was certain he'd seen a starling pick up a bee from the ground.

This rather puzzled him.

Mabel continued as a bee and there was an uneasy tension between the occupant of the cage and the little furry insect flying around now and again.

Mabel realised this state of affairs could not go on.

Smitan had to be allowed to get back to his normal self or he could not be handed over to the authorities. He could not do that confined in the cage.

He had to be allowed to come out and make his transformation to a human.

It would have been easy for the blacksmith to change into something small and work his way between the bars of the cage. Mabel wondered why he didn't. He could have been away in the blink of an eye.

Was it only her presence as a bee that kept him trembling on the floor of the cage?

In a heartbeat, Mabel decided to become herself again.

She turned deosil and stood before the cage in her human form.

"Simon, you are defeated. Accept you have been overcome and we shall let you out to be yourself again."

The starling squawked.

Outside in the garden, in the surrounding forest and wider world, everything was coming to life. Birds were trilling, insects were buzzing, flowers were opening. A soft summer day was unfolding.

Mabel, Gabriel and their prisoner looked at each other in the growing light.

"Will he keep a promise?" asked Gabriel.

Mabel gave a tired shrug.

"We have no choice. We cannot produce a caged bird to the lord as our culprit. And we cannot make him become a man again."

"If we don't feed or water him..." Gabriel too shrugged. "Surely he'll come to his senses."

At last the starling got to its feet. It flexed its wings.

"We'll shut the door and close the house shutters," said Mabel. "I think we shall try to contain him."

"Have you some rope?"

"There... in that chest," said Mabel.

Gabriel bounded over to the chest under the window and sought out some sturdy rope.

"And there should be string too."

"Why string? What do you need with string?"

"You think you will confine him with that?" She pointed to the thick rope, "As a starling?"

"Ah yes... I see."

Mabel reached into the cage and risking a few pecks with the long beak of the starling she grabbed the glossy black and gem speckled bird firmly.

It screeched and squawked but Mabel held on.

"Now tie the string to its legs and then the string to the rope."

Carefully the bird came out of the cage, tethered by one leg to the piece of string.

"Now Simon, we are giving you a chance," said Mabel. "Become a man again and we shall hand you over to the Lord's men. We must bind you, for you are too clever not to be bound."

The bird flew quickly from her but was brought up short by the string held in Sir Gabriel's hand.

He fell to the floor.

"We must trust you in this," said Mabel. "I have no wish to hurt you... but if I must I shall and I will do so with Elinor's name on my lips."

Gabriel threw her a strange glance. What did she mean? Surely she would not kill Simon Smitan. She had known him all her life.

The look she was giving this small bird sitting on the dust of the floor was decidedly frightening and quite steadfast. It seemed she had made a resolution.

The bird raised its wings and suddenly before them stood the six foot blacksmith, Simon Smitan.

"Bind him Gabriel. Quickly. Bind his wrists and do not let him be able to raise his hands above his head," said Mabel.

As Gabriel stooped to tie the rope around the man's ankles, Smitan lunged. Somewhere in his clothing had been a small knife.

It bounced from the maille under Sir Gabriel's surcoat but it was enough to unbalance him.

"I warn you Smitan," said Mabel as the man crouched to spring and pass again with the knife. "I will, I promise, end your life. I will do so in revenge for Elinor... gladly. You have a choice."

Smitan laughed and kicked Sir Gabriel down onto the ground.

As he turned his back to run from the cottage, Mabel turned withershynnes once more.

"I wish to be a bumble bee."

Her human body disappeared. She became tiny. She rose on silvery gossamer-like wings and followed the blacksmith.

He turned.

"No... you wouldn't... you know that you'll die if you do this... No! Mabel... No."

Mabel did not seem to hear. She flew at him and he flashed his hands before his face, whimpering.

He missed her and she stung him on the cheek.

He immediately slapped his hand to his wound.

"Argh!" His face was agonised "No!"

Mabel made another pass and stung him again on the wrist. And again on the neck, then on the back of the hand.

The man fell to the floor.

Mabel, completely spent, also fell to her house floor.

Gabriel jumped forward.

"Mabel! Oh no, Mabel."

Smitan tried to get up but all he succeeded in doing was paddling himself to the wall. He leaned on it and moaned in fear.

"Mabel!" cried Gabriel. "Mabel... no don't go!"

Gently Sir Gabriel picked up the little bee with his finger and thumb and set it into the palm of his hand. His lips gently stroked the tiny body as if he'd breathe life into it.

"Mabel pleeease."

Smitan was now having difficulty breathing. His eyes bored into Gabriel's but the knight was not looking. He was looking at the little bee dying on the palm of his hand.

"Mabel... why... all for Elinor? What about me? Mabel I don't want to do without you. Come back Mabel."

Mabel bee was still but for a little struggle of her tiny legs and a quiver of her antenna.

Smitan was now gasping. His hands to his throat.

Gabriel began to sob and slid down the house wall.

He cradled the little bee body of Mabel Wetherspring in his palms and put his head onto his knees and wept.

Smitan gave a gasp.

"Priest... I need a priest."

"Don't be such a weakling. Bee stings... that's all! And you have killed my love, you... Why should I help you?"

"No... no..." the man's face was white." She has killed *me*. I cannot abide the sting of a bee. It makes me ill and... and... several stings will kill me. For the love of God... a priest please! I need a priest. I need to make confession. She has killed me."

CHAPTER FIFTEEN
~ THE BEE ~

Father Ignatius was summoned and he just managed to get a confession from Smitan before the man convulsed and lay still forever, slipping away quietly, as croaked as a frog. The Lord Robert had already heard that the man had confessed to the killings and why.

And at last Father Ignatius and Lord Stokke organized the body to be taken away.

Sir Gabriel stood tall and bowed to his lord as he left the house. He could never tell anyone that Mabel had killed Smitan. Never.

Eventually alone in the cottage he set the tiny body of Mabel the bee, on the table.

"Oh Mabel. There was no need for that. You did not have to give your life."

He sat on the bench where he had once sat with Mabel while she tended his wounds.

"I know you think that Greathouse and Elinor are now avenged but I could have subdued him... I could... There was no need for you to... intervene... you frustrating... interfering, annoying, woman. You lovely, wonderful one of a kind ..." He wept into his hands. "Contrary woman, I loved."

After a while, with one look around the cottage and at the tiny body on the table, he got up, wiped his eyes and made for the door.

Suddenly there was a slight buzz.

Gabriel looked round.

No, surely not.

The little bee on the table was spinning round on its back.

"Mabel!"

In two strides he was at the table and he allowed the bee to crawl upright onto his finger.

It shook itself, used its legs to clear its two large eyes and then stared at him with a head cocked to one side.

"Mabel?"

He stretched out his arm and the bee flew up shakily and landed gently on the floor.

Once Mabel had turned deosil, they flew into each other's arms.

"Oh Mabel... Mabel!"

"Gabriel! I am so glad you're alright."

"Oh Mabel!"

"I take it Simon is gone?"

"How could you do that?" He pushed her at arms' length. "I could have managed... I would have..."

"I was afraid for you. I had to stop him from hurting you."

He took her hand and squeezed it. "He is dead Mabel. You killed him."

"I know." Her face was ashen with shock but also it looked as if she would sleep for a week. Her face was lined and drooping.

"I am so tired, Gabriel. That is why I was unable to wake when I had stung him. I could never have transformed and come back as Mabel. I needed to rest a while."

"You frightened me. I thought you were dead."

"Ah no." Mabel giggled a little. "I chose carefully."

"How did you know about him? That a bee's sting could kill him?"

"Something he said ... and did... once. I was not absolutely sure but I took a chance." She said again, "I couldn't let him hurt you Gabriel. Again."

He wrapped his arms around her.

"Oh you silly woman. You could have died."

"But I didn't."

"Yes... why didn't you? Because you are really a woman?"

"Ah no..." Mabel smiled up at him.

"Did you not know that it's only the honey bee which dies if it stings? It loses its sting in the thing it attacks and also part of its own body too. But a bumble bee, the placid, friendly little bumble bee, when *that* stings it can do so over and over, for it retains its sting and lives to fight again."

"Oh Mabel."

"Something I've learned on my... *travels* around the village," she said.

They stood close together for a while until Mabel said. "I must wash and change and..."

"We should go and make a report to the Lord Stokke."

"What shall we say?"

"The truth. That we confined him here and a bee stung him to death. But we must never say what that bee was called," said Gabriel with a wry look. "That the bee was named Mabel."

*****

Upon the fourth day, in the fourth hour of the sixth month of August and with forty heartbeats gone since they came together that day, Mabel and Gabriel stood in the garth of her house.

The Lord Stokke was leaving his manor of Bedwyn and moving on to his holding at Stockley near Calne. Then he would leave there to go to his manor at Rutishall for the autumn.

He would, they thought, return to Bedwyn in the Spring.

"Will you be with the Lord Robert when he returns here?"

"If he wishes it."

"Do you owe him the customary forty days knight's fee?" asked

Mabel.

"I do, though I stay with him over and above the statutory days, since I have only my father's home to go to and I am not welcome there for any length of time. At present."

"Oh?"

"It's a long story which I will tell you one day."

"Oh so there will be another day upon which to tell me?"

"You know there will."

They could hear the bustle of the sumpter wagons being loaded and the portable items which travelled with the Lord Stokke from manor to manor. People were yelling to each other, to servants and at horses.

"Then you must go."

"I... must... go."

He took her shoulders and kissed her tenderly on the forehead.

"I will write."

"Pah! I know you will not."

"I *can* write, you know."

"Pah… write poetry!"

He smiled. "Maybe I will write poetry?"

"You will forget all about Mabel Wetherspring."

"I will not. How can I forget the only woman I know, who can change into a peregrine?"

"Every time you look up and see that bird, you will think of me."

Gabriel chuckled. "I think I will. Take care Mabel."

He strode away and Mabel felt her heartstrings fracturing one by one as he disappeared through the trees; felt that invisible chord which attached her to him, snap.

She turned to go back to her home but something made her change her mind.

She spun withershynnes. "I wish to be a peregrine."

Up, up she flew until she could see the whole village below her. Down, down she dropped until she was flying over the manor yard.

The first wagons were already out of the gate. The ladies' carriage came next with their outliers and then the lord and his personal mesnie.

More wagons followed and at the very tail a raggle taggle of servants and hangers on.

Mabel located Bertran in the line of horses. It wasn't difficult. He was such a beautiful beast and he stood out from the rest because of his colour.

Mabel flew in a circle above the train of horses and gave out a mewling cry which, had she been human, would have been the cry she would make as her heart broke.

Sir Gabriel Warrener looked up quickly.

There was a tear in his eye.

"Ah... Gabriel!" said one of his young companions, looking up. "See! I think that bird rather likes you."

Gabriel smiled wryly. "Ah no, Sir Philip," he said sadly. "It's not that."

"What then?"

"I think... that bird loves me." And he watched until the peregrine was a mere speck in the blue sky.

~~FIN~~

GLOSSARY

Assarting - Grubbing up a piece of land from forest to convert it to arable use.

Bailiff - The men who were superintendents; they collected fines and rents, served as accountants, and were, in general, in charge of the land and buildings on the estate of a manor. Also see Steward.

Besom - A brush.

Bier - A movable frame on which a coffin or a corpse is placed before burial or cremation or on which they are carried to the grave.

Billhook - A curved knife used for cutting brushwood.

Buttery - A storeroom for beverages, the name being derived from the Latin and French words for bottle.

Braies - A man's underwear.

Cerecloth - Grave cloth in which a body is buried.

Cernunnos - An antlered God of the Celtic pantheon.

Coif - A close fitting cap worn by both men and women.

Consecrated Ground - Ground that has been made or declared sacred or holy, and is therefore suitable for Christian burial.

Constable - An officer of the crown responsible for a county or part of a county whose job, amongst other things, is to look into felonies.

Cotte - A long, sleeved garment worn by men and women.

Cuckold - A man whose wife is having an affair.

Dais - A raised platform upon which a lord dines and hears pleas in his manor court.

Daub - A mixture of mud, dung and chalk which is used to make walls.

Deosil - The direction of the sun's path. Left to right. Clockwise.

Distaff - Hand spinning equipment.

Filberts - Hazelnuts.

Garth - An open space with trees and vegetables planted. An enclosed garden.

Hauberk - A coat of maille.

Heriot - A tribute paid to a lord out of the belongings of a tenant who died, often consisting of a live animal or, originally, military equipment that he borrowed.

Horn in windows - Horn was heated and flattened and became almost transparent. It could then be used in windows in place of glass.

Hose - Stockings.

Kirtle - A woman's long dress made of wool or for nobles, silk.

Lymer - A large hunting dog rather like a modern greyhound.

Madder - A plant which gives a red dye. *Rubia tinctorum.*

Maille - Links of metal formed into a garment worn by knights and fighting men.

Mantle - A bird of prey covers its kill with outstretched wings to keep it from competitors. This is known as mantling.

Mattock - A hand tool used for digging, prying, and chopping. Similar to the pickaxe.

Mesnie - A medieval household with a feudal lord. More narrowly, a group of knights who travel closely and fight in tourney and war with a feudal lord.

Midden - Place where all rubbish is disposed of.

Napery - Tablecloths and other domestic dining cloths.

Nightjar - a medium sized nocturnal ground dwelling bird.

Pope's prohibition - The Interdict - pronounced in 1208 till 1214; a sentence debarring a person or place from ecclesiastical functions and privileges.

Reeve - A man of lower rank chosen by the village who takes care of all business which affects all the peasant inhabitants of a manor.

Rouncey - An all-purpose horse.

Servitor - One who serves at a lord's Mediaeval table.

Shift - The underclothes of a woman; a long linen dress.

Smoke Hole - In Mediaeval houses, a hole in the roof where the smoke from an open fire would escape.

Steward - A man who is in charge of the finances and general running of a lord's manor.

Supertunic - A sleeveless garment, usually of wool or silk, which adds another layer to Mediaeval clothing worn by men and women.

Tenting Ground - The open space where cloth is stretched to be dried when it's been fulled and dyed.

Titmouse – a small bird.

Tumbler's cure all - A mixture of herbs which was applied to bruises and scrapes. Named mainly for entertainers who were often hurting themselves.

Unlawed - A large dog that has not had its claws amputated.

Villein - A feudal tenant entirely subject to a lord or manor to whom he paid dues and services in return for land. He is not able to move from the place he lives.

Wild Hunt - Typically involves a "soul-raving" chase led by a mythological figure escorted by a ghostly or supernatural group of hunters passing in wild pursuit.

Withershynnes - Sometimes in modern spelling Widdershins, turning against the path of the sun, anticlockwise.

AUTHOR'S NOTE

Most Mediaeval people believed in magic and in magical beings of all kinds. Werewolves and vampires are just two types often discovered in the pages of manuscripts and in legends.

Shapeshifters are people who are able, simply by wishing it to be so, to change into any animal they wish and back into human form and this change must be voluntary for them to be considered true shapeshifters. Transformation must not be accidental and it must not be subject to any particular rule or set of circumstances. They must retain their human mind.

This book came about by me watching a fly land on my car windscreen when I was sat in a traffic jam. Moments later I had the germ of the idea for withershynnes.

I had long wanted to write another series of Mediaeval books where my 'detective' is female and not noble.

There are, of course, other writers whose tales have female investigators at their heart. I loved some of those books but they just never quite ring true for me, for it's highly unlikely that a woman could do the things they are allowed to do in those centuries before emancipation. Women were at the beck and call of men and would never be allowed to roam freely gathering information about crimes. I wanted a woman who could come and go at will, never be beholden to anyone (except her lord, at times) and be free to investigate when and how she wished.

So Mabel Wetherspring was born; an independent, clever, literate, practical, woman who is from common stock, and with a special skill which proves extremely useful.

I am at heart a murder mystery writer. I am a Mediaevalist. And so I chose to set Mabel down at a time I am interested in, the beginning of the thirteenth century, in a place I know well, Savernake Forest.

You might think I have made a mistake when I say August is the sixth month. The Mediaeval year began in March, not January as it does today.

The poem quoted in this book is anonymous but sometimes attributed to William Cowper, 1731-1800, though many would argue, it's not his style.

I'm not really a writer of fantasy, yet Mabel will go on to solve other crimes, with her sidekick Sir Gabriel Warrener, in a fantastical way.

Susanna M. Newstead   May 2021

WITHERSHYNNES BOOK 2: CAT'S CRADLE IS AVAILABLE ON PREORDER FOR PUBLICATION IN 2022.

SAMPLE CHAPTERS AND MORE CAN BE FOUND AT SUSANNAMNEWSTEAD.CO.UK

USE QR CODE FOR SUSANNA'S SITE

ABOUT THE AUTHOR

Susanna, like Mabel has known the Forest of Savernake all her life. After a period at the University of Wales studying Speech Therapy, she returned to Wiltshire and then moved to Hampshire to work, not so very far from her forest. Susanna developed an interest in English history, particularly that of the 12th and 13th centuries, early in life and began to write about it in her twenties. She now lives in Northamptonshire with her husband and a small wire haired fox terrier called Tabor.

Susanna hopes to return fairly soon to her beloved Wiltshire downs where she will continue to write the Wythershynnes series, the Savernake Medieval murder series and her Kennet Valley mystery romances set in the area around Marlborough, Wiltshire.

ALSO BY SUSANNA M. NEWSTEAD

The Savernake Medieval Murder Mysteries

Belvoir's Promise
She Moved Through the Fair
Down by the Salley Gardens
I Will Give my Love an Apple
Black is the Colour of my True Love's Hair
Long Lankyn
One Misty Moisty Morning
The Unquiet Grave
The Lark in the Morning
A Parcel of Rogues
Bushes & Briars
Though I Live Not Where I Love

Kennet Valley Medieval Romances

Forceleap Farm
Hunting the Wren

Illustrated Children's Books

Tabor the Terrierble: The Gardner's Dog
Tabor the Terrierble: The Dark Knight

Please visit her website for further information
https://susannamnewstead.co.uk/

Lightning Source UK Ltd.
Milton Keynes UK
UKHW041211201121
394223UK00004B/148